Shanghai

Michigan Monograph Series in Japanese Studies
Number 33

Center for Japanese Studies
The University of Michigan

Shanghai

A Novel by Yokomitsu Riichi

Translated with a Postscript by
Dennis Washburn

Center for Japanese Studies, The University of Michigan
Ann Arbor, 2001

Published by The Center for Japanese Studies, The University of Michigan,
202 S. Thayer St., Ann Arbor, MI 48104-1608

Library of Congress Cataloging in Publication Data

Yokomitsu, Riichi, 1898–1947.
    [Shanhai. English]
    Shanghai : a novel / by Yokomitsu Riichi ; translated with a postscript by
Dennis Washburn.
        p. cm. — (Michigan monograph series in Japanese studies ; no. 33)
    ISBN 1-929280-00-9 (cloth : alk. paper) — ISBN 1-929280-01-7 (pbk. :
alk. paper)
    I. Washburn, Dennis C. (Dennis Charles), 1954– . II. Title. III. Series.
PL842.O5 .S513 2001
895.6'344—dc21

2001017281

This book was set in Bembo.
Jacket and cover design by Heidi M. Dailey
Jacket and cover illustrations from *Shanghai, a Century of Change
in Photographs (1843-1949)*, by Lynn Pan (Hong Kong: Hai Feng, 1993)

Printed in the United States of America

This translation is dedicated to my mother
and to the memory of my father.

Shanghai

One

At high tide the river swelled and flowed backward. Prows of darkened motorboats lined up in a wave pattern. A row of rudders drawn up. Mountains of off-loaded cargo. The black legs of a wharf bound in chains. A signal showing calm winds raised atop a weather station tower. A customs house spire dimly visible through evening fog. Coolies on barrels stacked on the embankment, becoming soaked in the damp air. A black sail, torn and tilted, creaking along, adrift on brackish waves.

Sanki, a man with the fair skin and intelligent face of some medieval hero, walked around the street and returned to the Bund. A group of exhausted Russian prostitutes was sitting on a bench along the strand. The blue lamp of a sampan moving against the current rotated interminably before their silent eyes.

"In a hurry?" One of the hookers turned her head toward Sanki. She spoke to him in English. He noticed white flecks in the folds of her double chin. "There's a seat right here."

Sanki sat down, settling himself next to the woman without saying a word.

"Got a smoke?"

Sanki took out his cigarettes and asked, "Do you come here every night?"

"Yeah."

"You look like you're broke."

"Broke?"

"Uh-huh."

"I haven't got a country, let alone money."

"That's rough."

"You bet it is."

The fog twined around the masts, flowing in like steam. The woman lit the cigarette. Every time the boats tied to the stone quay rocked in the waves, the roman letters of the ship's name floated up by turns in the flicker of the gas lamps. The dull clank of copper coins could be heard among the Chinamen gambling on top of the barrels.

"You want to go out?"

"Not tonight."

"Why not? Come on, let's go."

"I'm meeting someone here."

"Well, if you can't, you can't." The woman crossed her legs. A horse-drawn carriage was crossing a bridge in the distance. Sanki pulled out his watch. Kōya was due to show up soon. He was going to introduce Sanki to a dancer named Miyako. Kōya had come from the lumber trade in Singapore to find a wife.

The light of the gas lamps filtered through the spaces between the damp linden trees, making a striped pattern that flowed over the creased shoe-tips of the hookers. Soon the wispy fog, as though in a rush, began to billow indistinctly between the stripes of light and shade.

"Should we head home?" asked one of the women.

"Yeah, let's go."

The prostitutes stood and sauntered away one by one along an iron railing. A young woman at the end of the procession glanced back furtively at Sanki with her pallid eyes. Then, with a cigarette still between his lips, Sanki felt overwhelmed by a dream-like sadness. When Kyōko had announced that she would leave, she had looked back at him in the same way as this young woman now.

Stepping over the black ropes that moored the boats, the hookers disappeared among the barrels. All they left behind was a banana peel, which had been stepped on and crushed, and some damp feathers. A pair of booted feet was sticking out from the entrance of the patrolman's tower at the end of the wharf.

As soon as Sanki was alone he leaned back against the

bench and recalled his mother back in his home village. He thought about her circumstances, about how she continued to struggle. Yet she managed to write letters to him that had grown ever more gentle over time. He had not been back to Japan in ten years. And all the while the only things he had accomplished were sitting behind the grille of a window in his bank and covering up the embezzlements of his manager. Eventually he came to realize that the only reason he had persevered in living this way for so long was to make the shady dealings of others look on the up-and-up. And once he confronted this reality, he did not simply consider it utter foolishness on his part. Instead he was increasingly attracted, almost unawares, by the allure of death. Once a day, without fail, he would contemplate methods of dying, even though he was never serious about it. It was as if these thoughts brought a peculiar kind of order to his life. When he was out drinking with Kōya, he would invariably seize the opportunity to say, "When you finally make a million yen, you'll think you're a success. But not me. I'll think I've made it when I put my neck in a noose and kick the stool away." As time went on, however, it was clear that he never intended to act out his thoughts. Whenever the image of his mother came floating up in his mind, the next day he would pull on his trousers and head out to work as usual. "I'm still alive because I'm a filial son. My body is my parents' body. My parents'. What do I know about this dirty business at the bank?"

The only times Sanki permitted himself to cry were when he reminisced about his old-fashioned childhood. And when he cried he would think to himself, "Yes, go ahead. It's all right to cry now."

At such moments he would go out, hands thrust into his pockets, and observe the near-desperate revelry of the teeming crowds of all nationalities. It was like watching a carnival.

For all that, when Kōya arrived from Singapore, Sanki definitely perked up for the first time in ages. The two had been friends since elementary school. Sanki had fallen deeply in love with Kōya's younger sister, Kyōko. Kōya did not learn about his feelings until after Kyōko had been married off. Kōya told Sanki, "You're an idiot. Why didn't you say something to me? If you had, then maybe I . . ."

But Sanki knew full well that if he had mentioned his feelings he would have put Kōya in a real bind. So he held his tongue, and thereafter kept his secret troubles to himself. And by now he had given up on everything—on the turmoil of his life, on Kyōko, on returning to Japan. Occasionally, when he gazed at his homeland from overseas, only his joy at the oncoming tide of Japan's steady progress stirred him to the marrow. Then recently Kōya broke the news that Kyōko's husband was dying of tuberculosis, and Sanki felt a sense of serenity, as though a nail had been pulled from his body.

Two

A district of crumbling brick buildings. Some Chinese, wearing long-sleeved black robes that were swollen and stagnant like kelp in the depths of the ocean, crowded together on a narrow street. A beggar groveled on the pebble-covered road. In a shop window above him hung fish bladders and bloody torsos of carp. In the fruit stand next door piles of bananas and mangos spilled out onto the pavement. And next to that a pork butcher. Skinned carcasses, suspended hoof-down, formed a flesh-colored grotto with a vague, dark recess from which the white point of a clock face sparkled like an eye.

In between the fruit stand and the pork butcher a deep alleyway supported by crooked brick pillars led to the entrance of a building with a sign, "Turkish Bath." Kōya, who should have been meeting Sanki, was inside one of the steam rooms listening to a phonograph and receiving a backrub from Oryū, the mistress of a prosperous Chinese man. Oryū was the Madam of the bathhouse, and her status was such that she really should not have been going in and out of the customers' baths. And it certainly was not economical for her to leave so many of the numbered steamrooms empty just to select customers that suited her tastes.

Before Oryū went into a customer's bath, she would always spread a rich lather of soap over her body. As she finished massaging Kōya, she began to spread the soap over him. Soon, they were covered up to their heads in rich white bubbles. Oryū asked, "Where to tonight?"

Kōya remembered that he had to meet Sanki. "Sanki's waiting at the docks. What time is it?"

"Why don't you just forget him? He'll be coming over here. It's much more important to me to find out when you're

7

going back to Singapore."

"That's hard to say. The way the overseas division runs things in my company, I guess I'll be called back once we've beaten the competition from Philippine lumber here."

"Have you started looking for a wife?"

"No, I'm in no hurry. As long as I have the Madam of the bath to hang around with there's no urgency."

Oryū suddenly slathered her bubbles onto Kōya's forehead. She turned a switch, and steam came billowing in from the walls, mingling with the sounds of a phonograph playing a popular tune. Kōya began to make short, quick steps in time to the music. As he did so the lather that had been so luxuriously squeezed over them to cleanse their bodies began to trickle down, dropping off like flowers. With each drop the vivid glittering tattoo of a spider emerged from Oryū's back.

"When the time comes for you to get married, you must talk to me first."

"What rule says you can keep secrets from me, but I have to share everything with you?"

"We're different sorts of people. After all, I'm a Chinaman's mistress."

"Oh, I see. Since you're going to be straight with me I have to tell you everything."

Sweat poured from the tattoo of the spider, its arms wrapped around Oryū's torso. As the steam began to fill the bath the Madam, her customer, the spider, and the bubbles faded smokily from sight into a pure white rectangle. Oryū's voice emerged out of the steam.

"Promise me you won't go anywhere tonight."

"But Sanki's waiting."

"Sanki! Why worry about him? He'll be hanging out somewhere."

"You'd better cut off the steam."

"No. Say you won't go."

"It's getting uncomfortable in here. Hard to breathe."

"Quit complaining and get used to it. Everyone has to have a bad experience here once."

"Madam . . ."

As two voices died away, the steam spluttered and shut off.

Three

Sanki got tired of waiting and went to the Turkish Bath. By the time he arrived, however, Kōya had gone off to meet him at the wharf.

Sanki sat quietly, sunk deep into the sofa in the waiting room. He could hear the laughter of the bathhouse girls from within entwined with some bawdy Portuguese song. From time to time sounds would emerge from the steam baths that rattled the walls, and the drooping heads of the tulips on the table would sway.

One of the girls came up and sat down beside him, glancing at his high-bridge nose from the corner of her eye.

"Sleepy?" asked Sanki.

She covered her face with her hands and looked down.

"I wonder if there's a room that's not crowded?"

She nodded her head in silence, and Sanki replied, "OK then, may I ask you?" Sanki had been fond of this taciturn woman for some time. Her name was Osugi, and whenever he dropped by she gazed longingly at his face over the shoulders of the other women.

The girls bustled around in lively confusion in the cramped, narrow hallway, letting in some fresh air.

"Well if it isn't Mr. Sanki. Long time no see."

Sanki was resting his chin on top of his walking stick and glancing suspiciously around at the girls.

"You always look so bored," chimed in one of the them.

"That's because I'm in debt."

"Name someone here who isn't."

"Oh, well in that case maybe I *will* take a bath."

The women burst out laughing. Osugi returned from preparing the bath. When Sanki entered he stretched out face up on a lounge chair. His skin began to grow puffy as it was moistened by the steam. He began to feel drowsy and thought he might try to sleep just like that with the steam flowing out around him.

He twisted the switch and, holding a towel in his teeth, closed his eyes. His body grew warmer by the minute. If he were to die in this condition . . . Just then, the image of Kyōko's face appeared. Then the agitated faces of debt collectors flickered before him. Then the gleeful face of his ruthless manager . . . He was the only one who knew about the manager's embezzlement. Sooner or later the bank would be shut down. The countless faces that had peered at him through the grille of his window swirled about like a typhoon. This would all come to no good. Everything that happened to him seemed to serve the sole purpose of creasing his brow with wrinkles.

The door opened. He didn't care who it was, anyone would do. Sanki lay motionless, eyes shut. The air swayed under the pressure of the door. All of a sudden his eyes were covered with a towel. If this were Oryū, it was her business to smooth out wrinkles.

The room remained still for a time. He felt as if the yellow spider on her back was staring at his prone body, and he was sharply on edge as he lay on the lounge. "Osugi?" he called out in a calculated way.

There was no answer. Sanki had been hoping that Osugi would come on to him, but Oryū was here instead. The urge to let Oryū know he was looking forward to a romp with Osugi was actually stronger than his sexual desire. He had never before yielded to Oryū's seductions, and by making Oryū angry he thought that he would be able to feel her lust for him growing more and more flamboyant. Snickering, with his eyes still covered, he stretched out both hands and began groping around him.

"Osugi! You can run but you can't hide. My arms are like a spider's, so beware!"

11

Sanki was embarrassed by his own clumsiness. His eyes were still covered. He did his best to laugh it off; but when he tried, contrary to his expectations, he sensed the door suddenly open and someone leave the room. Something was likely to happen in the void that followed. Sanki remained alert, gathering his consciousness in the touch of the humid air on his skin. Then he heard violent sounds beyond the door and suddenly a woman hurled herself on top of him. The next moment she was crying at his feet. It was Osugi.

Sanki immediately understood the incident he had caused. He felt violently angry at Oryū. But he knew that if he got mad now, Osugi would be fired. Removing the towel from his eyes, he looked at Osugi's hair, now disheveled by her sobbing. He quietly left her in the steam bath and got dressed. He then went into another room and called for Oryū.

She came in laughing, pretending to know nothing, and said absently, "You came late tonight, didn't you."

"So I'm late. What happened just now?"

"What do you mean?"

"I mean what happened with Osugi?"

"That girl is good for nothing. Doesn't make a bit of money."

"So that's why you want me to take care of her?"

"If you'd do that I'd be grateful."

Sanki realized that in a careless moment his joke had cost a woman her livelihood. To help Osugi now he had to grovel before Oryū. Yet even if he apologized, it was clear she had already decided to dismiss Osugi. That being the case, he wondered what he should do next. Sanki took Oryū by the arm and drew her close to the bed.

"Listen, Oryū. Lately I can't help thinking about anything but death. Until I see you, that is. Then those thoughts disappear."

"Why do you think so much about death?"

"Why? Well, I could explain, but I don't think you're

the kind who'd understand."

"I don't understand people who think about death, that's for sure."

"I pour all my emotions out to you and this is how you respond? I certainly can't think about death now. So tell me what's on your mind."

Oryū sharply patted Sanki on the shoulder. "If I listen quietly to you, you'll end up seducing me. And then I'll want to die too." Oryū stood up and started to leave. Sanki took her hand.

"Can't you do something for me? If you leave like this I might do something desperate."

"Go ahead. You can die and rot for all I care."

"But if I die, I'll be the one who suffers the most."

"Stop fooling around. And let go of me! Even I feel like dying tonight."

Oryū shook herself free and left. Sensing the ridiculousness of this insanity, his anger toward Oryū came full circle and he grew increasingly agitated. He plopped down on the bed and stroked the soft nap of the woolen blanket back and forth as though he was trying to soothe his heart.

The door opened again. Once more Osugi flew in and tumbled in front of him. She began to cry without once lifting her face.

Sanki could not bring himself to go to her. From the bed he watched the small movements of her sobbing back. The dusky nape of her neck gave a feeling of voluptuousness, like a black carp. He moved down to take a closer look at her neck, but then he had the feeling Oryū was peeping in from somewhere and drew back.

"Come here, Osugi."

Moving to her side, he put his arms around her and brought her to the bed. She sat cowering and continued to cry with her back toward him.

"Don't cry so," he said. He rolled onto the bed face up

and once more looked happily at Osugi's face.

As soon as his hand caressed her shoulder she shook her body as if to say "Don't touch me." She made no effort to move off the bed, but continued to cry with her face now buried in her sleeve.

Sanki stroked her arm. "Listen to my story, OK? Once upon a time, far, far away, there lived a king and a princess."

Osugi began to cry even harder. Sanki sat up, dangling his legs off the bed. His brows furrowed. He said nothing more. Staring at the blades of the ceiling fan, he wondered why it was that he could not touch with even one finger a woman he found attractive.

There must be some reason for this. He listened for a while longer to Osugi, whose weeping was now punctuated by hiccoughs. He thought about where he put his hat. And with that, he left the room.

Four

Kōya went down to the wharf, but Sanki was nowhere to be found. The only thing he could make out in the fog was the rustling of the slightly soiled red jackets of the street cleaners. Looking more closely, he could also see, on a bench under some linden trees, the beards of Indian men bunched together like so many birds' nests. He walked to the edge of a green. A small boat loaded with marble moved along languidly, jostled by waves created where the two currents of the river ran together. Kōya crossed a lawn where tulips were blooming in a kind of circular encampment. All at once he thought of the beautiful transformation of his own appearance. He turned back at once, hailed a rickshaw, and went to the dance hall where he would find Miyako. *What if Miyako says she won't marry me? . . . but no, everything in its time.*

Buildings had been erected right next to each other all around the dance hall. Vines had crawled into the cracks of their walls, covering over the tops of windows. Inside the dance hall a man named Yamaguchi beamed with laughter when he caught sight of Kōya through the sleeves of the dance girls twirling round and round.

Yamaguchi was an architect with strong pro-Asianist beliefs. He had been a pal of Kōya in the days before Kōya went off to Singapore. Kōya came over, sat down across from Yamaguchi, and said, "It's been so long. How're things going these days? Whenever I see you, you look like you're having a good time."

"That's my predicament exactly. Once you start down the path of hedonism you can kiss your humanity good-bye. I saw Sanki the other day, and he said you're here to look for a bride. Is that true?"

"It's true, all right. Know anyone? I'm counting on you

15

if you do. Only, don't send me your hand-me-downs."

"Now that you mention it, there is someone I can recommend. A Russian woman named Olga. How about it? I thought about her for Sanki, but he's too much of a Don Quixote. No fun at all. How about you? Feel up to marrying her?"

"Does that mean you can't marry her? Olga, I mean."

"No, no, I've got the will. It's just that it would be far more interesting to give her to someone else."

As Kōya listened to Yamaguchi prattle on he kept an eye out to see if he could find Miyako. But he couldn't, no matter how hard he looked.

"But if I marry Olga and you continue to see her . . . Well, that's just a little too interesting for my taste."

"Oh what the hell. If you think it's too interesting, you don't have to marry her. And if you get tired of her, well that's that. Nowadays a monthly stipend of about twenty yen will do."

Foreigners were filling up the hall at a leisurely pace. "Changing the subject," said Kōya, "what's up with Furuya?"

"Furuya? He goes around buying out geisha contracts. Pays them off in monthly installments. But then he switches geisha all the time."

"Does he still hang out here?"

"Yeah, he's around. He hasn't paid off his former wife yet."

"How about Mihashi?"

"He's doing fine too. The guy treats his mistress way too respectfully. It's not good. He's an idiot, just like Sanki."

Kōya was still wondering what had happened to Miyako. He nodded, "Hmm . . . and Kimura?"

"I ran into him just the other day. As always he's crazy about the horses. At the time he brought along six of his Russian mistresses to the track. He lost big. Still, he's in good spirits, because whenever he loses, he just sells one of his mistresses on the spot. That particular day he was literally wiped out, so he sold all six. For good measure he pawned his jacket and vest.

16

Yet he stayed so cool about it all. To him keeping mistresses is like having a savings account. Anyway it's been a real pain to me. This Olga woman I mentioned? She was part of Kimura's fire sale."

"So what are you up to?" Kōya continued to glance around the dance hall as it began to fill up.

"Me? Well I recently gave up my architecture practice. Now I deal in dead bodies. It's really hard work, but it's also the best way to make money. You should come in with me. I can show you all the angles of the business."

"What exactly do you do? Trade in corpses?"

"Since you put it that way, I guess I do. I run a kind of disposal service. I buy bodies from the Chinese and sell them. For what it costs for one corpse you can keep seven Russian mistresses. Seven. And that's Russian nobility, mind you!"

Yamaguchi's lips were twisted as if to say, *How about it?* Kōya looked at the dancing around him and thought that such a job was certainly no big deal for a man like Yamaguchi. The lines of dancers were like strands of *udon* noodles, and through the spaces between he caught glimpses of the band's shining trumpets, which were being waved about with abandon. Suddenly Yamaguchi caught sight of an elegant Chinese lady and whispered, "There's Fang Qiu-lan."

"Who's Fang Qiu-lan?"

"She's a Communist, for one thing. But she's also quite a woman. Your older brother, Takashige? He knows her."

Kōya glanced back to try to get a peek. But just then Miyako came down from the second floor and over to a chair next to Kōya.

"It's quiet tonight, isn't it."

"I suppose so."

"You don't want to dance?"

"It's not that. It's just that we're talking about wives."

"Then I'd better get out of here."

Miyako sidled around the bonsai palms and returned to

her seat. Kōya said, "Now then, that story you were telling me about corpses . . ."

"Huh? Corpses? Why don't you go off and dance instead? We can talk about the dead later."

"OK. Be right back." Kōya followed after Miyako. Pairing off, they flowed into the crowd of dancers. Miyako drew her mouth up by his shoulder and whispered, "Your legs are heavy tonight. When a person's legs are heavy they must be thinking about something."

"What am I thinking about?"

"You're thinking about finding a wife."

"Maybe."

Kōya had actually been thinking about one dead body and seven mistresses. What a weird way to make a living. It was the very essence of turning waste into wealth.

Up to the point when he heard Yamaguchi's story, Kōya had had an overwhelming desire to marry Miyako. But after hearing that the value of one dead body was enough to keep seven mistresses, all he could think about was the misfortune of the married man. When the dance finished he went back to his seat next to Yamaguchi.

"Let's hear more about your business."

"What's the hurry? Dead people always stay put."

"Yeah, and so does poverty."

"You don't look poor to me."

"Maybe not, but that's me. I had someone more like Sanki in mind. If I don't do something he's going to die."

"Sanki? Going to die?" Yamaguchi jutted out his jaw.

"These days it's all he thinks about."

"Then he'll be a money-maker for me."

Kōya suddenly spread his feet apart and laughed in an extremely loud voice. "That's right. It just occurred to me that Sanki might make a certain profit for you."

"I guess I'd better make him president of the company in that case."

Kōya detected a trace of friendly feelings toward Sanki in Yamaguchi's exaggerated laughter. He felt glad about that. "What's the name of your company?"

"I haven't come up with one yet. How does 'Dead Bodies, Inc.'" sound? You should mention it to Sanki. Since he wants to be a stiff, he ought to be attracted to the trade."

"But what does your company do with corpses."

"Preserve the bones, of course. I get 200 yen for each skeleton I export."

Kōya considered the thickness of lumber that would fetch 200 yen for his own company. "But can you sell that many bodies?" he asked.

"Look, you sell them to doctors. They're free to buy them anywhere through their agents. I got started when an English doctor approached me and told me that he needed them for teaching."

Kōya tried imagining Sanki in charge of a skeleton manufacturing company, and it occurred to him that good fortune befitting Sanki would come in the guise of dancing skeletons. "When you watch the dancers, doesn't everyone look like a skeleton?"

"That's become a problem lately. My house is full of skeletons. Now whenever I meet someone the first thing I look at is their ribcage."

"Then I must look like a skeleton to you."

"Actually, you do. Come to think of it, everyone has a frame just like a shoji. It's funny."

The next dance was starting. Kōya got up and said, "I'm going to go dance. You watch the waltz of the bones for me."

Kōya paired up with Miyako again and flowed in among the backs of the men and women who had begun to undulate beneath the passementerie. Kōya whispered into Miyako's cool ear, "It's up to you tonight."

"What are you talking about?"

"Oh nothing. Just something very natural."

"You're being a little fresh, aren't you?"

19

"If you don't marry me, you'll be the one who's fresh."

"If you keep on talking you'll just be breathing dust."

Either way, we're both skeletons. Kōya pulled Miyako around among the other dancers as if he were steering a borrowed car. Then suddenly Miyako whispered to him exactly what Yamaguchi had said: "Look there. Fang Qiu-lan."

Reminded of the woman Yamaguchi had mentioned, he looked back. However, Fang Qiu-lan had already disappeared into the circle of people moving about.

"Pull me around so I can see. Yamaguchi was telling me about her a little while ago."

Miyako led Kōya and turned into the stream of dancers flowing the opposite way. At the mercy of Miyako's searching eyes, Kōya had his head turned this way and that when unexpectedly a pair of Chinese faces, man and woman, appeared from among the shoulders of the crowd. Kōya gazed at the couple and had the sensation that a breeze was blowing on him. He asked Miyako, "Is that her?"

"Yes."

Kōya now led Miyako in the opposite direction, moving around behind Fang Qiu-lan. By doing so, each time they spun around, Qiu-lan's face would leap up, peeking out from behind the man's shoulder in Kōya's direction. He couldn't help smiling faintly when he thought that his own brother knew the beautiful woman before him. Qiu-lan's perfectly clear eyes continued to move about calmly in front of Kōya's smiling face until the dance ended.

When they've had enough of music and dance, then come the smiles and laughter. And when the smiles and laughter fade, then come the amorous glances.

Kōya recalled a line of a verse on a beautiful woman by Xu Jiao-tao as he handed his ticket to Miyako. "She's really beautiful. A rare one," he said.

"Yes, she's a rarity."

Looking with pleasure on Miyako's pouty, swollen lips,

20

Kōya went back over beside Yamaguchi. "You know something. That Fang Qiu-lan lady is a rare one. How did you come to know her?"

"You may not know it, but I've become an authority on pro-Asianism. I know just about every famous Chinese person in Shanghai."

"I guess I'll have to treat you with more respect from now on. So how about introducing me to her?"

"That's out of the question." Yamaguchi raised his hand. "Why?"

"Introducing you to her would expose Japan to shame."

"If you've been a representative for Japan, then you've already exposed it to shame. So it won't matter a bit what I do, will it?"

Yamaguchi exaggeratedly widened his eyes, as if Kōya had touched a sore spot. "But in my case I was introduced to her by Oryū's husband, Qian Shi-shan. So I'm afraid there's nothing I can do."

"OK, I'll forget about it tonight. But what a waste."

Kōya and Yamaguchi grew quiet, their eyes drawn to Fang Qiu-lan's table in the corner. Their silence was filled by the usual uproar created by some foreigners competing over Miyako. Yamaguchi tugged at Kōya's arm and looked over at Miyako. "See, you like Miyako, don't you."

"Yes."

"Well, she's too much for me, so you may as well give up on her. Those foreigners there? Look closely and you'll see she has them all under her thumb."

"Did she put you down once?"

"She won't have anything to do with Japanese people. I suspect she's a spy."

"All the better," said Kōya.

The two smoked for a while, looking over at the chatter of the foreigners bantering with Miyako.

"Americans?" asked Kōya.

21

"Yeah. Those two are from Palmers Shipbuilding, and that one is from Mercantile Marine. Things are on the quiet side today. Sometimes a war among the European states breaks out over Miyako. To tell the truth, the only reason I come here is to enjoy that. Still, even I don't get what she's up to."

Yamaguchi slowly turned his head away from the Westerners and back toward Fang Qiu-lan's table. "Huh?" he gasped, raising himself partway and looking around in confusion. "Where'd she go? Qiu-lan?" he said to Kōya.

Kōya stood up and left Yamaguchi without a word. He went out the front. He spotted the yellow jewels in her hat flickering atop a rickshaw. He hailed a rickshaw as well, and went off in pursuit of the woman without even bothering to put on his own hat. He leaned halfway out over the front and exhorted the runner to go faster and faster. In his mind it wasn't Qiu-lan he was chasing but the image of Miyako receding steadily in the distance. *She's really beautiful. If she married me, the world would be a very sweet place.*

Every now and then Qiu-lan's high-bridged nose would turn toward the shop fronts on her left and right as her rickshaw slipped in and out of the shade of the trees lining the street. Beggars spitting phlegm. Rickshawmen pitching pennies on the pavement. Customers coming out of restaurants with lips and chins glistening. Fortune tellers with pipes in their mouths looking intently into the faces of clients. All these people turned to stare at Qiu-lan's face as she passed.

Noticing so many people turning to look, Kōya thought again about Qiu-lan's beauty, which he had momentarily forgotten. And like the others looking at her, he felt revived. Compact lips. Large dark eyes. Swept up bangs. Butterfly necklace. Light gray coat and skirt. *And what about Miyako? All around her Westerners are vying for her attention, studying her tastes, following after the capricious flow of her gaze, counting in the dark the number of times she dances with a rival, and putting her higher and higher above them on a pedestal. If I brought such a woman to Singapore, where true beauties are rare, the Japanese there would likely fall over themselves in the excitement.*

Kōya snapped out of his reverie and noticed that Qiu-lan's rickshaw was pulling up behind a waterworks truck and coming to a stop. His own runner cut ahead into the space that had opened up, passing Qiu-lan and slipping in alongside the truck. Kōya's efforts to catch up had ended with them stopping in that spot. He glanced back at Qiu-lan. She was accompanied by a young man wearing a Western suit who was in a rickshaw behind her. As she crossed her legs she noticed Kōya.

For a moment Kōya thought he detected a slight movement in her face suggesting that she was calling up a memory of the dance hall. The truck next to his rickshaw began to speed away, and Kōya's runner took off at the same time, running even faster now. Gradually the distance from Qiu-lan began to widen. Kōya looked back again, but this time she was nowhere to be seen. All he could see beneath the light of the gas lamps was a pale line of bluish walls leaning in the shade of the acacia.

Yamaguchi got tired of waiting for Kōya, so he left the dance hall. Metal fixtures on a gold-colored divan. The bumpy flesh of ducks, cuts of bright-red arrowhead. The luster of rows of bluish green sugarcane. Women's shoes. An iron-barred window in a money exchange. Cabbages, mangos, candles, beggars. The street was crammed with these things. Yamaguchi paused and considered where he ought to go. He conjured up Osugi's face, a face that blushed in embarrassment each time he had her massage his back at the Turkish Bath. For Yamaguchi, who had seen so many shameless, debauched women, Osugi's dusky, softly lambent skin, her dark eyes beaming moistly in the shadow of her eyelashes, her lithe arms and legs, all gave the impression of a young plant growing alone and healthy in the forgotten shade of a rocky crag. *Hold on now, you're not the only one to have sniffed that girl out.*

He quickly made up his mind to hurry over and visit Osugi. He stopped and raised his head and immediately a crowd of rickshawmen who had been observing his behavior came rushing over from every corner of the street. *Ah, these urchins. Can they tell already?*

Yamaguchi chuckled to himself as he looked over the faces of the runners, then got onto one of the rickshaws.

Arriving at the Turkish Bath he came into an empty waiting room. The vibration of the walls as the throbbing vents poured out steam penetrated his body. He leaned back on the sofa and lit a cigarette. Staring into a mirror on the opposite wall, he stood up and tried twirling his mustache. The sound of the clock over his head made him think of Olga, who was left alone at his house. Olga had suffered a sudden spasm of epilepsy last night, digging her fingernails into his wrist. *Oh no. A girl like Osugi will assume I was scratched by another woman.* Yamaguchi pulled the wrist with the nail marks out from his cuff, then covered it up again. Olga's throat, arched back as she had writhed in agony, her belly thrust out, was transformed in his mind to Osugi's throat.

"Is that you, Yamaguchi?"

The face of Kōya's older brother, Takashige, appeared unexpectedly in the doorway. Yamaguchi turned around and raised his cigarette.

"How are things going? I was hanging out with your brother over at the Saracen earlier this evening. It won't do to leave him running around Shanghai."

"I've been looking all over for him. You think he'll come here tonight?"

"Hard to say. Your brother cut out on me to go chasing after Qiu-lan. His feet are apparently as quick as his hands."

"Qiu-lan was at the dance hall?" Takashige's eyes widened in surprise.

"She was there. To be honest, I was tempted to chase after her myself. But your brother beat me to it."

Takashige and Yamaguchi sat side by side on the sofa. As he pulled on his thin, bristly mustache, Takashige furrowed

24

the eyebrows of his dark face in deepening skepticism. "What would she be doing dancing at the Saracen? It's really strange. Was someone escorting her? Was a Russian there?"

"A young man was with her."

Takashige was the labor manager for Far East Cotton Mills. Fang Qiu-lan was one of his employees. Yamaguchi could see Takashige was puzzled that she had gone to a dance hall operated by Japanese.

"Qiu-lan is a spy, after all. She pops up everywhere," said Yamaguchi.

"Perhaps. But Russians have infiltrated my factory. I can't stand them. Who knows when trouble will explode? It makes me uneasy. Agent Fang is spoiling for a fight."

"Russians, huh? What a strange lot. I can't understand them." Yamaguchi stood up again and peeked into the mirror. "How about it, Takashige. Up for a drink this evening?"

"Of course. That sounds great."

"Well, then . . ." Yamaguchi's face, round like a monk's, brightened up as he went into the hallway. There he glanced into the bathgirls' room, hoping to catch a glimpse of Osugi. But she wasn't in. He climbed up three or four steps to the second floor, but it did not seem a very popular place judging from the fact that no one was there. He went around peeking into the steam baths. "This is no good at all. My plans tonight have completely fallen through."

"What are you shuffling around there for?" Takashige asked.

Yamaguchi didn't answer. He started to leave by the front, but ran into one of the bathgirls, Shizue. When she saw Yamaguchi she came up close to his chest and spoke rapidly.

"Did you hear? Osugi was fired just now. The Madam got jealous and threw her out. The poor thing left sobbing."

"Where did she go?" Yamaguchi instinctively started to go out.

"If she had somewhere to go no one would be worried,

but she hasn't got anywhere to go."

Yamaguchi paid no heed to Takashige, who was following after him, and walked hurriedly three or four paces toward the street. But there was of course no way for him to know which direction to search. Realizing this, he turned on his heels and went back to Shizue. "If you find out where she is, let me know right away. Got it?"

Turning again into the dark, Yamaguchi put a five-dollar bill into Shizue's hand and went back to where Takashige stood.

"This is turning out to be an expensive night."

"What was that about? Who's Osugi?"

"This is a fine mess. When your brother went chasing after Fang Qiu-lan, I thought all right, I'll just come here for Osugi. But now the Madam of the bath has fired her and tossed her out."

Takashige could see how much Osugi's eviction had agitated Yamaguchi, and he tried to imagine what kind of woman she was. A long time ago, when his sister Kyōko was a girl, Takashige had considered marrying her off to Yamaguchi. At the time Yamaguchi was fond of Kyōko, and, like a lot of other men, he would hang around and pursue her when he had the chance.

Coming out onto the main boulevard, Yamaguchi looked right and left around the streets as the fog began to thicken.

"We might try the Saracen, but I doubt if Kōya has been too concerned about waiting for me this long."

"If he is really chasing after Qiu-lan, then it's possible he's being done in right about now. She always carries a pistol."

"You may be right, but I've never heard of anyone who was shot after being nice to a woman. Anyway, forget about your brother. What about you? She's a real stunner. After all, you work with her everyday. You're not a bronze Buddha, are you?"

"No I'm not, but I'm safe. I decided to pretend I don't

know who she is."

"You're afraid that perhaps she'll run out on you when she finds out you know who she is?"

"Hey, this is no laughing matter. I feel like I'm carrying the weight of Japan on my back. If I allowed myself to be attracted to her even a little, the factory would collapse. It's all fine and well for you to be pro-Asianist, but you ought to give us ultranationalists our due."

"Ultranationalists? Oh, I get it. Let's discuss this over a drink. Hey!" Yamaguchi raised his walking stick and hailed a rickshaw.

Five

After Sanki left that evening Oryū called Osugi in and fired her. This showed in no uncertain terms the inflexibility of Oryū's mind, which Sanki had surmised as he was lying on the bed.

Osugi of course did not understand what was behind this. Leaving the entrance to the Turkish Bath, it dawned on her that from this moment on she would not be able to come back.

As she exited the alley, she passed by the wheels of a rickshaw stopped on the pavement, then retreated back into the alley. The pillars there, swallowed up in the fog, were lined up like a gallery. An old woman came out of the darkness coughing, her earrings about to fall off.

Osugi halted and cried, halted and cried as if she were counting the pillars. Passing through the alley, she moved alongside a canal that flowed through the back streets. Pitch-black bubbles gurgled up on the surface of the canal water. A bluish green quietly lapped at the oil floating on the surface along the walls of the canal. The mortar encasing the walls was beginning to peel away.

Osugi arrived below Sanki's lodgings. She looked up at the darkened second-story window. She had come here just to gaze aimlessly at Sanki's face one more time. Then ... when she thought about what would become of her next, she didn't know what else to do but cry.

Osugi leaned against the mortar railing and pressed one hand to her forehead. A gas lamp stood next to her, tilted to one side amidst pork bones and scraps of sugarcane that had been gnawed on and spit out. Perhaps she would not move until the light of the gas lamp went out and the window to Sanki's room opened. From above the canal she looked down on the black waste spewed up by the bubbles. Garbage gradually drew together and formed an island. The yellow corpse of a chick and the swollen body of a dead cat, their heads touching, and a chamber pot showing its underside, and shoes and greens formed a damp, stagnant pile in the middle of that little island.

The night deepened. The fog came flowing in more and more thickly over the canal. It branched between roofs and twined into recesses. Still leaning on the balustrade, Osugi started to nod off when all at once she woke with a start at the sound of footsteps. A solitary figure, shrouded in the fog, came slowly toward her. Osugi made eye contact with him.

"Osugi?" a man's voice asked. It was Kōya. After pursuing Fang Qiu-lan he had gone from dance hall to dance hall getting drunk, finally ending up at Sanki's place.

"What are you doing here at this time of night? Go on up!" Kōya took Osugi's hand and pulled her up the stairs. Osugi passed through to the second floor, but Sanki wasn't there. Kōya undressed in the room and threw himself onto the bed, just like he was rushing into the Turkish Bath.

"It looks like Sanki's still out, so I'm going to sleep. I'm tired. You sleep over there, Osugi."

No sooner had he spoken than Kōya closed his eyes and fell asleep. Not knowing what to do, Osugi wordlessly folded the clothes he had thrown under the bed. The smell of a man rose like a wave through the room as she moved about. Tidying up, Osugi timidly caressed the silver fittings on Sanki's beloved cornet. She then gazed in the bookcase at the spines of the Western books she could not comprehend. Catching a glimpse of her own sleepy face reflected faintly in the glass of the bookcase, she involuntarily pulled away, then peeked at it again.

There was a thud and she straightened up, wondering if that could be Sanki. But he had still not returned even when the clock chimed two. Presently she fell asleep, her body drawn up against a pile of sheet music, and dreamed about waves and fish and children gathered in a crowd.

Osugi suddenly awoke in a haze. The room was pitch-

29

black. And in the darkness she could feel arms curling themselves around her body. She struggled painfully. She was still dreaming about children jostling her, and she gathered more and more strength in her body to try to get away.

She wanted to shout "Stop it! Don't!" over and over to someone—anyone. But her voice caught in her throat. Osugi was soaked in sweat as she got to her knees and tried to stand. Just then she heard a man's voice next to her ear. She caught her breath in surprise and stopped moving. She could feel Kōya's body. All at once, in the darkness that now seemed to spin in a dance around her, Osugi heard the sound of the sheet music tumbling as the pile collapsed around her head.

When Osugi awoke the next morning, she saw Sanki sleeping in the bed with Kōya, and recalled what had happened during the night. At that moment it occurred to her that even though she thought it was Kōya who had taken her, it might have been Sanki. How could she ever ask them about such a thing to find out what happened? She had at best only a vague recollection of what had taken place in the dark last night when she had been so groggy from sleep.

Osugi compared the two men's sleeping faces, which seemed to drift in the stripes of the morning sun. She stood up, craning her neck.

The voices of flower vendors mingled together and filled every corner of the alley. "Meekuihō! Deedeehō! Pārehohho! Pāreho!" Osugi hung Sanki's clothes on the wall and boiled some water. She thought that she should try to ask whoever got up first if they would let her stay here. But then again, she did not really know who to ask.

As the water was heating Osugi leaned out the window and stared at the alley below. A barge loaded with coal, its black sail raised, had stopped on the canal she had been looking at last night. Scraps of straw and stockings and fruit peels gathered, clinging to the boat's motionless rudder and to the exposed iron pipes that stuck out from the streets as though they were trying

30

to stop the boat. Countless bubbles churned up, thickening into mud and flowing back leisurely into a narrow back canal that reflected the morning sun on half its surface.

Osugi stared at the bubbles. It occurred to her that her own body was hung over that railing like some human commodity. If she left here, she would have no idea where to go. Presently, garbage was tossed from windows that faced onto the canal here and there. Each time a flock of birds spread yellow wings and fluttered over the back fences.

At about the time the water came to a boil she could see laundered Chinese clothes being hung out between the houses sandwiching the canal. Now the mangos and white lotus flowers that filled the baskets of the vendors moving around below were partly obscured by the clothing.

Kōya got up. Seeing Osugi, he draped a towel over his shoulder and asked, "How are you? Were you able to sleep?" Then Sanki got up. Chuckling sleepily, he asked her, "What happened last night?" Osugi laughed but did not reply. The two men disappeared into the washroom, and she was now even more confused about who had ravished her.

Six

Sanki went out with Kōya, leaving Osugi at his place. It was rush hour and rickshaws filled the streets, flowing like a river. Riding atop their rickshaws, the two drifted along with the crowd. As if by mutual understanding they kept their silence about Osugi. In fact, Sanki was certain that Kōya had brought Osugi home, and Kōya was sure that Sanki had called her over to his place.

Other streams of rickshaws flowed out from between buildings. When those streams combined at street crossings, the figures of the rickshawmen disappeared as their cars squeezed ever more tightly together. The passengers formed a silent throng, their upper bodies floating on waves that slid past all at the same speed. To Sanki it didn't seem there could be rickshawmen hidden beneath that crowd. Running along the walls of brick buildings, he gazed on this lively flood tide of people of all nationalities and searched for faces of acquaintances. At that moment Kōya, who had been drifting behind Sanki, pulled alongside.

"Hey! What's up with Osugi?"

"You don't know either?"

"Didn't you bring her back?"

"Don't be ridiculous. When I got to your place she was standing in the entrance."

"Oh, I see. Maybe she didn't have any place to go after she was fired." Sanki remembered Oryū's attitude and felt that he was undoubtedly the cause of Osugi's misfortune. That left him in a black mood. Even so, it was unsettling that Osugi made no effort to leave his apartment. Had Kōya done something to make Osugi stay, as though she were nailed in place? If Kōya and Osugi were in the same room last night, well, then, knowing Kōya . . .

32

He glanced at Kōya's face. Sanki detected in the area around those beautiful, resourceful eyes a resemblance to the face of the younger sister, Kyōko. Immediately he felt a disturbing calm at the fact that the person who had hurt Osugi wasn't he, but the older brother of his beloved. *Especially now that it appeared that Kyōko's husband would die soon.*

"What went on last night?" asked Kōya.

"Last night? I got drunk and fell asleep in some alley. What about you?"

"I met Yamaguchi at the Saracen, then chased after a woman named Fang Qiu-lan."

Rickshaws filled with flowers and vegetables flowed past carrying housewives home from the market. The scent of roses and Chinese cabbage rose and swayed around Sanki and Kōya. Each time those flowers and vegetables slipped out of the shadows of buildings they were struck by the morning sunlight and shone vividly with a rustling freshness.

Sanki took this stream of funereal flowers as a sign of the death of Kyōko's husband. Then it struck him that his own unhappiness might be due to his envy of others' good fortune. If he had been as fortunate as Kyōko's husband, no doubt there would have been someone as wretched as himself, someone wishing for his death just as he wished for the death of her husband. He looked around at the flow of humanity. An exhilarating river of the living rushed forward in torrents. *Where does sadness exist here? Where is there unhappiness? Weren't these merely sad-sounding words elegantly arranged on the way to the graveyard?* In the next instant Sanki dismissed his own sentimentality, and with the morning sun striking his face he had to smile in spite of himself.

Seven

Kōya left Sanki mounting the steps to his bank and had the rickshaw go on to the Muramatsu Steamship Company, which was located in the very center of the business district with its imposing edifices lined in a row. It was the controlling company of Kōya's firm. As he rode along Kōya thought about his improper actions toward Osugi last night—actions that resulted from having missed Sanki and chasing after Fang Qiu-lan.

Oh well, what's done is done. If I give her five yen that'll be the end of it. If having a conscience was such a big deal, then Shanghai would be full of unproductive people doing nothing.

With that, Kōya's reflections about the incident were over. Instead, he felt valiant, a sense of pride of conscience that by snatching Osugi away from Sanki he had, for the sake of his sister, deflected the temptation pressing in on the man who loved Kyōko.

Entering the business district, Kōya headed for a row of banks. A group of horse-drawn carriages that belonged to currency brokers galloped by at full speed. The carriages, with their horses' clattering hooves reverberating like countless stones hurled on the pavement, raced in a line through the boulevards and side streets. The speed of the Mongolian ponies pulling these carriages moved the currency markets in New York and London. The wheels would occasionally bounce up and the carriages would float like nimble yachts. The brokers who used these carriages were almost entirely Westerners, who ran from bank to bank armed with smiles and nimble wits. Their trading margins, which expanded and contracted moment by moment, were the wellspring of activity between West and East. It had long been Kōya's dream, a dream he shared with practically everyone in this harbor town, to become one of these exchange brokers.

He decided to drop in at the nearby gold exchange and have a peek before going to the Muramatsu Steamship Company. At that moment the exchange was in the midst of its trading hours, and a human whirlpool, spinning about with a roar, was squeezed into the middle of the hall. A wall of telephones slightly darkened the interior. The throng of people, smeared in oily sweat, chests pressed together, flowed back and forth between the two centers of buying and selling. The swirl continued round and round, back to front, left to right, amid a constant careening and shouting. It folded back on itself and then moved again, inscribing a circle and colliding with the wall. Repelled, it surged back. Spectators sitting on rows of chairs along the walls that surrounded and looked down on the trading pit silently cast glances toward the center of the whirlpool.

Kōya thought, *just one more year. Another year and I'll try to seize my fortune here.*

Looking around the hall from his chair, it was hard to conceive that every minute this place influenced the gold exchanges in New York and London. He left his seat and went over to the wall of telephones. A young man, who had extricated himself from a receiver, was leaning heavily against the wall of telephone lines behind him, sucking his stomach in as he rested and smoked a cigarette.

Kōya arrived at the Muramatsu Steamship Company at ten o'clock. He cut through the center of the imposing office building. With the lower part of his body passing through an aisle of desks that formed a passageway, he uniformly tossed greetings right and left to the workers he knew until he entered the last office, the Forestry Division. In place of the travel expenses he had expected from the home office in Singapore there was a special delivery telegram addressed to him: "Market increasingly perilous. Warehouses full. Fear decay. Eagerly request your utmost efforts."

Upon reading this, Kōya's hopes of searching for a bride

disappeared. Under these circumstances it would be virtually impossible for him even to request travel expenses. He knew that he would soon get the order to return at once. It had never occurred to Kōya that the British government's declaration lifting export limits on rubber would so quickly affect his search for a wife. Of course he knew Britain had to repay its war debts to the U.S. And that it had been relying for some time on tin and rubber from Singapore to do so. Thus, the Singapore market was now in a panic, and the lumber trade halted. And for that reason he probably would have to put off looking for a wife.

So be it, thought Kōya. He went back down the stairs, where some beggar children came running up beside him. He wasn't thinking about Miyako. Or Fang Qiu-lan. Or Osugi. And he certainly wasn't thinking about the beggar children. Sturdy cuts of Philippine lumber were the only thing on his mind. He considered what kind of tactics he could use to put pressure on his rival. *Why was Singapore lumber losing out to Philippine lumber?* *"The length of the cuts are no good. The lengths . . ."*

It was a fact that the lengths of Sumatran lumber from Singapore were as much as five inches longer than Philippine lumber. The Chinese did not like the fact that this extra five inches took up warehouse space, and they thought the longer cuts were good only for increasing the draught on loaded freighters. The longer Singapore lumber took more transfer time when it arrived at the warehouses on the continent, and when the lumber rotted it was tossed out on the ground, as if it were more convenient to store like that. Philippine lumber merchants took advantage of this weakness and made inroads in the market by focusing on physical properties rather than the psychology of sales. Therefore, Kōya had to adjust his tactics accordingly. First of all he would make the rounds of the lumber companies and determine if their key factions were Chinese. Once he had learned that, he then could devise a suitable strategy for each company. He always kept his collars spotless, a sharp crease in

36

his trousers, and a smile on his face, hiding the anxieties of the home office beneath a smoothly knotted tie. Now, he thought, he would have to draw out the people in these companies, casually inquiring after their health without coming across as too pushy. As he mulled over these thoughts he finally noticed the beggar children following persistently after him.

To steel himself for his struggle he walked down to the piers to gaze at the power of Philippine lumber as it came upstream. On both sides of the river poles were arranged vertically and horizontally in empty boats the length and breadth of the banks as if arrayed for battle. Tattered clothes hung like flags on every boat. Sampans, their torn brown sails hoisted, came slowly upstream one after another from the port. Boats loaded with raw cotton. Freighters crammed full of peanuts, coke, rice, coal, clay, rattan, scrap iron. Mixed in among these, floating serenely upstream, the white and red Philippine lumber vied with greenish yellow lumber from the Yalu River and with red sandalwood from Siam. However, there was not one length of Singapore lumber—no quince, no tamarind, no mirabelle.

This is no good. This will not do.

He noticed a large raft coming downstream with vegetables on it. Sampans waltzed like insects on the water around the raft. A boat loaded with bluish bananas shimmered like verdigris in among the poles and tattered clothes as it slipped beneath the vault of a bridge.

Suddenly a shot rang out on top of that bridge. More shots followed in rapid succession. The glittering window panes of the reddish Soviet consulate across the bridge shattered, and a group of White Russian soldiers sprang from the top of the bridge. They drew their swords and, shouting wildly, rushed pell-mell at the consulate. Someone fell head-first from a window. Plunging into a hedgerow of Bengal quince, the body dangled there an instant before completing a somersault and tumbling into the river. Shots continued for some time inside the building, but presently the red flag was ripped down and a white flag hoisted high. The white hands of applauding Westerners rose like a wave from the crowd of onlookers. The applause continued to swell from the opposite bank, from windows of nearby buildings, and from boats. Kōya shouted "Banzai!" three times, all the while picturing in his mind those clear eyes of Fang Qiu-lan he had seen the previous evening. Swords drawn, the brigade jumped up on a truck and fled into the crowd. The only ones watching the event who did not make a fuss were the Chinese, whose silence seemed to say that the same old thing was happening again in the same old way. Kōya went over to the front of the consulate, now riddled with holes. Some Russian prostitutes and British sailors were puffing on cigarettes as they passed by the wounded, who were being supported on the shoulders of Indian policemen.

Eight

That day a disquieting rumor began to spread very near closing time at the Jōryoku Bank where Sanki worked. Word leaked from one of the employees that a group of robbers knew the mark of the Jōryoku Bank and were plotting to hit the bank's car as it was transporting cash to a correspondent bank.

When Sanki heard this he was delighted. No one would want to transport the shipment of cash, and so he figured that his manager would be in a real bind. His speculation turned out to be right on target, for when it came time to prepare the shipment, the person in charge abruptly resigned.

Things began to get tense inside the bank, with the manager at the epicenter of the tension. He gathered everyone in a special room and tried to recruit a new person to take charge of the shipment by offering a 24 yen bonus. Of course no one valued money more than life. The employees refused the offer because they could envision gangs hiding in the recesses of the numerous back alleys of Shanghai—criminals for whom taking a life was no more significant than smashing a tea cup. The manager upped his offer to 50 yen, but there were still no takers. 50 was raised to 100, then 120. Even though the bonus shot up, no one said a word, partly out of interest to see how high it would go. Sanki broke the silence. "With things as they are, no one is going to go no matter how much you pay. Given your skill and experience as a manager, I think it's proper that you go yourself."

"Why is that?" asked the manager.

"It's natural to expect the manager to be the most knowledgeable. If a shipment of money can't be made, that's the time when a manager must assume responsibility and take action."

"I know what you're up to," the manager said. Opening

one eye wide he drummed his fingertips nimbly on top of a chair. "Of course you realize what will happen to this bank once I am gone for good."

"I know all too well. But when you talk about being gone for good, what you're really saying is that you expect to be killed. If that's so terrible, then it's just as terrible for any of the rest of us. Right now the bank has an emergency. For a manager to shift responsibility to someone else at such a time . . . well, I think that shows a lack of understanding of what it takes to be a manager. Especially when you consider that the manager profits most at this bank, and . . ."

"All right, I get your point!"

In the silence that followed the manager glared arrogantly at the scenery outside the window, one of his arms twitching ever so slightly.

Sanki thought his unscrupulous manager would never be able to fire him, so he felt a certain pleasure at having aired his resentments.

"Given the situation," said the manager, "Mr. Sanki should leave at once."

Sanki quietly walked toward the entrance. As he grasped the doorknob he looked back. "Then you're saying I shouldn't come back anymore?"

"Do as you please."

"If it's up to me, I might come back."

"Do your best to resist the temptation."

"I see."

As Sanki left the bank he thought happily, *At last I've done it!* He considered taking revenge by exposing the manager's embezzlements, but he knew that would cause a run on the bank. *The depositors would be hurt by a run more than the bank. In any case, the manager was hiding his embezzlements by making worthless collateral look like something of value. The mounting losses would sooner or later come to light. How many more people will deposit their money there by the time those losses appear? If the amount of new deposits were enough to cover the manager's misdeeds, that might actually help all the depositors.* Sanki found himself at the edge of a river wrestling with his conscience over the matter of taking revenge. These pangs of conscience were in effect an admission of defeat. From tomorrow on the specter of starvation would begin to loom larger before him.

Nine

Osugi wandered from street to street, then returned in the direction of Sanki's place. Wondering if there weren't some place that could use her, she looked for walls plastered with notices. Coming across a fortune teller at the entrance to an alleyway, she stopped in front of him. She was all the more confused about who had ravished her last night. Sanki or Kōya? Before her a young Chinese woman who had received a reading from the fortune teller was leaning against a wall crying. Next to the fortune teller a stall, which was nothing more than a table with its legs about to fall off, was covered with pale yellow, translucent pork grease smeared in a wavy pattern. The oil sucked in the dust that floated from the alley, and constantly trembled from the far-off reverberation of carts and footsteps. A little girl, stretching up to peer over the top of the table, stared so closely at the grease that she got some stuck on the tip of her nose. A flaking gold sign dangled above the child, and beyond that a brick pillar chipped by bullets seemed to curve under the peeling remains of countless layers of weathered posters, which now resembled papier-mâché. Next to the fortune teller was a locksmith. Rusty keys spread around the shop, climbing the walls to the ceiling like vines. The keys, together with the heads of ducks hanging down in the poultry shop in the next building over, encased the entrance to the alley. Presently, several women, pale from opium, eyes dull and listless, emerged unsteadily from that entrance, which glistened with pork and poultry fat. Seeing the fortune teller, these women assembled behind Osugi's shoulder and peered down at the tin board.

Out of the blue someone tapped Osugi on the shoulder. She turned to find Sanki standing behind her smiling. She bowed a little, and her whole head, especially her ears, gradually blushed.

"Let's go eat," Sanki said as he walked off.

Osugi followed quietly after him. Soon it was evening and they found themselves out on a street where a cloud of steam flowed refreshingly from a black urn sitting in front of a stall that sold hot water. Just then someone tapped Sanki on the shoulder, and he turned to confront a male Russian beggar extending his hand.

"Can you spare some change? I was ruined by the Revolution and don't have anywhere to go or anything to eat. I'm in a real mess, and will probably die by the roadside. Please help me."

"Would you like to go by carriage?" Sanki asked Osugi. Osugi said yes in a tiny voice. In front of the carriage stand the owner's wife stood by the head of the horse and ate her rice gruel. They boarded an old, rococo-style carriage and lurched out into night streets that were corpulent and heavy with the damp.

Sanki thought he should tell Osugi he had been fired. But if he did, it would be tantamount to tossing her out on the street. Since he had been responsible for costing Osugi her job, he felt he ought to keep quiet about his own. Sanki pretended to be in a jovial mood, saying "You haven't made a peep. Did you lose your tongue when you lost your job?"

"Well, I lost my job right after you left."

"Not to worry. You can stay at my place as long as you want."

Osugi did not answer. Sanki did not know what she was trying to say as she fidgeted. Still, he thought that even if she were to utter something at the moment he would not likely be moved much. In the rear of an alley firecrackers exploded incessantly. Some American sailors were brandishing a stick and striking a rickshawman in order to make him run faster.

Their carriage came to an intersection and halted for a while. The smell of pigs came wafting in the dust down one road, and from the opposite direction some prostitutes came swaying, their torsos sparkling. From yet another direction came a confusion of bare feet and rickshaws. At the change of the traffic light the wheels of the vehicles and the wave of humanity raised a great commotion as they blurred into a single, pure pale blue current. Their carriage moved out, but the light quickly changed back to red. The polished road they were heading down seemed to float up. The groups of hookers and the cars and the houses, all bathed now in the bright red illumination, had become a river of blood.

They got down from the carriage and again walked among the crowd. As a throng of people stood immobile, spitting saliva and chattering, they climbed the porcelain steps that led to a restaurant and settled into a room. A large leaf of tobacco, sagging and verdant, was stuffed in a vase on the table.

"How about it, Osugi? Do you want to go back to Japan?"

"I guess so."

"But even if you go back there's nothing for you, is there?"

Waiting for the food, Sanki leaned against the railing and chewed pumpkin seeds. He hadn't figured out yet how he was going to make a living now. But considering everything, his problems would be worse if he went back to Japan. This was true for just about anyone of any nationality who had gathered in this colony in China. If they went back to their homeland they would have absolutely no way to make a living. That's why people who had had their livelihoods taken from them in their native countries had gathered here and were creating an independent state unique in the world. Another way to look at it was that each respective race of people made their living here as suckers on the tentacles of a giant octopus, pulling in a huge amount of wealth for their home countries. Thus, with the exception of the Russians, even people who were idle, unemployed, or simply aimless could be thought of as an expression of patriotism simply by their mere presence in Shanghai. Sanki laughed at the thought. The truth is, if he were in Japan the

44

only thing he would be good for is reducing Japan's food supply. But because he was in Shanghai, the space his body took up was always a territory of Japan.

My body is a territory. This body of mine. And Osugi's body.

They had both been fired and were trying to figure out what they should do now. Sanki thought of the former Russian aristocracy drifting all around them. Their women made a living wriggling under the thighs and crotches of men of every nation. And Russian men were, among all nationalities, the lowest class of beggars. Sanki blamed the Russians in Russia. They were the ones at fault, since they continued to force their compatriots in a foreign land to lie under men, or to become beggars.

People are more comfortable whoring or begging from foreigners than from their own countrymen. *Well, then, so be it. These Russians don't need my sympathy at all.*

Still, Sanki had to wonder if he and Osugi really caused trouble for other people. At that moment it occurred to him, like the idea of China that was now emerging as an irresistible wave, that his manager was someone he really should hate. And yet he had forgotten that hating his boss was the same thing as hating his mother country. Once the mother country was rejected, the only activities left for a Japanese in Shanghai were begging and prostitution.

Ten

By the time the *samshu* was brought to Sanki the meal was already half-over. The quivering lips of a carp and some ear-shaped mushrooms were left on the table untouched by chopsticks. Gutted domesticated duck, pork kidneys, baby mice soaked in honey, longan soup and fried apples, blue crab and scallops. Sanki thrust his ivory chopsticks into a duck egg that resembled cloudy jade and sang a Japanese song in a low voice.

"How about you, Osugi? Can you sing or are you too embarrassed? What? You want to leave? Don't be silly. That's foolish." Sanki pulled Osugi next to him and tried to rest his elbow on her knee. But his elbow slipped off and he fell over, his jaw bumping her knee with a thud. Osugi blushed and she held up Sanki's head with her trembling knees to keep him from falling.

A plate heaped with thick steaming shark's fin was presented by an expressionless waiter, who brought it in round a slightly darkened chiffonier. Sanki stood up, grasped the balustrade, and looked down on the street. There in the crowd a prostitute was swaying on a rickshaw, crossing her small embroidered shoes above a blue lamp. As she moved along between the signboards and banners the jewels in her necklace glittered like fish.

After they left the restaurant Sanki walked with Osugi for awhile. Each time they passed the entrance to an alley a prostitute would tap him on the shoulder: "Come over here, sugar."

"Not this time. I've got one." Sanki would point to Osugi behind him.

It occurred to Sanki that Osugi might end up standing at the entrance of an alley like that, and he would become a beggar squatting in the middle of the road. And yet the thought did not make him sad in the least. He took Osugi's hand as they walked along. Unsteady on his feet, he leaned from time to time on her shoulder.

"Listen, Osugi. Starting tomorrow I'm likely to become a beggar. If I do, what will you do for me?"

Wide-eyed, Osugi laughed as she supported Sanki. A Sikh policeman, rifle slung upside down over his shoulder, stared at Osugi's face. A group of near naked rickshawmen, faces scarred by smallpox, were squatting in a row on the cushions from their cars, absorbed in closely examining their copper coins. Bright red arrowhead flowers, with dew poised to drip from their petals, were piled up on the road around the globe of a lamp that gave off an oily smoke. A Chinese man casually sauntered over to Sanki and pulled out a photograph.

"What do you say? Ten pictures for three yen."

Indistinct shocking images began to emerge from the photo concealed between the two men's chests. Osugi looked at the photo over Sanki's shoulder, then immediately turned her head and walked away. Sanki walked after her quietly. He felt that the purity of their past had crumbled, like dried mud, in a single instant.

"Osugi."

She looked back, still blushing, then took off again. Sanki sensed danger, as though a hand were stretching out for the body of the woman in front of him. Tonight is dangerous, he thought.

"Osugi! I have some business tonight, so you'd better go home ahead of me." He whirled around in the opposite direction and walked off sadly. Soon he entered a tea house where the women didn't look like women to him.

The large hall was as noisy as an exchange. A brightly colored group of call girls was bunched together like the seeds of a pomegranate that had burst open. He tried to walk silently among the tables, but some woman surged toward him, hanging on his shoulder like a tassel. He proceeded forward, pushing with the shoulder on which the woman clung past the torsos and earrings of women gathered in groups around the tables. Wristwatches entangled above his head. A plate of squash was moving between torsos that rubbed together.

The more Sanki bathed in these women, the more his sexual desire disappeared. He sat down on a chair and lit a cigarette. A group of women, crowded around a table like a canopy fluttering pliantly, glanced at his face. He placed a coin on the palm of his hand. Whereupon the women fell over themselves as they came down on his palm. Flattened like a pickle under the crush of women, he roared with laughter. Hands groping for the coin struck each other on his chest. Earrings tangled up. Pushing away a woman's body with his knee, he managed to stick his head out from some boots that were glittering in the air. He finally struggled to his feet, but the women were scurrying around, clawing under the legs of the chair as though they were all jamming their heads into a single hole. He put copper coins down the necks of the women gathered there. The wave of wasp waists began to surge more violently. Looking away from the women clinging to him, he tried to head for an exit. As soon as he did so, a new group of hookers assaulted him between a pillar and a table. Stiffening his neck ramrod straight, he made his way forward, pushing the women aside with the corners of his squared shoulders. His neck embraced by the arms of women front and back, he felt as strong as some sea creature cutting through waves. Perspiring from the pressure of pulling women along, thrusting his shoulders forward as though he were swimming, he saw a gap in the women and plunged through. But the sea of women would simply wash over him again with new hands each time he managed to shake them off his body. He moved the whole length and breadth of the hall, constantly thrusting with his elbows. A woman he pushed staggered, but was carried off clinging to another man's neck.

Sanki got out and looked for water. He was physically

exhausted. He thought of Osugi's body waiting for him.

"Dangerous," he muttered, groaning to himself.

He was convinced that he should not touch Osugi's body until Kyōko's husband died and he had the chance to see Kyōko's face. If he had sex with Osugi he thought it a foregone conclusion that he would end up marrying her. Until then, how should he purify his body? He had grown fond of old-fashioned morals. China, as it was here and now, made his fondness for the old morality about sex seem like an idea as fresh as the sun.

Out of nowhere, Sanki was tapped on the shoulder again. He turned to see standing behind him the man who had shown him the photo earlier. "Come on. Ten pictures for two yen."

Sanki felt afraid of this kind of Chinaman and glared at him. Once more he walked off in silence. If he looked at the photograph once, he would be done for. He walked along looking so closely at the decorations in the display windows it appeared that he was about to stick his head through the glass. Bright scarlet candles hung from the ceiling like teeth growing down. A peach-colored bed surrounded by mirrors. The prison-like gate of a pawn shop. The shank of a cow, hoof pointed up, among the noodles of an *udon* shop. He was tapped on the shoulder again.

"OK, OK. Ten photos, one yen."

At that moment, seized by a single, glittering notion, Sanki grew excited.

In order to become truly objective toward humanity, people have to have the act of others copulating thrust right before their eyes. He ducked down an alley as though he were being pursued. In the depths of the alleyway some women, trembling from opium, were clinging to the walls like a line of geckos.

49

Eleven

Petals fell in a blizzard from the plantain flowers. Miyako walked arm-in-arm with Kōya. Soldiers from Annam were lined up, bayonets and rifles arrayed. Beyond their helmets, which looked like flattened chestnuts, a French wireless telegraph office flickered blue as it scattered flowers of sparks. Miyako, reminded of Michel's refined, amorous look, said to Kōya, "I've danced with an engineer from this telegraph office for thirteen days, now. His name is Michel. It's just like everyone says, Frenchmen are superior people."

For a moment Kōya forgot completely what he was trying to discuss. This was the first time he had accompanied a dancer so far from the dance hall. His competitive drive was stimulated when she compared the size of the bouquet of flowers he had given her with others she had received.

"How many times have I said I love you? I've been so busy lately that I haven't had time to keep my diary properly."

"I've been busy too, as you can see. Every time you see me you always lie, saying 'I love you, I love you.' Italian men, being Italian, are always trying to find my soft spots. Oh well, anything goes. It's best to live day to day as pleasantly as you can."

"So now I'm in competition with an Italian?"

"I'm competing with Yōko, aren't I. I'm not as good as she is. Still that Italian guy is always irritating Yōko and me. From now on I'm dancing with Americans only."

"So you'll never raise the Japanese flag?"

Miyako pulled her head into her fur and laughed. "That's right. The foreigners are customers, after all. Aren't people like you in league with dance hall girls like me? After all, we're all conspiring to take money from the foreigners. So no matter how much you chase after women like Qiu-lan and me, it won't get you anywhere."

A philosophy of life can take many forms and sprout just about anywhere. And Kōya was being brought to grief because Miyako's philosophy took account of the pigment of his Japanese skin. Women he had known in the past had always praised him by saying he was just like a foreigner. However, competing with foreigners by striving to come across as foreign did not work to his advantage with Miyako. He had shown up at her dance hall for ten days now, but her eyes always told him, "Oh, a Japanese. He can wait."

The vanity of the dance hall girls in Shanghai was determined by how many foreigners bought their tickets exclusively. By this calculation, Miyako was almost always number one.

About a third of the time over the last ten days Kōya had competed with foreign businessmen in his fluent German and French. Another third of the time he concentrated on spending his money and chatting at the dance hall. However, the Japanese Kōya, who had fallen under the spell of Miyako's haughty pride, became too obsessed with his self-esteem to be able to puncture Miyako's arrogance. Because he was losing confidence, Kōya felt compelled to reach out farther and farther to Miyako.

Some plantain flowers, blown about by a soft breeze, swirled around and clung to the trunk of a linden tree. Blown together from three directions, these white petals clutched at the lawn and tumbled like delicate kittens on the gravel of the pathway.

"It's pitch-black up ahead," said Miyako, snuggling close to Kōya.

"It's all right. Just rely on me and you'll be fine."

Kōya cut across the lawn of the park and headed toward an overgrown spot untouched by the lights. Miyako knew what would happen beyond those thick bushes. She recalled how she and Michel had forgotten all about the time for an hour there beside the pond. It appeared that men preferred the same kind

of locations. She knew what Kōya would do there. As Kōya
guided Miyako along and stirred her remembrances, they came
up to the side of a pond choked with water plants.

"Let's head back," said Miyako. She walked away from
Kōya and turned toward the gate, gazing at the profusion of
buds the shrubbery was putting forth.

Kōya stared at the retreating figure. He knew instinctively that the sturdy long-legged foreigners who gathered around
her were attracted to her legs. *Why should a Japanese man be scorned
in this way?* Lamenting his own short legs, Kōya strolled up to
the front of the park gate. It was too much of a bother for him
to ask why the only legs not permitted to enter the park from
this gate were Chinese.

Flickering in the light of the gas lamps, Miyako waited
for Kōya under the fresh leaves of the pruned linden trees.

"You and I can always be good friends in a place where
there are gas lights," she said.

Her triumphant smile made its way through a tunnel of
green leaves that continued on into the distance. A road shining
like a flat whetstone. A hedge of roses. Cars sliding by, their
bellies reflected in the light. An alphabet of signs marching on
toward this citadel of illumination. When he reached this point,
Kōya had to admire the manners of the foreigners who continually gave him trouble, even if it was only because his admiration
showed that he, at least, was not Chinese. He took Miyako's
hand and asked, "Where should we go next?"

"The Palace Hotel."

Alongside another pond Kōya smiled broadly as though
proud of his skill in not mussing the crease of his trousers.

"When I hold hands with you this way, my life seems
totally bright. It's really a marvel."

"We're dancers, you know."

"But you girls . . . is dancing your real purpose? If I
were to compare you to something else . . . Well . . ."

"Enough of this. If we dancers got married, you'd probably think it was a degradation of marriage. If you're concentrating on looking at Fang Qiu-lan, that should be enough."

"But I'm asking what it means that we're constantly making fools of ourselves by chasing after you?"

Turning her face away from Kōya, Miyako flashed a smile vivid as the scales of a fish. "It's really hard to answer, isn't it. Look at a book on the rules of social dance. It's written that a woman has to pose as if she's following the man. That's why we dancing girls have to act freely, in our own way, when we aren't dancing."

Stung this way in rapid succession, Kōya felt the need to politely maintain a stodgy composure. He wanted not so much to be loved by Miyako as to discover the vulnerable spots of the woman, who to him was a spectacular beam of light. He recalled Osugi, who had pliantly yielded her body in the darkness three nights ago. Osugi, Miyako, Oryū and the Chinese Fang Qiu-lan. *The difference among the varieties of women is glorious,* Kōya thought, eager to introduce Miyako to an incomprehensible Don Quixote such as Sanki.

When they reached the Palace Hotel, which overlooked the river, Kōya and Miyako sat facing each other in chairs in the lobby. Splendid walls like a Buddhist temple. A tall ceiling in a sky pattern. Gleaming walls and pillars. A thick crimson Afghan carpet. Hidden from view in a space between round pillars, two foreigners played dice in a elegant posture. The only sound was the dice rattling from the cup and echoing in the hushed marble space. Miyako pulled out her compact and said, "A German is coming to meet me here soon. Could you please go home on your own?"

"Who's that? The lover you always talk about?"

"Yes, well, one of my lovers. Look, I'm sorry. I wanted to tease you a little tonight, so I misled you. He's coming soon."

Kōya suppressed a sigh and said nothing. Miyako laughed. "But I'm off today. If I don't entertain as many of my clients as I can on my days off, then it wouldn't be a day off, would it?

What I mean is, this is the day when I really work. It's exactly the opposite from what most people do."

"A German, huh? Is it that bastard, Pfilzer?"

"Yes, and I'll have you know he is a prominent employee of Allgemeine Elektrizitäts gesellschaft. He and Mr. Cleaver, who works at General Electric, are always fighting over me. Tonight I'll meet Mr. Pfilzer. And then of course I'll have to meet Mr. Cleaver."

"Oh, why of course you will. So you don't know when you'll go home?"

"It wouldn't do to go home. After that I still have a tough schedule. I have to see Mr. Luce of Palmers Shipbuilding briefly, then Mr. Boswick of Marine Company. Really I am quite overworked tonight."

Kōya glanced at the clock and stood up.

"I think I'll run over to the Saracen and have a carefree night of dancing. Bye-bye."

"Good-bye. Maybe I'll bring someone along there to dance too."

Twelve

Coolies slept on the pavement of the slumbering street. In the gaps between their hardened shoulders their tattered clothes swayed like plants in a gentle breeze. A blind dog was tugging at a sleeping beggar's pouch beneath the flaking vermilion of a closed gate. From time to time the barrel of a policeman's gun could be seen drifting along, glittering sharply between the gloomy piles of buildings.

Sanki had to accompany a young Russian woman back to Yamaguchi's house. After slipping away from Osugi on the street three days earlier, he had been staying with Yamaguchi. During this time he had been ordered to entertain and comfort the lonely Olga, who was one of Yamaguchi's women.

"She's a bit of a lonely-hearts, but she's honest. She likes music from the age of Czarist Russia. Since you're free now, I'm asking you to look after her. While you're doing that you have the right to do what you want with her."

Sanki knew all too well that Yamaguchi was sneering at him. All the same, it was a lot more pleasant to talk about music with Olga than to listen to a lecture on Asianism from Yamaguchi.

"OK, I'll borrow her for a while. In the meantime you can find a job for me."

For three days Sanki passed the time talking about the life of a provincial governor in Russia, about Chekov and Tschaikovsky, Bolsheviks and Japan, about sausages from the region of the Caspian Sea. However, when he considered how he should deal with Osugi, who had been left behind at his place, he fell into a depression at odds with the lively atmosphere of their talk.

When Sanki's face darkened sullenly, Olga moved at a quicker pace as if to cheer him up. Speaking in English she said,

"This really won't do at all. Even when you should be happy you look sad."

"You're just not used to the facial expressions of Japanese people."

"You're lying. I understand you perfectly well. Yamaguchi told me all about you."

"A guy like Yamaguchi doesn't know anything."

"That's not true. I heard it from Yamaguchi. He said that you're the type who goes around saying that you want to die, and that I should try to have as much fun with you as possible."

"That's ridiculous. He told me you were lonely and that I should show you a good time."

"Really? That Yamaguchi is clever. At first I was lonely. But I've gotten used to things this way. . . ."

"It's the same for me. Since things have come to this . . ."

In the depths of the slumbering street Olga's delicate face rippled vividly like concentric waves. Gas lamps wrapped in acacia leaves. Geckos with legs stretched apart, immobile. An arched gate with its light extinguished. The oil-soaked iron latticework of an oil shop. Down a tunnel-like alleyway the ring-shaped door handles stood in silent array.

Olga sighed. Staring at the line of paving stones, she drew close to Sanki.

"Don't hide anything from me, Mr. Sanki. This Yamaguchi? He has five women, doesn't he."

It was probably more than five women. Still, Sanki had been ordered by Yamaguchi to comfort Olga. So he answered, "I really don't know anything about Yamaguchi. And he doesn't know anything about me. But what you said just now . . . well, aren't you mistaken about that?"

"Don't get me wrong. I don't care how many women Yamaguchi keeps. I was just thinking how happy I am that you'll be staying with me a little longer."

Sanki was exhausted from three days of dealing with broken English. And now for the first time they were having a conversation drenched in Olga's sighs.

"We talked about Bazarov, didn't we? You know, Turgenev's character."

"Yes, yes. That materialist was a forerunner of the Bolsheviks."

"But that's what I am now."

"Then you don't know how many hardships we were forced to endure, do you?"

"Of course I know. But Bazarov isn't a Bolshevik. And his isn't a materialist or a nihilist. He's a physicalist. That's something I don't think the Russian people understand very well. The Chinese understand it best. The Chinese are physicalists. They've advanced beyond the materialists."

"I don't see what you're getting at," Olga responded. Sanki thought that what she meant was that whenever she heard someone beginning some amorous banter she held to the principle that it was best to talk nonsense. He became desolate at the thought.

Olga walked on even more dispirited than usual. Beneath the gas lights on a street corner a metal ladder cast a reflection in bluish water puddled on the pavement. Under some buildings crowded darkly together, a tofu maker had opened the door to his shop and was up and about. From under the eaves of the shop only the pure white liquid of the curds came oozing out into the night from a stone mortar turning sluggishly.

"Ah, I want to go home to Moscow," said Olga.

Thirteen

When Sanki got back to Yamaguchi's house he went to his room. As soon as he was alone, he fell face up on his bed and thought immediately about Kyōko in Tokyo. If her husband was about to die, then a telegram would certainly be sent to her older brother, Kōya. But he hadn't seen Kōya in three days, and if he went back to his place to meet him then he would run the risk posed by the temptation of Osugi's love.

What are these phantoms flitting across my heart. Osugi, Kyōko, Oryū, Olga. And he was Don Quixote, always brushing aside the women close to him for the sake of clinging to the idea that Kyōko was his secret lover. Beyond all that, he wasn't sure if he would be able to marry Kyōko or not, even if her husband were dead. And now he had lost his job.

He thought Olga had left a little while ago, but she came back to his room. "Yamaguchi's gone. Could you go look for him? I have to go home by myself now. I hate this place. I want to go back to Moscow."

She plopped down on the bed where Sanki was lying and started to cry. As he considered whether her decision should make him happy or sad, he started to stroke Olga's back. Olga lifted her head and said angrily, "Get off the bed! I want to sleep by myself."

Sanki quietly got off the bed and put on his shoes.

"Good night. Good-bye." He paid his courtesies and was about to leave the room when Olga jumped up and flung herself around his neck.

"Don't leave!"

"I have to stand here like this all night?"

"Bolshevik! Demon! You've all treated me badly."

"I'm not a Bolshevik."

"Oh yes you are. You're a Bolshevik. If you weren't, then you couldn't be so cold-hearted."

"At least a Bolshevik wouldn't come in when I'm sleeping, wake me up, and take the bed for themselves."

Olga bit her lip and cried silently. She pulled at Sanki's arms with a strong jerk. He resisted her force, but his feet slipped and he was pulled toward the bed. Fastening one hand on the bedpost he found himself bending like a shrimp. "Olga! If you keep pulling like this you'll rip my clothes."

"Monster!"

"I've lost my job. If you rip them, tomorrow . . ."

Sanki began to find the whole situation ridiculous and burst out laughing in mid-sentence.

Grunting and turning red, Olga clasped Sanki's neck with one arm and tried to pull him down. His neck started to ache and he pushed on Olga's throat.

"Stop it, Olga! I'll hit you!"

By now Olga was clenching her teeth as she fastened on his neck. It was hard for him to breathe and he began spluttering.

"Olga! Olga!"

Sanki lifted Olga to his shoulder and threw her down on the bed. Her feet did a complete somersault, tracing an arc through the air onto the shuddering bed. As soon as she could get up she threw a pillow at Sanki.

"Demon! Monster!"

She was deathly pale, and again lunged furiously at his head. In this whirlwind he blocked her body, but teetered backward, placing his hand on a mirror on the wall. Olga bit the top of his shoulder and shook her head. Sanki felt as though he were being stretched out as he was squeezed between the undulations of her muscles pressing on him and the surface of the mirror. Perched on a line between frenzy and existence, their groaning bodies intertwined indistinguishably. Then, in an abstracted state, like glass in which it is impossible to tell who is who, they fell with a thud to the side of the bed.

Fourteen

For some time Sanki left it to Olga to do as she pleased. Stretching and flexing, full of life, she murmured at his forehead, "You're sweet, Sanki. Go to sleep now. Here, look. Not on the floor. You'll catch cold there."

Olga tried to raise his head, but couldn't. So she plopped down on the floor again and said, "You mustn't forget me, Sanki. You'll take me with you to Japan, won't you? I'd like to see Japan. Please, Sanki, say something." Her lips moved like a brush over Sanki's face. Then she stood up and patted out the wrinkles in the bedding.

"You're certainly strong, to have tossed me here like that. My head was spinning after you did that. But I'm all right now."

Olga jumped into the bed, wrapped a blanket around her head, and began to dance on her knees. Lying to the side of the bed, Sanki did not get up. Olga raised her head and peeked out at him from under the blanket.

"What's wrong?"

Sanki finally got up, turned away from Olga, and started out of the room.

"Where are you going?"

He said nothing and started to open the door with his shoulder. Olga dashed over to him dragging the blanket.

"Don't! If you're going to leave, take me along."

Sanki gazed at her face as though watching her fully stretched-out legs. He started out.

"Don't go. Please don't. If I'm left alone, I'll die."

"You're really annoying."

Sanki pushed her away. She shuddered and broke out crying in a loud voice. He quickly opened the door and fled outside. Olga lurched out and ran after him, bending forward like a folding screen. She grabbed his arm at the top of the landing.

"You're running away from me, Sanki. I can't stand it."

She stamped her feet and pressed his hand to her moist face. He remained silent for a few moments. Shaking his hand free he started down the stairs again. She caught him by his shirt. Her body bent over, she was facing down.

Clutching the banister, Sanki continued on.

"Sanki! Wait. Please wait."

The tips of her arched feet slapped each of the stairs as they were dragged along. Sanki's shirt was pulled up, exposing his navel, which was twitching painfully amid the sweat on his stomach. Carried by his momentum, Sanki smacked into the wall in front of him at the bottom of the stairs. When she turned at the landing, Olga fell sprawling at his feet. He bent over to help her up. All at once he felt the desolation he experienced when looking up into an empty sky. Standing astride Olga, who was moaning now, he stared blankly at her hair.

Fifteen

There was a river at the far end of the street. Its calm water was deliberate and cloudy that evening. The pitch-black sail of a junk drifted along between the walls of the buildings like a sneak thief prowling.

From time to time Osugi sensed the beating of bat wings at her ear. Glancing up, the chill of multi-storied buildings overpowered her. She had waited three days for Sanki to come home. He wasn't the only one who had failed to show up. Kōya didn't come back either. During her wait all she could do was boil water and watch it cool, clean the room over and over, and stare out at the canal. Realizing at last that the two men must dislike her, she grew more distracted than angry. Osugi resolved that she would not meet Sanki again, and so she had walked as far as the river bank.

A set of cranes suspended at rest over the mud bared the rusted teeth of their gears. Stacks of lumber. A crumbling stone fence. A mountain of greens spilled from a cargo hold. White fungus grew like skin on a small boat split open on the side. A dead infant, one leg sticking up, floated amid the stagnant bubbles puddling on the keel. Moonlight tumbled down everywhere, lusterless as though bred in the dust.

Puoco tempo somente

Depressa de cima abaixo

A Portuguese sailor in a cocked hat passed by singing a song from his homeland. Osugi looked at the moon and became like the moon. She looked at the canal and became like the canal. She had absent-mindedly passed the whole day in this state. Out of nowhere, she remembered her friend Tatsue. *If I had a room I could get customers like Tatsue.* That's right, if she could get customers, she thought. . . . Standing on a bridge, she felt vivid pangs of hunger. She recalled the food she had eaten since morning—some duck's leg, lotus fruit, pork rind, bamboo shoot.

In spite of her hunger Osugi couldn't shake the image of Tatsue's silk stockings, which gleamed in her mind like sacks stuffed with rare pleasures. The crimson of her lips looked puffy, holding secrets like the tongue of a special man. At that image Osugi once more wondered in confusion who had taken her, Sanki or Kōya. The incident that night—because of the will power it took to worry over which of the two had ravished her, she felt she had lost the core of her being, like a whirlwind spinning out of control. Osugi no longer understood anything, and in that state she began to travel swiftly down the path toward that ultimate livelihood available to a woman.

Far away, from over the mud, she heard the sound of a Chinese fiddle. She crossed a bridge and gazed at the faces of men in the manner of the prostitutes she had seen. A Chinese man slept with his mouth open amid sticky, wet entrails in a butcher shop she passed. A young woman with flowers in her bangs was selling glass chimneys for lamps beneath the broken chains of a crane. A coolie, his hair in a queue, emerged from the piles of rotting tires along the river bank and came up to Osugi, laughing.

Osugi hunched her shoulders and walked on. The man followed after her. Trembling, she looked back at him.

"You've got me wrong. I'm not like that."

In a panic, she ducked into an alley and anxiously turned corner after corner. In the recesses of that alley she spied a swollen naked back through a hole of sharp, broken glass. She came to a halt. She had lost the way out. Above her head laundry was hanging in a row like fish bladders soaking the walls. A woman leaning against a pillar was coughing, her bony shoulders twitching. On the floor behind her a naked man and woman with diseased eyes were squatting around a single red candle. Osugi glanced up and saw silent faces peering out from each of the windows in the walls that pressed in on her from all sides. She stumbled like a trembling stick across the paving stones and got lost farther and farther in the labyrinth of walls. Lights gradually disappeared. And in the darkness a mountain of countless rags she assumed was a pile of rubbish began to creep from the corners of the alley. She was suddenly stopped short by a wall, and her legs would not move. A pile of those black rags, stuffed between the narrow walls, swept over her like a thick wave. In an instant Osugi saw human nostrils lined up like dots before her eyes. As she fainted she was sucked into a hardened wave of rag-covered backs and disappeared.

Sixteen

Shopkeepers in the alley bustled to wash away the dust. Boiled eggs stacked high on bamboo baskets. Heads of birds slumped over in stalls. A monkey trainer in among fermented tofu and cayenne pepper. Pork fat trembling at the sound of footsteps. Foot-bound housewives wandering idly among mangos that had rolled between sets of old shoes ripped open. Shining coal, broken eggs, swollen fish bladders.

A Brahman temple in a recess of this disorderly street corner towered over everything. Today, however, the way to the temple was blocked by the bayonets of Chinese soldiers, and Indians were not allowed to partake in the celebration of the birth of the Buddha. The Indians clearly understood that the road was blocked at the instigation of the British authorities, and they filled the street corner with its glinting bayonets and glared up at the pointed spire of the temple.

Presently a company of British soldiers clad in dark-green, together with some White Russian soldiers, came marching behind a military band down an English-style street, where the residents obviously disliked the crowd of Indians. Behind the company a red armored vehicle, its machine gun barrel rotating like an insect antenna, moved past the crowd of Indians, who were darkly sullen.

Yamaguchi received a phone call from Amuli, an Indian patriot, and walked over to the scene with Sanki. When they arrived, all they could see were the Indians, their eyes flashing in silence, and the tip of the black barrel of the machine gun. Despite the presence of the machine gun, Yamaguchi, as an Asianist, felt angry at the Chinese soldiers who were as responsible as the British for blocking the Indians. Then he realized why Amuli had called, and he laughed. *It's just like him. Calling me over here to stir my anger like this.*

He quickly noticed that the road cut off by the Chinese soldiers, across from the street corner where they stood, led into a zone under Chinese jurisdiction. *That Amuli. He wants to say to the Japanese "consider this." Well, don't try to make a fool of me.*

Then, in the next instant he noticed that Sikh policemen, employed by the British garrison, were pressing in on the crowd of Indians who stood face-to-face with the Chinese soldiers.

Yamaguchi no longer understood Amuli's purpose. *Does he think it's good for me to see the shameful conduct of these stupid Indians? Or is he asking me to look at the faces of the Chinese soldiers, who support the violence of the English soldiers?*

In the end Yamaguchi, who belonged to a movement that sought to unite Asia against the White Calamity, could no longer see any humor in the situation as he watched the powerless faces of his Chinese and Indian comrades. He noticed a pile of hard-boiled eggs in a nearby bamboo basket. The eggs had utterly no bearing on this incident, where different races were clashing on the street. Yet those eggs reminded him of the faces of Chinese people. Seeing the slit necks of birds lying darkly in the stalls at his feet, he thought of the Indian people. He muttered as though Amuli were next to him, "Your so-called numberless people are nothing more than a shield against bullets."

"That's right," Sanki replied unexpectedly, as if he were the one who had been addressed.

Whenever he met Amuli, Yamaguchi had the habit of trying to tear apart the phrase "the numberless people of India" that Amuli boastfully used. And when he brought it up, Amuli would respond by satirizing the Japanese militarism that was Yamaguchi's pride. *But isn't Japanese militarism a unique weapon for rescuing Asia from the White Calamity? What else was there? Look at China. Look at India. Look at Siam. Look at Persia. To recognize Japanese militarism was to confront an axiomatic fact of the Orient.*

As Yamaguchi walked along the pavement by himself, he got worked up recalling a past gathering of Asianists. That

66

day Li Ying-pu of China took the "Twenty-One Demands" of the Japan-China Cooperation Treaty as the pretext to denounce what he called "this clear case of Japanese militarism." Yamaguchi responded right away, arguing, "Once China and India accept Japanese militarism, then the union of Asia will be possible. What's more, if you consider the extension of Japan's leasehold on Manchuria for ninety-nine years unfair, then we have no choice but to kill off the concept of East Asia. We must all recognize that with Japan's ninety-nine-year lease of Southern Manchuria now a reality, East Asia is guaranteed its existence for the next century."

To which Amuli replied sarcastically, "Thanks to Japan's ninety-nine-year lease of Southern Manchuria, we can at least be sure that, just as Messrs. Yamaguchi and Li are arguing in this way, Japan will be arguing with its East Asian comrades for the next century. However, no matter what disputes arise between China and Japan, India will be independent. And when that day of independence comes, India must strive to expel all foreign powers from China. For India's sake. For the sake of peace in Asia."

Yamaguchi thought about the force that would destroy China long before India ever gained independence.

That force was clearly not Japanese militarism. It wasn't British capitalism, nor Russian Marxism, nor China's own militarism. It was definitely opium from India or Persia.

Walking beside Yamaguchi, who was striking a serious patriotic pose, Sanki had been mulling over what he should say to explain to Yamaguchi his encounter with Olga last night. He had called Kōya and arranged to meet him at two o'clock that afternoon. He had to ask Kōya about Kyōko and Osugi. In the meantime, how should he deal with Olga?

He wondered how much he had really resisted Olga. He thought about how Olga had forced herself on him. The result was that he was now in a quandary over how to handle her.

The more he thought about it the more he was convinced that the most important thing was to figure out a way to forget about Olga.

"I won't be going back to your house any longer," Sanki announced.

"Why? Are you afraid of Olga?"

Sanki could not parry Yamaguchi's question, which hit his weak spot.

"Yes, she's scary."

"But she told me not to let you slip away. If you run out on me now, I'm in for it. So don't do it."

"Then I'll have to beg your forgiveness."

"What a pain. This is more complicated than the problem of India."

Sanki watched as Yamaguchi broke into a guffaw, and in the pit of his stomach he grew afraid, sensing some sort of subterfuge.

"Let me go for today. I have to meet Kōya at two o'clock."

"What an idiot. Running away from such a fascinating woman. You're an idiot."

Turning his back on Yamaguchi's sneering face, Sanki hurried off to the Parterre café. All he wanted to know was whether or not Kyōko's husband had died.

Seventeen

That very same day Kōya wrapped up contracts with three lumber companies. He sent his upbeat report to the headquarters in Singapore.

"Activities as follows. Have taken care of Philippine lumber. Expect competition to panic."

Remembering the call from Sanki that had come to his company, he picked what looked like a speedy rickshaw and hurried to the Parterre café. He felt really happy as he sat on his rickshaw. If he could push on in such a favorable way, he would soon be made branch manager here. Then he would try his hand at the gold market with a sure-fire method. Then he would go into silk, then currency, then into cotton on the Bombay futures market. Then the exchange in Liverpool and finally . . . The fact that he had lost Miyako to foreigners had been the main source of his melancholy agitation; and so at the core of these fantasies was a raging, heroic ambition aimed at attacking the very heart of the power of the foreigners who had taken her away from him.

In the face of Chinese land and money, which had become the source of the economic power of foreigners, he thought that he had to disrupt as much as possible the sharp vertical trusts they directed.

To do that, first I have to shoot the horse of Philippine lumber. Shoot that horse.

Wharves lined up like blackened teeth beside these wild fantasies that flamed inside him. A motorboat, metal fixtures gleaming, sped back and forth beyond an area where cargo was being lazily off-loaded. A fleeing sampan was eating the wake and exhaust of the motorboat. Masts propagated prolifically. Ships ran on like a castle wall. Tattered sails danced above the point where the river and ocean mingled and the color of water changed. The whole scene seemed to release its brilliance as it neared Kōya's speeding rickshaw.

What's Philippine lumber, or lumber from the Yalu River? What can they do in Vladivostok, or Qilin?

He entered the Parterre café under the stilled blades of a ceiling fan and found Sanki in the severe quiet of the place listening to the sound of sugar dissolving in milk. Kōya threw up his hands in resignation at the entrance and proceeded in.

"I haven't been home once since we last met. It's a little awkward."

"Same here. And after all this time, I don't want to go back yet."

"Me either."

They simultaneously thought of the abandoned Osugi. But Kōya was unable to contain the joy that was bubbling up in him.

"Listen, now," he said, "today I managed to knock off three companies. Thirty thousand yen just like that."

"Don't tell me how happy you are. I was fired the day I left you."

"Fired?"

"I said something that annoyed my manager."

"Didn't I say you were a fool? A fool!"

Some former officials from Czarist Russia, their permanently melancholy faces lined up beneath the heavy pendulum of a clock, were sunk in private conversation. A silent crowd of coiled napkins. The sunken marble of the fireplace. The powder of dried confections scattered on the carvings of the thick tables. The dark-green curtains drooping in secret folds. Kōya realized that right now the Parterre, this oppressive haunt of Russian Imperialists, was utterly unsuited to his own cheerful mood. Everyone he looked at was subdued, and the dignity of misfortune, like some overwrought rococo elegance, washed over everything, including the dissolutely curled edge of the carpet.

70

"Can we get out of here?"

"Sure, but I like the calm here. This kind of place is best when you've been fired."

"This place suits you perfectly. A gathering place for the unemployed."

"Don't treat me like an imbecile all of sudden. As things stand, I'm going to hit you up for money."

"Oh for god's sake, now I get it. I'm not sure anymore who the real Czarists are here. Let's try asking those Russians over there."

Seeing Kōya laugh in such a delighted way, Sanki knew he couldn't rely on him today. Kōya said, "So how about? I just said we should try asking those Russians. Will you do as I say today?"

"Serving you is no fun. Will you hand all your money over to me?"

"Ah, well I have something to ask of you on that score. You'll understand what from the look in my eyes."

"And you should understand what I want from the look in my eyes. I didn't go to all the trouble of getting fired just to be your servant."

"You're a stubborn one. Isn't it a virtue in China to be obedient to money? You're a fool not to rid yourself of the old Yamato spirit. Well, they say never give a sucker a break. Boy!"

A waiter came over. Kōya got up and repeated, "Now listen, you. Today, just for once, let's both be as foolish as we can. There are a lot of interesting things in life. But you always go around frowning, you get fired, and lately you play at being Don Quixote."

"Thanks, but no thanks. I'm going to your older brother's house later. You can make fun of me all you want, but I have to get your brother to find me a job."

Sanki went outside. Without paying any attention to Kōya, he headed off toward Takashige's house. Kōya continued to talk, as if chasing after Sanki.

71

"Don't go there! Come here! I'll show you Fang Qiu-lan. Fang Qiu-lan!"

Eighteen

"It sounds as though Kyōko's husband's in critical condition. The last time she came here she said she'd return to Shanghai if her husband dies. She seems to like China more than Japan. Anyway, as things stand I'm the one in danger these days. I'm not sure who'll be the first to go, her husband or me. Can my wife hear us? The most dangerous thing for me is her overhearing us." Takashige said, glancing at Kōya and Sanki.

"Why are you in danger?" Kōya looked at his older brother in surprise.

"Some Russian workers have infiltrated the factory. I'm plant manager, right? So I'm in the riskiest position. Some day, in among the machinery, someone will do me in. Soon this will be nothing to joke about."

"So the strike has started?"

"Not yet. That's why this is the most dangerous moment. The Bin Zhong labor union is a bunch of thugs."

"That is dangerous, isn't it? Still, it doesn't really affect me."

"It doesn't affect you?"

"That's what I said. Today I just concluded three contracts for thirty thousand yen. At this rate I'll be branch manager within six months."

"I'm jealous that it doesn't affect you. Isn't there a story in some textbook about an older brother sweating it out as a plant manager while his younger brother lives the sweet life? In any case, if I were Chinese I'd go through with it. I'd start by fighting the plant manager, then I'd throw guys like you out."

"Oh, that reminds me. I saw a woman named Fang Qiu-lan at the Saracen three days ago. Yamaguchi insisted that you know her. Do you? Fang Qiu-lan? She's incredibly beautiful."

73

"Yes, I know her. She's a worker I hired."

"An employee?" Kōya sounded stunned. "She can't possibly be a worker. That can't be right."

"She's working under an assumed name. Drop by sometime and you'll see her. I don't dare say anything about it, so I keep quiet and pretend not to know. She has a lot of influence in the Communist party here and that's frightening. When the strike takes place she'll probably kill me first, so I'm under a lot of strain on this job."

"If you're killed, that'll be the end of our sibling rivalry."

"You got that right. I have to defer to the workers, the directors, and to the Japanese people. And on top of all that I have to defer as an older brother. Maybe it would be better after all to be done in quickly. What's your opinion, Professor Sanki?"

"I'm at the same point myself," Sanki replied.

"Oh that's right, Sanki's been fired. He's got his eyes on my wallet now," added Kōya.

"Fired?"

"A man who gets fired is a fool," Kōya added.

"Fired, huh? Of course, anyone who's been fired feels like they want to be killed. Not just Sanki."

"So how about it?" asked Sanki. "You must have some job where I'll be killed. Anything will do. I came here just to ask you that."

"There are plenty of jobs like that. Like I just said, this factory's the place to get popped off. If it suits you, come over anytime."

"With things having turned out the way they have, I think you're right. It's best to be done in quickly, with a bang."

The three men laughed in unison, as though they had reached some punch line.

As the room grew quiet, Sanki glanced around. Kyōko had been raised here. He had fallen in love with her here. And it was in this room that he had resolved so many times to die on account of her marriage. Now, in this very same room, he was

74

being given a job by her older brother so that that he could go on living. And for what purpose? Simply to wait for the death of Kyōko's husband.

Sanki thought that the one spot on earth that brought him so much heartache was this drearily common eight-mat room. The moment the word common sprang to mind it took on a strange appearance. What's more, if Kyōko were to return, this room would once again silently resume its strange activities.

Sanki stared out the window. The tents of British troops were lined up, ropes dangling like a clump of jellyfish. Arms stacked. Coal piled up. Simple cots. A football flying up amid the undulating peaks of the tents. Sanki recalled an article in the *Times* that deplored the fact that the livelihoods of these troops would be lost when they were repatriated. And what about the Japanese in this land? Except for doctors and restaurants the Japanese here consisted almost entirely of people trapped by debts who couldn't move away.

Sanki said, "I've been thinking lately that given the way China is now it's best not to hold onto any genuine hope or ideals whatsoever. What do you think?"

"I think you're right," said Takashige. "There's just no way to hold onto hopes or ideals in a place like this. For one thing, they don't understand such things here. The only thing they understand is money. And they won't even accept that without first checking the bills one by one in the presence of someone else to see if they're counterfeit."

"Maybe, but Sanki hates accumulating even counterfeit money, so there's nothing that can be done for him," said Kōya.

"Sanki and I are alike on that score, since we both prefer to use up counterfeit money. People who try to make money in China work under a handicap, since it's impossible to accumulate anything. That's where the Chinese are clever. They've devised ways to make sure that all the money made here gets spent here. That they think of us as human at all is proof of the kindness of the Chinese."

"Are you saying the Chinese aren't human? That they're gods?" asked Kōya.

"They're avatars of men who aren't human. There's no place on earth where the people have mastered the art of lying as well as in China. But lies aren't just lies for the Chinese. They're a source of righteousness for them. If you don't understand this inversion in their concept of righteousness, if you don't understand the Chinese, then of course you won't understand the future course of the human race."

In the paradox that overflowed from Takashige's horseface Sanki sensed the kind of philosophical clarity he had lacked for so long. He said, "Have you ever had the experience as plant manager of being caught in a bind because you thought the demands of the workers were justified?"

"Oh, I've had that experience. But on those occasions my cunning, smiling face appears spontaneously, as is the custom of our class. I'm smiling, but a smile is the primary weapon we use to subjugate the Chinese people. They can't understand our smiles, because they're communicating with nothing. The moment they're off guard you grab their money behind their backs, and you smile again. Then they fall. One of these days they won't fall, no matter how much we smile. And when that happens we'll be struck down by righteousness, and no longer able to smile. Japanese people are weak and frivolous when it comes to righteousness. Now you tell me what other countries lie for the sake of righteousness? Now that lying has become a form of righteousness, as it has with the Chinese, it's impossible to subjugate them. They're able to put everything in the swivel-chair of justice and spin it around. You tell me where there's a more mysterious country?"

Takashige, exercising the privilege of age, began to get worked up in front of the two of them. Sanki sensed a curious physics at work in the phenomenon that his youth, more than Takashige's story itself, continued to serve as the raw material that stirred the passions of the older man.

Nineteen

Copper coins flowed out from the seaport to the provinces. Silver coins in the seaport began to disappear. Brokers' carriages raced between Japanese and British banks. The gold market soared in response to copper and silver. Sanki's pen grew weary with calculating the conversion of British pounds. On Takashige's recommendation he had found a position in the Trade Division of Far East Cotton Mills. Next to him sat a Portuguese typist who was preparing a report on the Manchester market. On the bulletin board was a note that the American cotton market was up because of storms. The raw cotton market in Liverpool was being propped up by the Bombay futures market. The smaller speculators' markets of Kutchakhandi and Tejimandi were in turn supporting Bombay. The main responsibility of Sanki's division was to track the fluctuations in these two smaller Indian markets to determine where they should purchase raw cotton. The decision as to where to obtain resources had a great impact on the productivity of the company. Thus small markets such as Kutchakhandi and Tejimandi, which were usually overlooked, were a hidden whirlwind that could wreak havoc sometimes on the worldwide cotton market.

Sanki had been aware for some time that Indian cotton could put pressure on Chinese cotton. However, the rise of the strength of Indian cotton in the market had coincided with the rise of England in East Asia. Soon the controlling power of Asian financial markets would fall completely into the hands of the Bank of England. It was necessary to guarantee the savings of those who had prospered in China, regardless of who they were, and so China had to safeguard those institutions that secured savings. And the institutions that were the most strongly protected in this way were those like the Bank of England.

Sanki fretted about conditions in his motherland each time he considered Britain's great financial power, which bloomed from cotton plants. The motherland reflected in his eyes was a nation with an explosive population growth. A nation whose productive power relied on raw materials that it could obtain for the most part no where else but China. What about its financial power? Japan's pathetic economic power flowed into China and lost its way. And its ideas? Even as it seethed in its little boat, it was screaming out to capsize that boat.

Sanki thought that countries without natural resources were all alike, however much they tried to overturn the system. All countries gradually evolve, to be sure. Yet as long as England was not overturned, then all countries would be at a disadvantage. For that reason, first and foremost, everything would follow from India's independence. Justice would come from India. Until then, Sanki thought, Japan would have to find its own way through all the hardships in order to prevent unrest.

Until then, Sanki would have to continue exchanging Chinese currency for British pounds.

At noon he went out into the plaza to smoke a cigarette. Some female workers flooded out of the factory gate. Cotton dust drifted around their bodies like a halo as they ate noodles in front of a shop. Delicate cotton dust flitted up like a column of swarming mosquitoes above the young women, who were making a racket. Catarrh-induced coughing reverberated sharply in the bowls of steaming noodles. The women stamped and danced around hurriedly, blowing on the noodles. Earrings shimmered, ebbing and flowing amid piles of refuse.

The glass of a power plant glistened among embankments of coal that stretched on into the distance. Inside the mill, amid the rotating machines, the ideas of the Chinese labor unions calling for resistance was putting heavy pressure on Takashige and the others. Takashige and his cohorts were but a single layer of humanity with nothing more than a smile to block the intrepid workers they faced.

Sanki looked toward the river. Warships from many nations expressed the aims of their homelands by spreading out batteries of guns poised and linked together like a fortress.

Sanki considered what he should do. Kyōko was definitely coming up this river soon, like some spawning salmon trout. But so what? He had to love Japan, so what was the best thing for him to do? *First, make Japan the ruler of Asia!* So Sanki thought. Gradually, standing in the light of the sun wishing for the death of Kyōko's husband, he appeared absurdly to himself like a salmon trout.

Twenty

The cherry trees outside the dance hall began to sway with the final jazz number. Trombones and cornets swung about. Teeth were exposed from the dark skin of a band from Manila. A wave of glasses with drinks enveloped the hall. Dust settled on a grove of bonsai trees. Dancers twined around their bodies the downpour of streamers that had been strewn about. Each time his hips bumped someone else's Kōya would drunkenly murmur, "Ah excuse me, excuse me."

Some American sailors appeared at the darkened entrance of the stairs and waded into the stream of dancers. The hall gave off the aroma of the sea as it began to sway more and more furiously. As a piccolo squealed out, there was a tramping of footsteps. A song of ecstasy. Weary legs cut by the sharp edges of spinning skirts. A tri-colored spotlight flashed over the melody between legs, shoulders, and waists. Necklaces sparkled, lips turned up, legs slid among legs.

"Ah, excuse me. Excuse me."

Miyako waded through, a tide of tape clinging to her head and torso. Her eyes washed over the face of Sanki, who sat immobile in a corner of the hall. An American was holding a German. A Spaniard was holding a Russian. Portuguese bumped into people of mixed blood. A Norwegian kicked at the legs of a chair. Englishmen caused an uproar with a shower of kisses. Inebriated people from Siam, France, Italy, Bulgaria. Sanki alone, his elbows resting on the back of a chair, was staring like a frog at the voluptuousness of people of all nationalities entwined in the strands of tape.

When the dance finished people leaned on one another and slid like an avalanche out the door. The revolving doors turned each time a dancer disappeared. The lamps began to go out one by one. The legs of the chairs, upside down in rows on the tables, stood out vividly. Someone softly turned the key to the safe, while another person closed the cover on the piano, which was concealed in the shadows behind the musical instruments and slowly sinking into the darkness.

Sitting on the floor under the only lamp that remained lit, Kōya at last spoke to his own shadow. "Ah, excuse me. Excuse me."

Sanki took sharp pleasure in the exhaustion of this hall, suddenly sunk in silence. With no sign of movement, he stared at Kōya's listless, drunken body and listened to the sound of a clock. Smoke and dust drifted lightly in one corner of the ceiling and then evaporated.

Clutching a handful of scattered tape, Kōya shook his head and began singing in a low murmur.

> Casi me he caido,
> Traigame algo mas,
> No es nada no toque,

Even in song he wanted to continue drinking. Watching Kōya sing this mix of Spanish and Portuguese, which had become his recent pride, Sanki felt he had to stand up. Grabbing Kōya around his shoulders, he walked him out, staggering through the blizzard of white streamers that lay in the deathly quiet hall. A curtain rustled somewhere and a blue shaft of light suddenly flashed out from a mirror like ripples on water.

"Too bad, Kōya. Didn't Qiu-lan come? Cheer up!"

Miyako, who was preparing to go home, came over from the door and stood beside the two men. She supported one of Kōya's arms, which dangled as he walked, and said to Sanki, "Where do you plan to go?"

"I haven't thought about that yet."

"Then come to my place. It'll be dawn soon. You can stick it out there for a while."

"If you really don't mind, I'd appreciate the help."

"It doesn't bother me. Oh, he's really heavy, isn't he."

"He's always been heavy."

Miyako raised her eyebrows and spoke to Sanki over the back of Kōya's drooping neck.

"Do you have to look after him like this?"

"I guess so. But there's a reason for it. It causes me a lot of grief."

The three trudged down the stairs and out onto the street. Some rickshawmen, who had been pitching pennies on the paving stones, came running over in front of Sanki. Soon three rickshaws were hurrying along.

Twenty-One

"You look a little embarrassed. It's safe here. Relax a little. I know all about your bad luck." Miyako stretched her tired body out on a divan in the room next to where she had put Kōya to bed.

What was she insinuating? Sanki narrowed his eyes in the tobacco smoke, the tip of his nose tinted by the shadows of a reddish yellow table.

"You probably think I don't know anything about you. But for a long time I've wanted to see what kind of person you are. And tonight, meeting you for the first time, you turned out to be just as I imagined you."

Sanki wondered about the figure he had obviously been cutting for some time inside the head of this sophisticated woman. No doubt it was a tattered figure drawn as a patchwork from the images of many other men.

"Has Kōya been putting me down?"

"Yes. I've heard about you every day. The truth is, I look down on you a little because of that. After all, you're the kind of man who despises a woman like me."

"But I've only just met you."

"That doesn't matter. I can tell right away, with just a glance, what a man is thinking. That ability is my pride, so don't try to deny it. Anyway, we can discuss all that next time. It's just that I look down on you because I know that even though you love that person you don't do anything about it."

"What are you trying to say?"

"Oh, nothing. It's not my business. Why did I bring it up? Never mind. Please eat up. This is a sarsaparilla. I always have it after I dance. Otherwise I'm no good to anyone."

"So Kōya told you all about Kyōko?"

"Now look at you, making such a face. Does it really matter what Kōya says? I'm just happy that you're here. I'm not going to sleep tonight."

"You look exhausted."

"I'm usually worn to a pulp. Forgive me, acting like this. Still, if I lie down this way I can talk with you longer. I'm chattering on tonight, but if you get sleepy, please lie down in Kōya's room. I may go to sleep here like this."

"OK, do as you please. It won't tire me a bit to sit here."

"No, no, it's all right. If I start to put you to sleep, then borrow this divan. I'm only lying here because I want to keep you up. You understand, don't you? Now come on, stop staring around the room as if it were so unclean. You know what a dancer's life is like. As you see, it isn't very proper."

Miyako twirled a powerfully stimulating white orchid around in her fingertips. Its faintly rose-colored petals scattered into her drink. She took the flower vase from a round red-sandalwood table and began to mimic the vendors that appeared each morning, calling out the names of the flowers.

"Chîtsūhō, Dêdêhō, Meikaihō, Barêhō, Pârêhohhō, Mêriho! . . . It's sultry tonight. I always dream about white fruit on a night like this."

She raised her cup, now covered in white petals, and drained her drink. Arching her body, she began searching for a cigarette behind her. Her knees shifted below her turned-up robe. Her tired torso undulated as it carved out a space. The swelling of her breast was smoothed by an indolent hand.

Unawares, Sanki was swirling in his drink the calyx that had been removed from a white orchid.

"I just remembered something I wanted to show you. Right now I have five lovers, all of them equal in my mind. A Frenchman, a German, an Englishman, an American, and a Chinaman. That doesn't mean there aren't others, but for now I'm being frugal and only let them escort me arm in arm."

She held the cigarette she had just lit between her knees

84

and pulled an album out of a drawer.

"My French lover is Michel. There's the American. Take a look at the others. They're all fine specimens, and the special characteristic they share is that they're sweet as lotus fruit. They would never be attracted to your Japanese woman. That's because they've been bullied by their wives. So I pretend to be innocent and treat them as if they were important."

Sanki did not look at the faces of Miyako's lovers, but out of curiosity he shifted his seat nearer to her. She drew in her legs and said, "Come over a little closer. My lovers' faces must look completely dark from over there."

"No, I'd better not. If I see them too clearly I might get frightened."

"Suit yourself. Though you ought to look at superior faces once in a while. Do I have to scold you to get you to come closer?"

Sanki began to wonder if Kōya was being stifled by her, and he gazed into her face for some time without responding.

"I know you're jumpy and afraid of something. But please relax. The five men lined up here are my kind of lover. I could never take a lover like you. Someone who goes all pale at having his love stolen from him."

He looked at Miyako with upturned eyes. Controlling the emotions that flared up furiously at the edges of his body, he affected a smile. She put her feet up on one corner of the table across from Sanki and said, "Isn't it about time you got a little angry? I know all about the kinds of things your love is doing with her husband. That's why I think you're pathetic. Beyond help, really. My lovers are always competing to be with me. You see the rug here? And the Khurasan? Michel brought them to me. And the velvet for these cushions? My English lover came trundling in with it asking me how I like it, since it's from Usküdar, and what do I think of the Byzantine? Of course these aren't the only things. Why just yesterday, they were falling over themselves to play golf with me."

85

"I couldn't care less about such things. Could you not lift your legs up like that?"

"Oh, I put my legs up without thinking. A dancer's legs are important, but not that important. I'm sorry. When I get tired I start to do things. I guess I've really become just another dance-hall girl."

"Do you act like this when one of your lovers comes by?"

"You're making fun of me now, aren't you. Do you think my boyfriends are the type who would allow me to act this way?"

It struck Sanki that Miyako had been coming on to him. At that point he had to reconsider how foolish he himself had been. He compared Olga's legs with Miyako's. He was soon sitting beside Miyako with the album in his lap.

"So what's next?" Miyako took the album from his hands.

The ridicule dripping from her lips was palpable to Sanki. On an impulse he put his arm around her neck. Her Marseilles-style hairdo came undone and rolled onto the back of the divan. Her body emitted a wave of laughter as she slapped Sanki's face.

"So you're not above that sort of thing after all. If I let my guard down that easily, I'd be lost."

She put petals from the white orchid in her mouth, and blew them one by one into Sanki's face. The cushions, which gave the divan a shiny texture, began to slide. Her elegant Chinese slippers rose without a sound and trembled. An embroidered silver squirrel bent at their tips.

Sanki realized that he was recklessly crossing a dangerous boundary. He jumped up and looked into a mirror. He thought the reflected face was somehow vulgar. No doubt she had sniffed out the dirtiness within him. With that thought in mind he stood up straight and glared at Miyako's face.

Clutching a cushion to her side, Miyako loudly burst out laughing.

"You do nothing but fret. But there's nothing you can

do to hurt me. You're mistaken if you think I should be pitied by people like you. So come back over here. And save your fierce expressions for the mirror."

Sanki knew he was being toyed with. Knowing that his face had nowhere else to turn, he wondered about the source of his own wretched ugliness that overpowered him. He sat down beside Miyako quietly again.

"It'll be dawn soon."

"It was good of you to come. From the moment you looked at me all you could think about was how you did not want to be defeated by me. And from the first moment I saw you I thought only that it would never do to love you. I suppose it's no use. From now on all you and I can do is fight."

His heart was continuing to be dragged along. He considered the danger to his own spirit, which took priority over his flesh. He stood up and said, "I should be going now. Good-bye."

Miyako was silent, as if she had been slapped unexpectedly. Sanki started to leave the room.

"Sanki? It's dawn, and I don't want to stay here by myself. Don't you know when you're being rude?"

Sanki turned around. He stepped on the album that had fallen onto the carpet.

"I've had enough for tonight. Forgive me. I'll see you again soon."

He hurried out alone amid the greenery that was starting to lighten, exhibiting his chronic condition of running at once from anything that troubled him.

Twenty-Two

In the depths of the rainy season the tram rails were distorted by evening mist. A hooded carriage on the verge of breaking down crept like a shadow through a valley of brick buildings. A Eurasian prostitute rested against the wall of an arched gate, staring into the rainy street. Acacia flowers placed around the cover of the gas lamp in front of her were rotting and oozing. Headlights spouting fog between narrow buildings passed by carrying a drunken man who was asleep, his mouth agape.

Sanki walked by the prostitute and into the alley. At a soot-blackened bar near the back the sweetbreads he favored were simmering in a pot. The place was almost deserted. The bar's Madam stood by a miniature lamp cleaning her eyes with gauze soaked in boric acid and listening to the sound of the rain. Sanki ordered samshu and decided he would drink until Takashige arrived. Then the two were scheduled to check on the night shift at the factory. The shaved head of a Chinese man on the other side of the pot with the simmering sweetbreads remained motionless, emitting a dull sheen like a piece of Seto porcelain. The watery sound flowing from the gauze pressed against the Madam's eyes, together with the liquor, sent a chill up Sanki's spine. In front of the bar a Chinese man, smoking a pipe with his eyes closed, leaned on a brick pillar. On the tip of the needle of the pipe a toffee-colored bulb of opium trembled and gave off a sizzling sound. Pigs' feet with coarse hairs here and there thrust out cloven hooves.

"Hey!" Takashige arrived behind Sanki, greeting him out of the blue. Sanki turned around as though a rock had been thrown at him. His breathing strained, Takashige continued to stand as he talked.

"Listen, now. Someone's been following me, so I'm

counting on you. Tomorrow is going to be very dangerous. It looks like it will start tomorrow. Tonight I have to go over to the police and humor them. I feel like my head's spinning."

The strike would finally begin.

"So then you're going straight away."

"Yes, let's go." Takashige grabbed Sanki's glass and gulped down the drink.

"The strike is about to start. Once it does we'll just have to manage somehow. That's the spirit of China. It's a peculiar thing, but even though my company is about to be taken down, I'm more concerned with the photos of water buffalo I developed last night."

"If you can do your hobbies and still manage to get by, then why can't we just sit here and have a drink?"

"If you talk like that, it's all over for us. Once a strike happens at my company, other companies will fall like dominoes. I feel like I'm holding the balance of power between China and Japan in my arms. If you coax me into having a drink, you'll be committing treason."

"That may be, but I'm going to have one more."

They ordered a round, and their heads were soon bent over their drinks. Takashige rolled up one of his sleeves and sipped at his glass, glaring at the bulb of opium still trembling, ready to fall.

An insect was feasting on the liver piled on a plate. The smell of opium permeated the liquor. The sleeping shaved head with the thin dull sheen slipped off a corner of the pillar, catching on a protuberance. The man woke with a start. The miniature lamp began to make noise inside its sooty glass globe.

"I forgot to mention it to you," Takashige said. But then he furrowed his eyebrows and kept his silence. Sanki stared for a moment at Takashige's lips, which were pressed to his glass.

"Kyōko's husband died."

Sanki felt as though his heart had suddenly stopped spinning. A surge of great vigor flashed out and galloped around inside his chest. He hung his head in opposition to his emotion of joy. Then, in the next instant, he felt like a board sinking little by little.

Even if I take his place as Kyōko's husband, I have no money. I have no status. I have no abilities. The only thing I have is some shapeless feeling of love.

He interpreted Takashige's silence as a sign of pity toward him.

Then anger reared up in the pit of his stomach. He was inflamed by an act of pity that pushed aside Kyōko, Takashige's younger sister. The behavior of the women he had rejected until now for her sake came floating to his mind in confusion. Oryū, Olga, Osugi, Miyako—all of them came surging up.

"We'd better head off for the night watch. Listen to me again. Tonight is going to be dangerous. Stick beside me or you'll be done for."

Takashige got up, touching the pistol he carried in his pocket. Sanki went out behind him. At that instant he resolved to take his leave of the wasted time in which he had secretly loved the married Kyōko.

I should just go ahead and cry for joy as much as I want.

A Japanese military patrol, bugles under their arms, passed through the rain. Takashige leaned toward Sanki and whispered, "This next strike will be a big one."

"Bigger and more interesting."

"That's for sure."

They got into a rickshaw and hurried off.

Twenty-Three

A waterfall of cotton crashing from round tubes. Rollers spinning. The night shift began its work amidst a stream of cotton that soon became a torrent. A cavern of machinery and scaffolding rumbled, stirring up a breeze. Cotton dust danced and drifted up like down from flapping feathers. A vaporizer spewed out mist, which obscured the rows of belts. A huge quantity of thread formed a procession speeding past interlocking cogwheels.

Sanki followed Takashige on his rounds from the carding to the drawing sections. Mist twined around metal branches of a densely overgrown forest of steel pipes. A lumbering mountain of haphazardly stacked rollers rotated.

Sanki covered his ears against the roar that assaulted him. Currents of air twisted about and formed numerous layers that came at them out of the midst of the steel.

Cotton dust fell on Takashige's face. He pointed to some female workers nearby and said, "What do you think? They make forty-five sen a day for this."

Women huddled together, moving as a group, their shoulders covered with cotton. They seemed to be mingling, fish in a waterfall of cotton. Bobbing earrings sparkled, visible through spaces between the machines.

"In the corner over there is the slapping. And to the side . . . Look, turn this way." Takashige fell silent and looked to the side.

Among the tangled vines of pipes a chillingly attractive woman worker was glaring at Sanki. Sanki could feel in her eyes the sharpness of a drawn pistol, and he asked Takashige in a whisper, "Who's that?"

"That's Fang Qiu-lan. I told you about her recently. All she has to do is raise her right hand and the machines in this

91

factory will grind to a halt. Lately she's begun to make peace with the faction of Oryū's husband. She's really a vicious woman, a real problem."

"I understand that, but why do you let things go on like this?"

"I'm the only one who knows her identity. To tell the truth, I get a little pleasure out of the competition. At any rate, she'll end up being killed as well, so look at her while you can."

Sanki struggled with Qiu-lan's beauty, staring at her movements. Sweat and cotton began to trickle down his neck. Gloves smeared with oil came squeezing out from under some spinning shafts and flapped between Sanki's shoes. Takashige tapped Sanki on the shoulder and spoke to him in Chinese. "The wages in this factory are higher than in other foreign companies. In spite of that they're demanding a ten percent raise. You see the problems I've got?"

Sanki nodded, getting a sense of Takashige's difficulties. Takashige had spoken to Sanki, but of course he was really speaking to the female workers around him. Then he turned to Sanki again and spoke forcefully in Japanese.

"When you make the rounds of this plant, sharpness and clarity are forbidden. Your only weapon is a splendidly obscure nihilism. Get it? Might makes right. You win and you're the government army. Lose and you're the rebel army. That's what drives things around here."

The two men came round from the drawing section to the scutcher. Sikh policemen, their turbans lined in a row, were concealed amid the cotton stacked up in the hallway.

"There are a lot of dangerous people in this section, so keep your hand on your pistol."

The impassive faces of male workers flowed in and out among sets of handles that formed an arc. The swell of cotton was a raging billow that bit at and shook the machines.

With the cotton swirling about him, Sanki came back to the question that was always on his mind. *Was this a factory for the sake of production or the sake of consumption?* This idea fluttered about like an exhausted moth between two dynamic, rotating powers. He had sympathy for the Chinese workers. Still, if as a result of that sympathy the natural resources buried beneath China were allowed to remain untapped, there would be no advances in production, no possibility for increasing consumption. For the sake of progress capitalism employs all methods to extract natural resources. And if workers hate the expansion of capital, then they must be resisted at all cost.

Sanki grasped the handle of his pistol and looked around at the workers. The following occurred to him suddenly. *If Japan did not use these Chinese workers, then certainly Britain and America would step in and use them. And if the British and Americans employed Chinese workers, Japan would inevitably be used for their benefit as well.*

Sanki recalled a telegram from Lancashire that arrived at the management division today. A meeting of manufacturers had convened in Lancashire to construct a policy for promoting British cotton. The result was that a group of Manchester manufacturers, in cooperation with Lancashire, had demanded that the government raise the tariff on the importation of cotton cloth to India.

Sanki knew what this mercantile activity in England meant. Obviously it would put pressure on Japanese cotton mills. The British were deeply concerned that the development of Japanese capital in China would steadily assail the largest market for British goods—that is, for Lancashire-produced goods—in India. And now a wave of Marxism had arisen in China among the workers in the Japanese mills. Japan's capital was under attack from both sides. Gloating American faces appeared in Sanki's mind. Then the faces of Russians rejoicing even more. The fall of laissez-faire and the rise of Marxism. And Japan, like an insect, was flying between these two currents. For Sanki there was nothing else to do about this now except wander around with his hand on a pistol. In this contemplative state the only thing he would be able to aim at and hit was the sky over his head. However, the danger closed in on him only so long as he was in this factory. So why did he have to undertake this useless adventure? For the sake of the older brother of the woman he loved. Each time he looked at Takashige's shoulder, he proceeded a step forward trembling at the unpleasantness forced on him by Takashige.

A hallway facing the river to the south suddenly turned bright red. Takashige whirled around as the window panes shattered in succession.

"Rioters!" shouted Takashige, sprinting off to the carding section.

Sanki raced after him. The light bulbs had all been smashed in the carding section and the female workers were wailing. Lapboard, shaped like truncheons, was flying about. Hemmed in by the machinery, a group of women turned round and round in confusion. A policeman's whistle continually punctuated the wailing.

Sanki watched a large, powerful Chinese man running wild among the trembling women. He was waving a white pennant as he threw a top roller into the machinery. A Sikh policeman sprang at the man from behind and as they toppled to the side, his turban fell off. A crowd of women came rushing headlong toward the exit. Jostling through two narrow doors, they jammed together and were caught. As bulbs were smashed, the lights went out one by one. In place of the electric lights the fire from burning cotton that had fallen in the hallway shone through the shattered windows. The scaffolding on the rollers, surrounded by groups of people grappling hand-to-hand, gleamed and flickered. Sanki looked around for Takashige from the hallway windows. People's mouths seemed to burst open among the mingled stripes of lights and shadows. Clumps of cotton flitted over the confusion of heads. Stones struck meters and spewed out glass. When the needle cloth on the carding machine ripped, needles came raining down from limply waving bags. The crying of the women rose in crescendo. As people fled amid the shower of needles, heads collided with heads. Mist billowed out from the vaporizers and into the stirring stream of humanity.

When the women who had fled into the hallway saw the flames of the burning cotton in front of them, they turned and rushed in Sanki's direction. The crowd pushing out and the crowd pushing back in collided. In the whirl of women workers he caught a glimpse of Fang Qiu-lan's face. If this riot had been started by the workers' group, why did she look so exhausted? Sanki concluded that this was definitely an unexpected invasion by outside agitators.

Sanki stood along the wall of the corridor as he watched Qiu-lan, who was now close to him. The women workers who engulfed Sanki once more ran into a group pouring in from another entrance. Sanki felt himself squeezed amid the scent of hair as the women ran into each other. Staggering, his eyes followed Qiu-lan. She was shouting as she rose and sank among the faces, strained from wailing, that floated around her. He tried to make for the center of the whirlpool to get closer to her. The fire had spread from the cotton to the roof of the corridor. A throng of women, having no other outlet, crashed into the steel door of the emergency exit. The door repelled the crowd, sending it shaking backward toward the roof in flames. Sanki sensed the danger to himself. He fled the whirl of people and tried to go back to the riot inside the factory. However, his hands could not force their way through all the shoulders packed together. Each time he heard a groan behind him, someone would claw at his head. Thin clothing soaked in sticky sweat clung together. He searched again for Qiu-lan. Atop waves of disheveled hair spinning about, one adorning flower spun round madly in the opposite direction. Her earrings glinted in the flames and roiled like fish leaping up and turning on their bellies. The crowd again overwhelmed him as it turned back again. He felt as though a pendulum was swinging wildly against his body. One edge of the whirlpool in front of him collapsed. A line of people fell like dominoes into the hollowed-out space opened by the collapse. A new whirlpool formed and began to run mad. Bodies jumped up and slipped in among the crowd of backs. Backs fell on top of backs that were trying to get up. From the edge of a wave that had collapsed in front of him, Sanki spied Fang Qiu-lan's face adrift. He inched forward over slackened backs and stretched out toward her. His chin ended up on her shoulder. The overpowering tremors of the crowd caused his body to list like a ship. He could not resist the pressure coming from behind him and slipped diagonally between shoulders. Right after that Qiu-lan began to fall. He tried to get up, holding onto her. But someone fell on top of them. He was kicked in the head. Aiming for a space among the oscillating bodies, he felt himself sinking. He took Qiu-lan in his arms. But his arms were pinned in among feet. Shoes were thrust under his sides. Yet for Sanki, the riot behind his back had now passed. Like shellfish sunk to the bottom of the ocean, they had to wait until they could drift up from the depths of this ocean of people. He flinched as he fought the pain. Qiu-lan's hand was writhing at his stomach. His consciousness was turned toward her, moving like a needle in a world where sound had stopped. When the emergency exit finally opened, the swirl of female workers made a rush for the open space. Heads that had fallen got up one by one. Sanki got to his knees, trying to stand. Qiu-lan had grabbed onto his jacket and was screaming, "My leg! My leg!" He picked her up and dashed out into the square.

Twenty-Four

Sanki awoke in a room next to Qiu-lan's. Smoking a cigarette, he gazed down from the window. At an intersection basking in the morning sun, ivory cages containing small birds were stacked up to the eaves on both sides. The street of bird cages curved sharply, forming an aviary tunnel. Vendors lined up to the right of the intersection. Chinese in their spring clothes circulated around the street, carrying flowers and making their way through the ivory cages. The street wound around, following a stream as calm as listening to the sounds of whistling birds, and came to a focus at a pond in the center of the district.

Sanki had forgotten why the course of events from last night had brought him to this point. He had simply run along through the rain as Qiu-lan had instructed him. He had raced into a doctor's clinic. Although she had suffered only some minor scrapes on her leg and a muscle pull, he nonetheless put her into a rickshaw and brought her here. He had said, "Please let it take you as far as your house. Don't worry about it."

It occurred to him that being chivalrous to her was his best chance to rid himself of his thoughts of Kyōko. *Hadn't his prudence led to nothing but tragedy in the past?* Stirring himself, he followed Qiu-lan into her place. However, his joy had already proceeded him inside those walls. She pointed to the guest room and said, "Please stay here. This room is empty."

His ardor sprang not so much from his gallantry as from her eyes. She continued, "Please, take that room. I'd rather you not see this one."

"Perhaps I should be going."

"No, please. I'd like you to stay here awhile. Besides, this is a Chinese street. If you go home at this time of night I'd have to go with you."

Running away from something he desired was now an ingrained habit for him. A sail drifted by, fully hoisted. Sensing in the sound of his own steps a reverberation of evil, he went into the room next to hers and raised the curtain. Then he went to sleep, wondering how long it would take before he began to feel contempt at himself for waiting for Qiu-lan to lose her feelings of enmity.

Now it was morning.

The elegant shape of a pavilion in the middle of the pond curved like a Western-style umbrella. The porcelain steps of the pavilion were inlaid with mirrors that glittered on the surface of the water. The railing of a delicate bridge filled with people arched over the surface of the pond teeming with carp. A stream of people, as in a festival, came pouring out slowly under a gilded sign.

Sanki watched as the thin fog that trailed over the people lifted, and he felt the time had come to take his leave of Qiulan. He rustled the drop curtain to her room. She was wearing an old-fashioned aquamarine dress and opening a letter on a red-sandalwood chair. They greeted each other, and she told him that the pain in her leg was better and thanked him. "If you hadn't been with me last night . . ." She then told him that she was glad to have found a foreign friend, and would take him to a local restaurant for breakfast.

"But what about your leg?"

"It's all right now. We Chinese would rather not show our weaknesses to the Japanese."

As if to encourage him, Qiu-lan went out first. They went down to street level, where the narrow roads of stone paving wound around like a maze. The signs and banners above their heads blocked the sunlight. A forest of bent ivory was arrayed in the shops beneath the signs and banners. Sanki enjoyed walking down a street with no other foreigners. The white liquid produced by polishing ivory ran along the cracks of the stone paving. Turning the corner, they came upon a row of shops filled with jade, which was also hidden beneath the signs. In among the jade stacked high on plates, a man with diseased eyes was turning his face blankly toward the light.

Watching a worker wash the tips of his fingers with the dust of polished ivory, Sanki said, "Isn't there somewhere you should be hurrying off to now?"

She stared at him as though she were trying to fathom the hidden meaning of his words. "No, not today. Not with this foot."

"But since you've come this far, you should be able to go anywhere. Please don't put yourself out for me."

Sanki pretended to be ignorant of Qiu-lan's identity. He turned his gaze toward a shop where wind chimes were softly ringing. She glanced at his profile for a second, then blushed gently like someone whose weakness had been discovered. "You know exactly what kind of woman I am, don't you."

"Yes, I know."

She laughed quietly. He said, "I believe the riot last night was instigated from the outside. If you had anticipated it, there wouldn't have been so much turmoil."

"You're right. It was completely unexpected. We had hoped for that to happen in a Japanese factory. But we didn't plan the riot ourselves, so I think it inconvenienced the Japanese, like it did me."

He smiled. "Please, trouble us whenever you like."

She shivered and flashed a toothy grin. Sanki suddenly grew melancholy. *What am I after? Isn't chasing after her like a thief looting after a fire? Isn't the fact that I accompanied her a sign of my own baseness?* Still, when he toted up the balance sheet of all his introspection it was enough for now that he could be distracted by the pleasure of wandering among the sights of a Chinese street with a Chinese lady. *Apart from that . . . No, it wouldn't do to think about it.*

Chinese shoes decorated in jade and silver were perched on the shop fronts like small birds huddled together. Ivory combs, pipes, and opium jars were stacked under the eaves to overflow-ing. Ink sticks formed a little stone fence under a mountain of ink pads crammed against a wall. The sound of camphor wood being split reverberated from various shops that carved Buddhist statuary. Necklace vendors, pounding with a crunch on their gemstones, could be glimpsed between shoulders. Sanki looked at Qiu-lan. Her aquamarine dress swayed pliantly among the Chinese fans arrayed in the shops like feathers spread open. They climbed the smooth tile steps of a restaurant. He held her arm when she tottered, and she laughed, "It looks as though I am still putting you out."

"It's my pleasure."

"I'm sure you're amazed that I can be a worker even though I'm injured."

"You already have my admiration."

"Even so, I'm really pretty hopeless still. No matter how much I swagger, I can't help wanting to wear these beautiful clothes."

As they went up the steps Sanki felt happy that he had touched the delicate anguish of this Chinese lady. Her smiling face appeared at each step in the mirrors inlaid in the tile risers, changing from moment to moment as if he were watching a film of her. Then he was reminded of Takashige's words: "Even she may be killed, just wait and see."

The film broke with a snap and the chillingly attractive, smiling face disappeared. There was a balustrade of green tile at the top of the steps that was overgrown with white orchids.

"If my being with you is a problem, don't hesitate to say so."

"You're the one who shouldn't hesitate to speak up. I can't think of you as Japanese. Of course we have to struggle against Japanese factories, but I can't think of it as struggling against you personally."

Sanki sat on an ebony chair now suddenly aware of the Japanese man floating up within himself—a man with feelings of love for her. He became melancholy again. Hadn't he rejected Kyōko because he had thrown his life into turmoil for her sake? Wasn't he now doting on Qiu-lan because he had rejected Kyōko and fled? Now he was beginning to feel confused on account of Qiu-lan, to whom he had run. He was beginning to lose track of where he was. Striking a defensive posture, as though he were backing away, he turned to Qiu-lan and began to speak.

"I'm grateful that you don't think of me as Japanese. But to tell you the truth, I don't think being Japanese is anything to regret. I'm Japanese enough that, unlike a Marxist, I can't think of myself as a citizen of the world. It sounds like you Marxists assume that the speed of cultural development is the same for both the East and the West. I can't help thinking that the only product of that error will be the appearance of a superior breed of victims."

Qiu-lan's smile froze, and she faced him as if she were drawing a sword. "We have made many errors up to now, but I still believe there is a way to apply Marxism that fits the resources and culture of each nation. Rather than concentrate our strength on fighting factories run by Chinese, it is natural that we move first in a more forceful way to confront factories run by foreigners."

"Aren't you just creating a new Chinese-style capitalism? The more you put pressure on the productive capabilities of foreign companies, the more you promote Chinese capitalism."

"For now we have to tacitly accept that fact of life. It's natural to fear foreign capitalism more than Chinese capitalism."

Sanki felt his attraction to Qiu-lan fade. He shook his head more and more and wanted to cut deeply. "Of course, I feel that it's unfortunate you chose a Japanese factory. I love Japan. But I can't agree with you that your struggle will automatically become a struggle between Japan and China."

"That's because you're an Asianist. To us it's time to atone for Asianists who have been serving the interests of the bourgeoisie in your country. We can't count on anyone other than Marxists."

"It's too bad that you lump me in with your notion of Asianists. My regard for Japan is no different from your regard for China. After all, it's a little annoying to have my patriotism construed as a love of the bourgeoisie. I don't see any reason now why I should not love my country, but love China instead."

"I don't think you really love your country. You just make an ally of it. If you truly loved your country, then you'd love its proletariat. Our resistance to Japan is not aimed at it's proletariat. So when I talk about these things, what I mean is . . ."

"If the people of China strike out against the bourgeoisie of Japan, to my mind that's the same as bullying Japan's proletariat."

Qiu-lan's eyes flashed, as though bursting with the ideology she had been spewing out.

"Why is that? We believe we have to liberate China for the sake of Japan's proletariat."

"And what if the age of the proletariat doesn't arrive in Japan?"

"We're resisting Japan's bourgeoisie in order to bring about the age of the proletariat in your country."

"And what if the age of the proletariat doesn't arrive all at the same time, even in China?"

"But aren't we constantly working to bring that about? In the first place we're devising ways to stir up grievances in your plant. It may be that something is going on right now. So please, for the sake of your own country, I'm asking your indulgence for a time."

She lowered her head. Then a new question arose within Sanki like a cloud. "As I said, I don't know how to respond to your plan to shut down the machinery in our factory. The only result of expelling foreign capital from China that I can see is that Chinese culture will continue to lag far behind other countries. I know that my words are very rude, but I'd like to hear from you, as a ranking Communist, about this real, objective problem, since China has the greatest need for foreign capital."

Qiu-lan, looking proud that she had the opportunity to display her quick wits, lightly spread open her Chinese fan and smiled.

"Yes, that's a crucial problem. At the same time it isn't a problem to be resolved by the people of the International Settlement, which is, after all, the dumping ground for the bourgeoisie of the Great Powers. I know it's also rude of me to speak in this manner, but you believe, don't you, that there are ideologies other than ours that will provide a means of escape from the military power of every nation that pours into China."

When she voiced her resistance to this "dumping ground" he disagreed and shook his head as he had done earlier. *The problem isn't that it's a dumping ground. The problem is the morals of this dumping ground.*

The reality was that all countries were starting to decay, and the key to revival could definitely be found in the dumping ground of the joint concessions that made up this colony. Sanki stretched out over the steam of the soup that had just been brought to them, and smiled. "For some strange reason my mind has always had a tendency to go a little dull when I have respect and affection for the person I'm talking to. Please don't be offended."

For the first time the elegant beauty of a model Chinese lady came flowing like perfume from the collar of Qiu-lan's dress.

"I'd rather not have such a serious conversation with you today. I ought to entertain you in a more cheerful way."

"It's enough to have been called an Asianist by you."

"Oh?" She raised her beautiful eyes and stopped fanning.

"At first I didn't look after you out of some admirable intention. If that had been the case, I expect I would have been moved in the same way by the plight of others besides you. My actions were stirred by looking at you, and so I was driven by motives antagonistic to Marxism. In any case, the reason I've spoken so freely about my true feelings is that I doubt if you'll want to see me again. So for today I'll say good-bye."

Sanki descended the smooth tile steps, exhausted by a pride resembling that of a religious adherent who has finished a confession. Qiu-lan tossed her fan onto the surface of the round ebony table. It landed with a thud.

Twenty-Five

The crumbling entrance to the slum faced out onto the river. Garbage was strewn about. Osugi walked by on her way to Sanki's place, hoping to find him there. Once the shadows disappeared into the twilight, Osugi's makeup grew pale. Fog flowed over the mud. A long, pitch-black casket threaded its way among the hollows in the garbage. Next to a used shoe store, spread out on the flats of the riverbank, an infant who would be sold was peeking into the dark bottom of a shoe.

Osugi spotted Sanki's figure among an oily knot of coolies hauling cargo.

She spun around, flustered, and headed in the other direction. But there was nothing for her to be upset about. During the ten days since she had left his house, it was natural that she should have picked up the judgment that would allow her to read a man's secrets. And yet . . . Suddenly her breathing became agitated there in the twilight. Feeling the arms that would strike the chest of the cold-hearted Sanki the next time they met, it was natural to feel a sense of triumph, but even so Osugi's back began to tighten behind her breasts. Forgetting now about the many, many crowds of men, she was beside herself. A trained monkey, exhausted from dancing, was staring at a banana peel in a canal. An old woman with teeth missing came out of the slum after having had a rotten tooth extracted. She sat down on the edge of a boat and began licking a copper coin.

Sanki followed the riverbank and came up close behind Osugi. However, he did not notice her, since she was facing away from him. The two were walking parallel, then Osugi, against her intentions, looked down at the fog-shrouded river. Excrement that had been dumped out somewhere was floating turgidly on the surface of the water in among the boats that filled the river. Sanki passed her. She thought that she would walk behind him as far as his house. Then the lewdness of the past ten days, which Sanki knew nothing about, assaulted her gentle spirit.

Osugi felt there was a dignity in the space between their bodies. Her made-up face drooped heavily. Her hopes had been worn down by the time she had spent walking. Her feelings of love, entangled with Sanki's retreating figure, began simply to sink. She called over a passing rickshaw and hurried ahead of Sanki.

He saw Osugi quietly bowing and swaying on the rickshaw. For an instant he stood stiffly, feeling the fresh air slice through him. He called a rickshaw and had it follow her. However, he did not know why he should chase after Osugi. Assaulted by homesickness, which flared in him unexpectedly with the exhaustion of early evening, he shrank back again. Black rotting stakes stood out indistinctly from black bubbles along the bank of a canal. A wall at the intersection of two old streets obstructed the rickshaws, which then went their separate ways right and left.

Osugi got off in a street bustling with people. She headed toward the entrance to an alley and tapped on the shoulder of a passing Chinese man.

"Want to come with me?"

Steam rising from the mouth of a jar at a stall selling hot water coiled around the manes of the horses in a carriage stable. A string of fresh-looking white bait sparkled amid the depths of a ravine of dried foods that looked like firewood hanging down.

Twenty-Six

Sanki took his meal in front of a cracked mirror. A telephone that hadn't heard the sound of a human voice for some time was hanging on the wall, along with a calendar that was peeling and forgotten, its numbers bleached and faint. Sitting under some irises bent and withering in their vase, he tried to forget about Qiu-lan. Dangling his arms at the side of his chair, he closed his eyes and experienced a life simply focused on the aroma of food that wafted from the entry of a stairway. His hopes. After seeing Fang Qiu-lan, his hopes had all disappeared. As if he were staring into water, he searched for his own death mask in the silence around him.

A Japanese waitress, who looked utterly bored, came up the stairs coquettishly imitating an aristocratic lady. On the pavement visible from the window he could see bluebottle flies swarming like a mustache around the mouth of a girl chewing on a pork bone. A British army band sped past at eaves-level on a truck. A group of bare-footed rickshawmen, illuminated by the fire of burning tar, came through the smoke, breaking it up. He noticed in the twilight the bubbles of cider rising stealthily to the surface of the bottle on the edge of the round table in front of him.

How interesting. At that moment the bubbles reminded him of the circumstances at his company. The thought flickered in his mind together with an image of Fang Qiu-lan. This was no ordinary strike. As Qiu-lan had said, it would progress further and further. The strike was a turning point, pregnant with the danger that it would lead to a conflict between nations. He grabbed the bottle and shook it. The bubbles had the power to rise and explode because of the pressure of the carbonated water. He drew a picture in his mind of a series of vertical cross-sections. The capacity for unity among the Chinese workers, which Qiu-lan and others were leading, would start at the bottom of his company, break through the council of foremen who worked under Takashige, burst through the council of managers, destroy the council of division heads, and rush up to top management. The demands of the workers would be rejected by top management. The Shanghai General Labor Union would act, and under their orders the workers would walk out. Then a larger strike would begin and all Japanese textile mills in Shanghai would begin to suffer from its spreading flames. Soon a boycott of Japanese currency would take place. No doubt British and American companies, in order to expand their own markets in China, would join with the many churches that extended like a network to fan the flames of Chinese unity.

And Russia?

Russia would no doubt continue to try to fan the flames burning the markets won by Britain and America behind their backs. Sanki imagined the huge unprecedented riot that would cause a stir in the center of the International Settlement. If Fang Qiu-lan were killed, it would happen during that riot. She would likely lose her life at the hands of Chinese mercenaries who danced on strings pulled by capitalists in England and America.

The huge vortex of Asia did not appear enormous to Sanki. Instead it was, for him, a map folded up inside his head. He gazed at the dry loose ring around the leaves of the cigar he held in his fingers, and wondered if reality for him was this dried cigar or the map inside his head?

Twenty-Seven

When Kōya arrived Sanki felt free, as though he had escaped the phantom of Fang Qiu-lan, which had assaulted him since the previous evening. Sanki said, "Your face looks bright. Just like some kind of beast."

Kōya raised his stick and laughed as he swatted Sanki. "Does this make me bestial? After last night, I'm not used to being human. I've schemed to do all sorts of bad things, but if you're going to be really evil, you have to become human first."

Kōya sighed and leaned close to Sanki. "How's it going? Aren't my rivals all stupidly dispirited by now?"

"Dispirited? I don't know. Me, I'm done for. I've been infected with Marxism."

Kōya jumped away from Sanki and mockingly raised his eyebrows.

"Infected?"

"Infected."

"You're worse than a beast. You live only for human misfortune. What can you do for someone who's tasted misfortune? Being unhappy doesn't do any good."

"If people like you really understood human misery, there'd be no Marxism. Marxism is just a way to make people feel happy."

"That's nonsense. Happiness exists because there are unfortunate people. Who are we to make the unfortunate happy? If people make someone else suffer, that's OK. If I don't look after myself, who's going to do it for me? Let's go. Tonight I'm going to a place where there's a goddess. I'm counting on you to be resolute."

The two went down the stairs. There were blood stains on the paving stones in the narrow space between the walls. On the floor of the deserted garden exit a Chinese man had collapsed where he had been attacked. They stood still. Blood continued to ooze out silently around the blue carvings on a Spanish knife that had fallen to the ground. Kōya stepped over the corpse and went on out. He said to Sanki, "What a terrible nuisance. I wonder what his problem was. Marxism?"

The strength of Kōya's vanity gave Sanki a strangely agreeable feeling.

"You're saying that's how you'll defeat Marxism?"

"That's right. If you make a problem out of a single corpse, it's only because you've been infected by the Marxist bug. We're a little different race from those simpletons who think the profits of capitalists cause a decline in purchasing power. Marxists are always forgetting the dialectic that machines go on to produce machines. They place a lot of value on primitive machinery, but the progress of capitalism will not crumble. Anyway, let's get out of here. They might think we murdered that guy."

Kōya stopped a rickshaw and selfishly left Sanki behind.

"I'm going to the Turkish Bath! Bye!"

Now that he was alone, Sanki was assailed by the illusion that the shadow of a person seemed to be rising from his legs, which had just stepped over the dead man. He turned into an alley at a corner where sugar cane was stacked up like a grove. A peepshow of naked Russian dancers flickered in the dark space between the buildings. To shake off his memory of the color of blood he bought a ticket and crouched in a corner of the room. Before him a naked troupe of dancers from the old Russian aristocracy was expanding and contracting like some exquisite curtain. Beyond the dancers, in the surface of mirrors that enclosed them on three sides, numberless factories of skin spread out infinitely. The geraniums the dancers held in their mouths seemed to exfoliate from their skin, flowing to a bright crimson among the turning fleshy pleats.

Sanki now saw in the twilight corner of this street a

110

new aspect in the development of human degradation. These people no longer felt carnal desire. They laughed in high spirits in order to train for a new life as humans who would be habitually depraved. An architecture of skin. A dance of nihilism. Our precursors. Weren't they truly emitting a bright, living light? *Banzai!* Sanki involuntarily raised his glass to toast them. The factory of skin extended and contracted, then transformed into an arched tunnel. A Chinaman with a shaved head covered in oil stuck out his tongue and started to crawl inside the tunnel like a camel. A flower garden filled with figs was reflected at a slant on the bluish skin of his head, which glistened from the oil. If you didn't look up at the world and everything in it from below, then its beautiful cinematic spectacle would be lost. The tunnel started to collapse. Sanki glanced behind him. He saw a beast stuck hard like the suckers of an octopus on the faces of a crowd of onlookers clustered together. From among the wave of clothing that buoyed up that huge beast, he came to appreciate the architecture of a barbarous civilization.

Twenty-Eight

Kōya's body grew puffy in the steam of the Turkish Bath. Soap bubbles dripped from Oryū's body as she finished massaging her customer. The tiger-striped spider tattoo came drifting out of the steam, damply changing color to a pale red. Kōya stroked a leg of the spider with one hand.

"Why did you fire Osugi?"

"Osugi? She was no good. You haven't heard about the place she hangs out at, have you? 13-8 Shisenro, Minagawa."

"You mean a place she has to hang out at?"

"Yes, of course."

"Then you're responsible for that, aren't you."

"I should be thanked for making a woman of her."

Bitch. Suddenly the lather on Oryū's tattoo gave off a venomous brilliance. He wondered, just who was washing whom?

"Are you washing me, or your spider?"

"What a thing to say! Have I ever had any thanks from you?"

"But that's why I asked. It looks like I've been hired by you."

She slapped Kōya's cheek with her open hand. He drew back and kicked at her. As steam billowed out with a hiss the usual tussle began.

Kōya recalled the face of Fang Qiu-lan, who he had seen at the Saracen.

"Tell me, Madam, does a Chinese lady named Fang Qiu-lan ever come to your house? I heard about her from Yamaguchi the other day."

"Fang Qiu-lan? Oh, she comes to visit my husband. He's always talking to her."

"So she's an enemy?"

"Perhaps, but only because she's an enemy of people with money."

"Then she's dangerous, isn't she. I was really smitten by her recently and was thinking of asking your husband to introduce us. Is that out of bounds?"

"Of course it is. She comes here secretly."

"In that case is it unreasonable to do it secretly? No matter what, I really want to meet her."

Oryū quietly gave him a sharp pinch. "OK, come up discreetly to the second floor. I'll call for you."

"Madam? It's your husband." One of the bath girls called in a fluster outside the door. Oryū turned on the shower, and water began to pour over Kōya's head.

"Madam? Your husband . . ."

"I heard you already!"

"Are you all right?" Kōya stuck his face out of the shower and looked at Oryū.

"Don't worry. He likes to put me in these situations, which is why I have to carry on like this. But this place is ideal for me. I've already told my husband about you. By the way, he says he'd like to meet you. Why don't you come up later on tonight? He wants to hear stories about Singapore."

Some time passed after she left, but eventually Kōya was called out to the balcony off the husband's room. He went up the stairs. A Xian-shou pattern of eighteenth-century Ch'ing appeared in the inlay on the walls surrounding him. He was mulling over ways he could sell lumber to Oryū's husband, Qian Shi-shan, who was an important businessman. He glanced in where a maid was pointing.

"Fine evening of moonlight. Politely receiving guests."

Reading the inscription on a scroll hanging on a pillar at the front of the room, Kōya recalled the color of the spider on Oryū's back. He entered. Oryū was resting her elbows on a carved square, eight-person table, cracking watermelon seeds and laughing across from a hunchback man. Some large, heavy-looking peonies were lined up on red-sandalwood chairs along a side wall, their scentless petals wilting tiredly.

"Please come in. I hear you've come from Singapore. Even though I'm an experienced businessman, I like you Japanese so much that I've had nothing but losses this year."

Qian Shi-shan's hunchback quivered with laughter in among the peonies. Kōya said, "Since your wife is in the habit of making a fool of me, it's hard to come to such an exalted place."

Oryū flicked a watermelon seed at him and peered into her husband's face. "Just listen to him. He's that kind of person, so watch your step."

"Oh, I don't know about that. Youth is interesting. Singapore must be hot, no? I've been hearing about the successes of your countrymen there for some time. How are things going these days?"

"Whatever you've heard, we're still no match for Western capital. On top of that, the place is filled with Chinese merchants. There's not much room for those of us with only a little capital."

"But the activities of the Japanese have been very lively of late. Are you in rubber plantations?"

"No, I'm in lumber. But it's the same with rubber. Westerners invest in their plantations through debentures or stocks at very low interest rates. In Japan's case prime costs are high. Even currency funds have a high interest rate. Now that we have laws regulating the use of dividend reserves we can't compete with the Westerners' plantations at all."

"Hmm, hmm. Japan does seem to have been hurt by China's exclusion of its currency. If you don't break into the markets in Southeast Asia, then your government's policies will shift directions, like a weathervane. That reminds me, four Japanese cotton mills collapsed under the strike today."

Qian Shi-shan became supercilious and started to laugh

as if he had seen through Japan's weakness. Kōya forgot about the lumber he wanted to sell and turned his thoughts to the weakness of the Chinese people.

"Well, things aren't so good for Japan now, but the Chinese in Malay and Siam are also in considerable difficulty these days. Chinese Communists have infiltrated the Chinese community in Singapore and have joined with the Russian-led movement to expel the British. That's why the British are abandoning their policy of protecting the Chinese there."

"The policy's changing gradually, but if it's abandoned without taking the Chinese into consideration, there will be no way to enforce it and the British won't be able to do anything. I have an acquaintance who admires the superiority of the British in Singapore. He says that the British have been more successful in Singapore than in other countries because they make use of young men who have been trained thoroughly in the language, customs, and capacities of the Chinese. That's something other foreigners can't do very well."

"True, that's the strength of the British. Even I admire them on that point. But the good relations and unity between Britain and China on the Malay peninsula sacrifices the peace and order of East Asia for the sake of Europe. There's nothing that makes the Europeans happier. All the same, the movement to expel the British has gained momentum among the Chinese, even though not one of those Chinese recognizes that expelling the British is the same as expelling the Chinese. What do you think? Chinese have held real economic power in Malaysia, Siam, and Indochina for a very long time. That means the invasion of Malaysia, Siam, and Burma by the Communist movement is tantamount to urging the native peoples to resist the Chinese, who hold economic power in their hands, even though the Communists are led by Chinese people."

"I see. Well, that's not something we haven't considered," said Qian Shi-shan. He was a little flustered, spitting out a tea leaf stuck to his lip as though he had been taken by sur-

115

prise. "Nonetheless, we Chinese have to promote Chinese production by Chinese hands above all else. If we don't, then banks in Japan and China will never be able to shed British control. To accomplish that we may have to temporarily borrow Russian hands, otherwise the coast of Asia, from India to here, will be European."

Noticing that Qian had said what he was going to say, Kōya stroked the corner of the table as though he were about to take a step forward. "I agree with you completely. The Malay Chinese express their disapproval of imperialism in their own country and so they pour money into the Communist movement on a large scale. But I think that's the same as pouring money into the anti-Chinese movement of the native people who are at the feet of the Chinese. I was truly impressed by the courage of the Chinese there. As soon as the Communist movement gains momentum in Malaysia, Siam, and Burma, it will evolve into a nationalist movement. And there's never been a case where a nationalist movement has weakened. Conversely, as that movement flourishes, the Chinese in Malaysia and Indochina will end up helplessly watching their livelihoods disappear. And to prevent that they will have no choice but to join with the British and French governments. The cooperation of the Chinese and British in Malaysia is convenient only for the Europeans, who will brandish their authority all the more in China proper or in India. That's why the Malay Chinese are now acting as East Asia's safety valve."

Qian at last seemed to have grasped that the political tactics of the Chinese were being attacked in a roundabout way. Hurriedly sipping his tea, he said, "There is nothing inconvenient about the Chinese holding economic power in Malaysia, Indochina, and the Philippines. It's simply a historical matter. All these countries were originally vassal states of China. The Chinese improved living standards in its tributary states, and are not at all unreasonable like the Europeans."

Kōya recognized the familiar refrain that Qian had fallen

back on, and in it he could feel the pride of the Chinese. All right then, he thought, picking up his scalpel. "Of course, they've been far from unreasonable. If there were no Chinese, then the progress of culture would be far less advanced than it is now in Micronesia, the Philippines, America, Siberia, Africa, Australia. The Chinese are far ahead of other races when it comes to laying railroads, digging in mines, and farming the land. In fact, they have been so active that everyone has forgotten them and all the benefits they brought. Only intellectuals understand that the world revolves around China. That's why the world is ganging up on the Chinese and fighting them. After all, the Chinese are the most populous race on earth. Being the most populous means that they consume the most food and clothing. It follows that the race that consumes the most food and clothing is by necessity the center of the world. That's why China, which controls the most people, must be considered an enemy no less dangerous to all nations than England and America, which control the banks. That's the burden of the Chinese, and you must accept it proudly."

Kōya's rhetoric grew more sarcastic as he set forth this new interpretation of China. Qian thrust out his elbows as though they were being pushed out by the hump on his back and stared into Kōya's face.

Kōya felt his words had finally grabbed Qian's attention. Increasingly worked up, he rubbed the oil on his fingertips into the mane of the Chinese lion carved into the table, then glanced over at Oryū. She spit the husk of a watermelon seed on the floor and snickered, her thick nostrils twitching as if to say "What kind of rubbish are you talking?"

Surprised, Kōya grew cool as he turned toward her and said, as if to kick her, "I came here, Madam, because I wanted your husband to buy lumber. But that doesn't matter right now. Your husband is the first Chinese person who appreciates my research interests. In reality the intermingling of Chinese, British, and Japanese in Malaysia will have a deep bearing on the coming upheavals in Shanghai. It's certainly the case that we will not be as idle as we have up to now. Qian here knows that better than anyone."

"This all means nothing to me. It's a waste of time to think about it," Oryū kicked back. Kōya again thought of Fang Qiu-lan, just as he had done earlier in the steam bath. He shifted his gaze to Qian and said, "Mr. Qian, the other day I caught a glimpse at a dance hall of a woman named Fang Qiu-lan. According to an Asianist friend of mine she's an Amazon for the Communists. Is that true?"

"Yes, that's who she is. I've met her only once or twice. She's really rather strange."

"I'd like to meet her. I'm sure that organizations like the *Lin tui qian* and the *Huang zhoung han* back in Singapore are sending support money to her group to back the recent disturbances. The money sent to China from the Chinese in Southeast Asia amounts to billions of yuan each year. At least a tenth of that is used to fund the Communist party, so of course the Bank of England frowns on it. When it comes right down to it, though, isn't it people like you who support Fang Qiu-lan's faction?"

"No, I don't support either side right now. The only thing I advocate is closer ties between China and Japan. And for taking that stand I have to be on my guard these days. Otherwise I could be in danger. Even so, if the means of sending money from Singapore is all in the hands of foreigners, then it's perfectly reasonable for the Malay Chinese to encourage the home government back in China."

"That may be, but the anti-imperialist movement in China, which resists white people, is trying to grab real power from the Chinese government. The irony is that the more the movement flourishes, the more the peoples of Southeast Asia will rise up and resist the Chinese who hold economic power in those colonies. In the end it's the same everywhere. The only major issue left, then, is a physiological limitation. Some say the white man is not suited to live in Southeast Asia, or in other tropical lands that provide the resources to sustain the most abundant lifestyle. The Chinese, in contrast, are said to be well adapted, and this is a limitation the white race has feared a great deal. Recently, however, I've heard it's been proven that the tropics pose no danger to the body after all, depending on cultural arrangements. So this is a problem that won't last much longer for the white race. What remains is the question of interracial mixing. There's simply no way to get around this difficult problem, even for the superior Europeans."

Kōya became aware all at once that he was a yellow man, just like the Chinese, and so he felt that the yellow race would be happier if they made Europeans their common target. Oryū's lips were beginning to shine from saliva as she noisily cracked her watermelon seeds. She glanced bitterly to the side as if to say, "How long is he going to drone on so pompously?"

Sensing from her attitude that she felt put down, Kōya was pleased that he was getting under her skin. He deliberately adjusted his posture and smiled, as if to say, *All right, bitch, hear some more.* He then spoke to Qian.

"In the South Pacific and elsewhere the mixing of white and dark races generally gives birth to colored people, not white. The mixture of yellow people and black people, however, usually produces yellow. That's why the number of black natives who prefer to marry yellow people over white has increased over time. Naturally this phenomenon proves that the race that will continue increasing into the future isn't the white or the black, but the yellow. Thus the center of genuine power in the world lies with the yellow race. Once this phenomenon becomes clear, then the opposition between yellow and white will become increasingly conspicuous in our ideologies. The next world war won't be an economic war. It'll be a race war. That's why if China and Japan keep quarreling with each other as they are now, the race that will benefit most is the white. India will be caught in the middle and will definitely never rise. And the safety valve for the Europeans that hurts India more than anything else? The Chinese on the Malay peninsula who make their living with Singapore as their center."

Qian Shi-shan knew that Oryū was losing interest in the conversation. Looking around as if to shake off Kōya's speech, he sipped at his empty tea cup and spoke quickly.

"Your explanation is an extremely advanced way of thinking. But China is, after all, a great power, and there are many people who don't know that China and Japan fought a war. A great power has to constantly pay compliments, or smile, simply for the sake of soothing the feelings of surrounding countries. Otherwise the world would not rotate peacefully. To put it another way, the Chinese like compromise above all, so long as everyone is peaceful. They prefer to settle all disputes peacefully. Countries that don't have a long history or a highly advanced civilization don't esteem compromise much. But the Chinese understand the virtue of compromise more than other peoples. That's why others lord it over us."

Kōya had no response to Qian's cunning magnanimity, which was equivalent to a cipher. So he smiled meaninglessly and replied, "What a superb speech. I think it was Lao-tzu, the deepest thinker in Chinese history, who also espoused a philosophy of compromise. This excellent way of thinking, which makes compromise the wellspring of all virtues, is incomprehensible to Europeans. I think it is an especially difficult concept even for modern Japanese and Chinese who long for every aspect of white culture."

When Kōya finished speaking Qian grasped the side of the table and began shaking. Oryū stood up behind her husband, put her arms around his back and led him over to a bed.

"Excuse me for a few minutes. I'm afraid it's that time."

Qian apologized to Kōya and lay down. He narrowed his eyes and took in his teeth a pipe Oryū brought to him. His lips began to move like a fish, and the sizzling sound of opium began. Oryū looked back at Kōya and asked, "Would you like some?"

120

"No, not for me. But don't hold back on my account."

Lying beside her husband, she lit her pipe. Kōya suddenly realized that the two had no doubt invited him to this room for the pleasure of having him watch them. He felt angry. Then he sensed the pitifulness of his own face, which had been chattering away so earnestly. Soon the two of them closed their eyes like some enraptured insects. Oryū's voluptuous hair came undone, tumbling into an opium tray inlaid with mother-of-pearl. The nose of the hunchback expanded as he breathed softly in the space between rows of amber and jade.

"Fine evening of moonlight. Politely receiving guests."

The inscription of the scroll came vividly to mind for Kōya, and soon the two slumbering bodies lost all decorum. Having steeped himself in pleasure with Oryū without paying, Kōya realized that he was now being forced to make complete recompense.

Twenty-Nine

At the hall where Miyako danced the foreigners who were always hanging around her were discussing the strike at the Japanese cotton mill. Miyako came over after a dance and leaned on a table around which some slightly tipsy men were seated. She listened to the remarks of the German, Pfilzer.

"The factory is definitely in the wrong this time. Because they despise Chinese workers. Generally, people who don't get angry even when they're looked down on are people who have long been in the habit of despising others. Japan always sends overseas the kind of man who doesn't respect foreigners, and then they try to take exclusive possession of our markets It's the first step to ruin. By pushing their exports, Japan ends up in fierce competition with products from its own factories here. And by irritating the Chinese industrial world, the Japanese have succeeded only in having their own goods boycotted. We're the ones who benefit, thanks to them. But of course we're sad about the situation for the sake of Miss Miyako."

"Why do you benefit?" asked Miyako.

"Because I'm German—or didn't you know? Until the war we had markets in the Far East. Those were stolen from us by other countries. So it's normal for us to take an interest when the goods of another country are boycotted."

"But Japan isn't the only country at fault," Miyako protested. "Even Germany is to blame."

"Yes, Germany has plenty to regret. I'm American, and I can tell you that the superhuman vitality of Germany puts constant pressure on our companies."

Pfilzer's glasses suddenly flashed in the American's direction.

"Excuse me, but what company do you work for?"

"I'm Harold Cleaver from G.E. And you?"

"Herman Pfilzer of the A.E.G. branch. This is certainly unexpected. Miss Miyako, this man represents our strongest rival, G.E. Well, well . . ."

The two shook hands and Pfilzer called to a waiter, "Champagne please!"

"Things are getting complicated," said Miyako. "If you two work for rival companies, which one should I support?"

"G.E. of course."

"No, no, by all means you must be on my side. If you opposed us Germans, then reparations will never be paid to Japan. For that matter, we won't pay America either. In fact, Germany can do what it likes now. A benefit of having lost the war."

Cleaver put down the whiskey he had started. "Actually, I feel tremendous sympathy for Germany. I just don't have much for A.E.G. I especially dislike the recent syndicate your company organized."

"If that's a problem, then I'm sorry. But after all, the syndicate was our way of expressing grievances against you. You see, Miyako, G.E. purchased Marconi Wireless. But not satisfied with possessing only Rocky Point, they also took control of Federal Radio Company. Now they're attempting to grab broadcast rights for the whole of China. Isn't that right?"

Cleaver laughed bitterly and drained his whiskey. "I'm satisfied with your very precise analysis. However, the truth is I'd be happier if your analysis were wrong. You see, Federal Radio had its broadcast rights stolen by Japan's Mitsui. I mention this not because I'm envious of the strength of the A.E.G. syndicate. I think A.E.G.'s recent acquisitions are admirable, even if you are a rival. Your stock swap with Linkê-Hoffmann, the joint financing with Raunhammer, and of course your merger with Rhein Metal. The creation of A.E.G. Linkê-Hoffmann was impressive. There's the Germans for you, I thought at the time. Still, shouldn't we be mutually economizing, in case there's a

123

second world war? After all, frugality is a virtue, no matter what you say."

Miyako jumped up and took control. "Enough of this. The champagne is here. If German and American syndicates keep attacking each other, we won't be able to dance."

"That's right. We ought to dance, not fight."

Cleaver raised the uncorked champagne. "To the prosperity of our enemy, A.E.G."

Pfilzer stood up unsteadily. "As a sign of respect, I say cheers to G.E." He caught a glimpse of the light bulb over his head and, after staring blankly for a moment, shouted, "This light bulb comes from my company! Hurrah! Hurrah! Hurrah!"

Cleaver looked at the ceiling, then pulled down Pfilzer's raised hands. "Look there. G.E. That's G.E. *My* company's light bulb. Bravo General Electric!"

"But this one's A.E.G. An Emil Ratenou incandescent bulb! Hurrah!"

"You're both fools! The lamp is a Matsuda from Japan," said Miyako.

Just as they were about to throw their hands in the air the two men fell silent, staring blankly at the ceiling. Then Cleaver suddenly yelled like a child, "She's right! That's a Matsuda! General Electric's Japanese agent, Matsuda Lamp! Bravo!"

He caught Miyako's waist as if sweeping her up, and, lifting one hand lightly to say "Excuse me, excuse me," he flowed with her into the dance circle that had just started to circulate. Champagne poured from Pfilzer's cocked hand. Leaning toward the retreating figure of Miyako, he grumbled, "Japanese agent? A.E.G. has a Japanese agent too. Don't you know the Okura Company? The Okura Company signed with us in London. *In London.*"

At that moment Miyako's eyes were straying over Cleaver's shoulder and she discovered Sanki's face submerged among the shadows of the palm trees. When the dance was over she went up to Sanki and sat down beside him.

"Why are you in a place like this? Go home. This isn't a place for people like you."

"Move out of the way."

"If I move, you'll be able to see my lover's face."

"I've been watching that woman over there for some time. She's quite beautiful."

"Who are you talking about? Ohhh, Yōko? She's a killer. She's dangerous, so face this way. She's not open like me."

"Be quiet and leave me alone. I have things to think about tonight."

Miyako dangled her feet from the chair and took out a cigarette.

"I want to be here too. Let me just sit like this for a few minutes."

"Kōya will be coming soon. When he does, come over then. I've decided not to talk to you until you marry that guy."

Miyako burned the flower in the vase with the tip of her cigarette and smirked. "Thank you for your concern. But I've decided not to speak with Kōya until you marry me. So please give him my regards."

"I didn't come here to listen to your jokes. I came here tonight thinking I would do at least one good thing in my life. So please listen to what I say."

"That's what I'm asking you to do. Since I definitely don't want to marry Kōya, I'll make my request over and over. If I marry him and go to Singapore, my complexion will turn pitch-black."

"So Kōya has no chance? No matter what I say?" The laughter had disappeared from Sanki's eyes, and a chill light was flowing from them.

"It was over from the beginning. The only thing I like about him is that he doesn't recognize his own mistakes in English. If that's how he is, then the lucky lady who becomes his wife will be blessed."

Displeased by Miyako's sarcasm, Sanki looked off to the

side. A handful of chocolates was being passed around over the laps of a row of dancers, who were raising a cheerful ruckus.

"Please dance with me tonight. Lately I've grown sick and tired of living. Why did I become a dance-hall girl? Just once before I die I'd like to dress up as a Japanese bride and marry you. Just one time. Please."

"You seem to have nothing to do now. It's dangerous to speak to me that way."

"Yes, it's dangerous. When I see people like me, I get scared and feel cold. If you don't take care, you'll be in danger. It shows in your face."

Sanki was increasingly displeased, as though she had touched a raw nerve. He frowned. "Couldn't you please go over there? When people who are alike get together, it always ends up a fiasco."

"It's already a fiasco, so what difference does it make? If you go crazy, tell me. I'll be your companion anytime. I'm not lying. If I stay on my own, then it's a sure bet my life will be aimless. And if that happens I'll just become rolled out, like a sausage. I don't want such a trivial life."

Sanki gazed at her face as though he were crossing over some dangerous boundary that had already penetrated him. He recalled Kyōko's face, no longer the face of a young woman. He thought of Qiu-lan's face. Seeing her was the same as dying. Was there no hope? Only death?

"I feel like I'm slipping into an icy crevasse. Because I'm always caught in the space between people's bodies, my so-called lovers all seem like dirt to me."

Sanki felt his chilled bones melting, as though they were being licked. "Go dance for me. I'll watch you from here."

"OK, I'll go dance. But dance with me once."

"I'm no good at dancing."

"You just have to shuffle your feet. People who dance well in a place like this look a little ridiculous."

"You hurry out to dance. If you stay here we'll just get

depressed together. It's better over there. That seems like the place you belong."

Miyako turned to look at the crowd of foreigners Sanki was pointing to. She laughed. "Oh, so that's why you've been fuming all along. When someone's angry at me it's my disposition not to say anything at all. So good-bye. I'll go over there. By the way, those foreigners there? They're the people in the album you stepped on the other day. On the far right is Mr. Bremen of the dyestuffs company, Meister, Lucius, & Bruening. And the one looking this way? Mr. Ruth of Palmers Shipbuilding Iron. There's Mr. Boswick of International Mercantile Marine, and in front of him . . ."

"That will do. In any case I feel sorry for Kōya."

"The truth is that there was nothing between Kōya and me from the start. Just remember that, all right? All right?" Miyako walked off, her back rippling with laughter, into a whirling bath of English conversation.

Thirty

Operations for the most part ground to a halt at Takashige's mill following the evening of the riot. An anti-Communist faction of workers stayed on at the plant to protect the equipment. When a command from the Communist faction arrived, these workers beat the messenger and threw him into the river. Leaflets from both the Communist and anti-Communist factions struggled in the breeze inside and out of the mill.

Takashige had not seen Sanki since the night of the riot. If Sanki were uninjured, he thought, then he would certainly show up. However, he didn't show.

Takashige made his rounds. The machines had stopped rotating and began to show signs of rust as a result of a southerly breeze overnight. Workers remained among the silenced equipment, looking pale because of rumors that violence would soon sweep over them. Closed in by the equipment like so many lice in a row, they began removing the rust. The humidity caused the emery used to polish the machines to crumble off the sandpaper. As they unanimously cursed the worthless Japanese-made paper, the workers practiced resetting the belts. Cotton was all around them, clumping up everywhere as it grew moist like waste that had not been disposed of properly.

Takashige surveyed the area around the factory from the top of a flight of stairs. A searchlight flashing from a destroyer in the harbor was moving around, looming among the stratus clouds. Sets of cranes thrust up through openings in the coal beds that stretched on blackly. A broken sail from a smuggler's ship rose like an ebony feather slanting to one side. Along the surface of the coal, tattered rags crawled and spread out darkly as though they were oozing out. The searchlight scampered over their backs, and the wave of rags stuck flat to the bed of coal.

They've come.

Takashige crouched over and started down the stairs. A dark crowd was running among the warehouses, their voices low; they slipped inside the glass of the generator room. As they advanced, aiming like a powerful weapon for the most vulnerable spot, there could be no mistaking that this was a group to be feared.

Takashige imagined that Fang Qiu-lan was secretly behind that group. He felt the urge to go around behind them and infiltrate their plan. *What did they want?* Right now it looked like all they wanted was to occupy the factory.

He pushed the button to an electric buzzer. At that moment the entire factory was plunged into darkness. Cries went up in two places beside the gates. Coal began flying at the factory. When the searchlight beam came round, a crowd appeared like so many ants scaling the fence hand over hand.

Takashige thought that the best thing was to lead them into the factory. Once inside they would be like rats in a sack. If he could close them off from the outside, that would do the trick. And if they destroyed the machinery, that loss would soon redound upon their own heads. He climbed down the stairs. The front line of a group pouring into the factory collided with a group protecting the equipment.

A line of chests like a picket fence pushed forward, shouting, into the spaces between the machines. It pushed against the workers in the factory. A detachment of Indian policemen brandished the butts of their guns and pushed back. Fighting hand-to-hand, tearing up the machinery, the crowds advanced farther and farther into the factory. The lock of a spare stock room was broken off, and a band of people rushed in and grabbed picking sticks to use as cudgels. Spilling back out of that room, they raised these iron clubs in each hand and renewed the attack.

Bodies came flying down from the cotton gins onto the heads of those grappling at close quarters. Wooden pipes were thrown about, striking some. Shards of glass from a broken meter

129

sliced open bare skin as it tumbled down. The sound of lapboard slapping together was closed in on all sides by screaming. Gradually, the anti-Communist faction crumbled away.

Takashige ran to the telephone and requested an immediate increase in the number of police. When he got back the lights he had turned off suddenly flickered on brightly. For a second the turmoil of the crowd stopped. Then once more shouting voices, like a spasm of anger, shot upward. Using a scaffold of rollers that had not yet been invaded as his shield, Takashige avoided the stones whizzing over his head. He shouted, "It's the police! Stand firm! Machine guns!"

At exactly the same moment the window panes around him began shattering with an explosion. From large black holes a new mob came bubbling over like foam. He watched them jump up on the machinery and hurl stones and coals down into it. Another group jumped up after them, and soon they were massed on top of the equipment. Then, having run out of targets to smash, they came cascading down, aiming for the workers.

The anti-Communist faction was swept up in the force of the crowd whose ranks were gradually swelled by these new groups. When these smaller bands joined together they acquired anew the strength of a single large mob as they turned on the employees. All resistance was now futile. Joining up with the Indian police, the employees retreated into the factory yard closely pursued by the mob. As they headed toward the west gate another group of rioters cut them off and attacked. Crammed together shoulder to shoulder, they ran into a fence and broke it down. But beyond the toppled fence a new group brandishing weapons appeared out of nowhere. Their angry mouths screaming war cries, they closed in. With enemies front and back, the workers had no place to go. Takashige and some of the other foremen aimed their guns into the crowd.

It's all over now. This is it.

The limits of reason hung on his trigger, coiling and uncoiling like a spring in response to the movement of the crowd.

A sea of unkempt hair surged with increased velocity toward the front edge of the mob. Then the guns of the Indian police went off. Shouts went up successively from Takashige's group and from the front line of the mob. Some of the mob lost heart, like a bird with a broken wing. They tried to draw back but ran into people behind them pushing the other way. Two black currents described an arc before Takashige's eyes, causing an upheaval. A wave of backs and a wave of heads lost direction and began spinning about. The heads of those running away ducked in among torsos crammed together. Stumbling at the collapsed fence, people fell. Then a fencerow of people collapsed on top of them and they all came to a standstill, forcing the rest of the mob to flow around them.

When the anti-Communist faction saw that the Communists were on the verge of defeat, they bared their claws and sprang on the retreating figures. People who had fallen tried to raise their heads to get up, but they became entangled with the feet of those running over them, fell again, and crawled about. Heads were forced down as feet trampled on unkempt hair and were kicked by the tips of feet rushing by like a typhoon. Lapboard flew around like javelins. Coal flew about as well, thudding on the backs of the fleeing mob. The shadows of the mob changed, dilating and expanding, as it followed the angles of the warehouse and soon disappeared from the yard.

By the time the machine gun unit arrived at the front gate of the factory the mob was gone. The only thing that could be seen each time the searchlight beam swept through the air was pools of blood resembling pale black bruises on the ground.

Thirty-One

Yamaguchi left the Turkish Bath, his face plump and flushed. He thought he would go over to Osugi's place and pass the time till midnight. But then he passed by the jewelry shop of his fellow Asianist, Amuli. He peeked in to see if Amuli were there. At that moment Amuli, who had just seen a customer out, was returning to the display case shouting something angrily to his Chinese houseboy. His back was turned to Yamaguchi, and each time he shouted the pure white of his collar dug into the dark skin of his quivering neck.

Yamaguchi thought that if he talked with Amuli now he wouldn't have time to meet Osugi tonight. But that occurred to him only after he had called to Amuli and entered.

"Oh!" Amuli majestically turned toward Yamaguchi. He put one hand on the thick glass of the case as he shook Yamaguchi's hand with the other. They spoke in Japanese.

"It's been a while."

"Yes, it has."

"Things have gotten really bad, haven't they," said Yamaguchi, releasing Amuli's hand.

"Very complicated. It appears that China will expand the strike considerably this time."

"Have you met with Li Ying-pu?"

"Not yet. I thought about meeting him, but no one knows where he is."

Amuli led Yamaguchi to a chair and sat down across from him. As he spoke a single gold-capped tooth glittered from a row of white teeth. "This last incident is really explosive. The Japanese workers at Far Eastern Cotton Mills are insisting it was Indian police who shot first and killed the Chinese. If they keep persisting in that claim, we won't be able to stay silent forever."

132

"What does it matter who shot first? It was the Chinese who smashed their way in. Anyone would have fired."

"Then why blame Indians?"

"At the inquest the autopsies showed bullets from both Indian and Japanese guns. Now the sentiments that fueled the movement to expel the Japanese have been turned on the British. You're happy about that, aren't you?"

Amuli gazed out at the shining wheels of rickshaws flashing by one after another in the thin mist that drifted in the darkness beyond the entrance. He laughed. "We don't agree with the expulsion of Britain from China. The only thing the Chinese can do is expel Chinese."

"Will you close down?" Yamaguchi glanced at the gemstones under the glass case. "Those all came from India, didn't they."

"No, they came from a thief."

"Well then, you won't mind if I take one?"

"Please." Amuli opened the lid of the case. Yamaguchi pushed aside the shining black strawwork elephants made in India. Thinking about Osugi, he pulled out an amethyst ring.

"This isn't fake, is it?"

"I don't know," replied Amuli.

"Then why should I be grateful to you?"

"It's because I don't know for sure that I'll take five dollars please."

Amuli held out his palm to Yamaguchi.

"You want my money even though it might be fake?"

"Business is business. Let's have the five dollars."

Yamaguchi handed him the money and tried the ring on his finger. "From now on I start a one-man boycott of India."

"It's Britain that has made me this way."

"Speaking of Britain, they've been doing well again, I see. The Congress Party is in danger?"

"It's in danger."

"So what do you think about it? If the Congress Party

dissolves, which way will you go? Surely your leader, Chittaranjan Das, wouldn't switch to the Communists. Are things safe?"

"I don't know. Das won't just stand idly by if Jawaharal Nehru abandons the party, which looks likely these days."

"But it would be extremely reckless for Nehru to abandon Congress."

Amuli gazed silently at the door and did not answer. Yamaguchi pulled up his sleeves thinking that detailed reports from India must be coming to Amuli.

"If Nehru abandons the party it's the same as tacking on an additional fifty years to British rule. Don't you agree?

"Yes, I agree," said Amuli.

"In that case your enemies just increased by one."

"They've increased."

"Now your compatriots say that they must call on the strength of your young people to suffer and fight against Britain. But the real danger that assails you from the rear is that infighting will make India even more fragmented. Don't try to reform India, defend it! Your aims have changed. Isn't it time to change your tactics?"

Amuli continued to gaze into the mist, silent as though he had been exhausted by the violent new upheaval that had broken out in his homeland.

"Have you had any more news from India since?"

"No."

"Then there must be considerable turmoil."

"When the Communist party begins to rise in India, there is no need for us to fight them. Our common enemy is Britain."

Yamaguchi sensed that this feeble display from Amuli was an effort to obscure the difficulties in his country. Simultaneously, he felt as if he were looking back over his shoulder at the blaze of ideologies engulfing Japan.

"But if the Communists rise in India, then the capitalists who have been supporting the independence movement up to now will realign themselves to support Britain. And if they do, then the program of the Congress Party will be buried forever."

"Perhaps, but even in China capitalists have joined with the Communists to carry out the boycott of foreigners. So India has no way to go other than rely on Nehru and Das."

Amuli looked up at the clock and shouted to the houseboy, "Close up!"

"But if that happens the coastline from India to Shanghai will be utterly Communist, and that's no good. We Asianists won't be fighting Europe, we'll be fighting the Communist army."

"Russia is the scoundrel in all this," said Amuli as he drew the curtains on the windows. The houseboy pulled down the large front door with a clatter.

Amuli continued, "The way things stand, your militarism will inevitably lead to a clash with Russia."

"And if that happens, what will India do? That is the most important question."

"In such a case India would naturally divide. It's a grave situation, since the current power of Nehru is greater than Ghandi's among the young."

"And what will become of C. R. Das?"

"He'll fight the British to the bitter end. There are a mountain of unresolved issues. The right of supreme command of the national defense forces. The right to control the economy. The power to issue Indian bonds. The movement to repeal the salt monopoly. Above all the right of appeal for political prisoners. Of the 360 members of the national executive committee of Congress, 270 of them, 75 percent, are now in prison. 75 percent. Whatever else happens, things can't go on like this. Our jails are filled with righteous people. Another five years. Wait five years and then we'll see."

Amuli pulled a piece of mimeographed paper from an inside pocket.

"This is a beautifully written critique of the governor-general of India that arrived the other day from a colleague in

Lahore. It's a rare piece of writing these days. 'The attitude of the governor toward the genuinely moderate plan we have formulated for the salt monopoly exposes the true feelings of the government, which are suspect. A ruler of all India who has retreated to a plateau, to a chimera that dazzles the eye, cannot understand the suffering of the starving millions who live below in the plains. It is as clear to us as if we are looking up at the sun. That chimera can only be sustained by the constant toil of the teeming masses.'"

"Sounds like a passage from the Communists. Is Lahore in danger too?"

Amuli raised his eyes from the paper and looked at Yamaguchi. "Everything looks like Communism to you, doesn't it. If Communism is so frightening, then your Asianism is finished."

"It is finished. Shall we go out?"

"Yes, let's go."

Yamaguchi stepped out first and Amuli followed, grabbing his hat. Yamaguchi remembered his plans to see Osugi, which he had temporarily forgotten.

"This was a real blunder," he said out loud. He'd have to give up going to her place tonight.

Thirty-Two

Osugi got up in the morning and, resting her elbows on the second-story balustrade, gazed blankly at the peaceful bustling of the back street below her. From the railing on a bridge over the canal a Chinese woman who had been carrying some flowering plants was staring just like Osugi onto the surface of the water. A cobbler who was always on the bridge was seated on the ground next to the young woman's hems holding a support and biting into the sole of a clog, using his teeth to pull out nails with a keening sound. Coming and going in front of those two were a peddler with fiddles piled up on his back, soldiers on their morning return, prostitutes swaying on rickshaws, and footbound women waddling along like infants. The people crossing the bridge moved along upside down on the surface of the water, where dented cans, insects, jet black foam, fruit peels, and many other objects swirled about. A small boat that had probably come down the river last night from Suzhou was loaded with split firewood. It was stopped, as if stuck fast on the muddy water.

Osugi could see an old lady sewing inside that boat, and she thought of her own mother in Japan. Osugi's mother committed suicide when Osugi was still a child. She hanged herself, leaving her only child an orphan. Why had Osugi ended up drifting into Shanghai? Her memory was no longer clear. She thought about what her relatives had told her. Her father had been a colonel in the army who died suddenly during maneuvers. Osugi had been raised by her mother. One day an order arrived saying that the pension Osugi's mother was receiving was improper and that she would have to repay everything. Since she had received the pension for such a long time, it was impossible for Osugi's mother to come up with such a large sum of money. And she knew that without the pension she would not be able to make a living. Overcome by a surfeit of grief, she took her own life.

"Receiving money from complete strangers, and then having to give it back . . . it's too much. It's just too much."

Osugi remembered those woeful days for her mother as if they were yesterday. The peaceful morning air grew absolutely still in an instant, pressing chillingly in on her body.

Osugi felt her tears welling up, and she could only ask herself whose fault it was that her life had come to this. In this idle state, in which she seemed shameless, she continued to stare at the old woman on the boat.

Someone tossed garbage from a brick wall where grass was growing into the canal beyond the old woman's boat. The figure of Osugi's mother disappeared from her mind. In its place, one after another, came the faces of her customers, different every night. Watching a bundle of scrap straw spin quietly on the canal's surface, she wondered if she could find a gentle customer who would pay for her to go home to Japan. She knew hardly anything about Japan now. The only things she could remember were the stone walls of a castle that traced out long, splendid lines, the wind soughing in the branches of pine trees, the thickness of village roofs when a cold autumn shower fell, chickens crying forlornly beneath the sasanqua, and that black post that always stood alone on the corner, reminding her of a human face. She did not know where she had seen the vistas that flickered in her mind.

The street scene in China she was gazing at now was different from such scenes in Japan. There was something relaxed about it. There were many people there who, like Osugi, leaned from railings and gazed blankly at the canal without going to work in the morning. The sun on the water sparkled, entwining the shadows in among the supports of the bridge. Tea and scraps of straw, clinging to the oars of boats, dead still as though rotting, drifted in the foam amid wavy shadows of poles and inverted reflections of crumbling bricks. The purple petals of a discarded iris continued to bloom, vital among the yellow corpses of chicks and scraps of cloth.

Osugi continued gazing in reverie, lost in her random thoughts. After some time had passed she decided she would go out a little early today to look for customer. She also thought that more than anything else she'd like to eat some Japanese yellow-tail. *That's it. I'll go to the market today.*

Osugi cheered up as soon as this idea came to her. She washed her face, put on her makeup, and headed off to the market, her basket dangling, every bit a maid from some fine household.

It was already close to ten o'clock, but the market, which spread in all directions over several streets of three-story concrete buildings, was still bustling. The street where the florists were located was like a garden overflowing with flowers in full bloom. The street with the fishmongers looked like the bottom of a drained pond. Osugi passed by walls filled with dried cod, dried salmon trout, and mountains of eggs. As she made her way past vegetables that smelled of being freshly picked, she was startled and came to an abrupt halt. Kōya and Oryū were standing in front of her next to some huge buckets of turtles. Osugi ducked behind a crowd of people before she could be spotted. Her mind no longer on her shopping, she slipped away under hanging bunches of lotus root and sugarcane in order to escape their eyes. Then she asked herself why she should have to run from them. *Weren't they the bad ones? Who forced me to be a street walker? Who?*

Her vexation came boiling up in that bustling crowd, and she had the impulse to go back and display herself prominently before those two. If she did, they would be really flustered. She'd like to see their faces then. So she decided that's what she'd do.

Osugi summoned up her courage and proceeded through the crowd toward Kōya and Oryū. Unaware that Osugi was there, they peered along with her into buckets filled with octopus, red carp, angler, and gray mullet, ambling toward a flower shop. Osugi tried hard not to lose sight of them as she bumped and stumbled through the crowd, and finally came up behind Kōya.

But just then Osugi asked herself what her aim was in confronting them. There was no longer anything to say, and so it wasn't reasonable for her to spew out her anger or lash out freely at the two of them. If they looked at her and were frightened, her anger would be assuaged a little. But what if, contrary to expectations, they made fun of her? If the two of them looked at her body and laughed, it would be the most unbearable moment for Osugi.

She continued following them for a few minutes, keeping an eye on their backs. She stared at the muscles of Kōya's shoulders and the stretch of his trousers.

She remembered the dream that night at Sanki's place, when unexpectedly in the darkness she had her virginity taken. In that dream a white wave crested. A group of children and a school of fish came chasing her one after another. Then she awoke. *The man that night. Was it Sanki or Kōya? If it had been Kōya . . . Ah, that torso, those shoulders. And now, walking beside Oryū. Hadn't he thrust his shoulders against me the same way?*

Osugi brought the cuff of her sleeve to her mouth. Glaring at Kōya, she followed them some more. How long did she intend to keep up the chase? No matter how long she trailed after them, it made no difference. At any rate, if she pursued them, then like Kōya . . . *That's right. Since that night he had somehow cleverly got at Oryū. Just as I take money from customers, he was now swindling money from Oryū.* It occurred to Osugi just then that instead of chasing them she could be making money by targeting clients the way Kōya did.

Osugi grew homesick. She left the market, got on a rickshaw, and went to a main thoroughfare. She got off and walked along a street that seemed a likely place for foreigners to pass. Swaying her hips slowly, casting glances from time to time at the faces of the men she passed, she headed for a park at the foot of a bridge.

However, she did not meet a single man who returned her glance that day. The only ones who looked back at her were a butcher, whose eyes flashed across a large cutting block as he wielded his knife, a shop boy, who twirled his opium pipe in a frightening manner, his legs thrust out into the street, and the beggars who simply groveled before her.

Osugi came to the foot of a bridge. In the park, as always, prostitutes of all nationalities emerged from their hangouts, gathering quietly to bask in the sun. Osugi mingled with them, sitting on a bench and allowing the plantain flowers, which fell in a drizzle, to settle on her shoulders. She stared vacantly, along with everyone else, at the spraying fountain, which rose up in lines, then broke apart and scattered. When the breeze shifted, a rainbow would appear and disappear, appear and disappear, repeating over and over its showy revels before the faces of the women.

Thirty-Three

As the strike spread through the port the production of cotton dramatically declined. The exchange rate began to rise against the yen. The value of silver fell and the gold market continued to advance. Western exchange brokers applied the whip to their horses ever more quickly as they raced their carriages between banks. Following the jump in the price of gold, silver began to flood the port. Then the value of cotton cloth began to rise. The shortage of foreign goods continued, and the price of cotton products from New York, Liverpool, and Osaka jumped suddenly.

Sanki took an interest in the phenomenon of Japan's domestic boom, which was indicated on the bulletin board in the management division of his company. If Japanese firms in China were suffering, those in Osaka were prospering. And even for Sanki's mill there was some good news, since remnants that had accumulated over a long period began to fly off warehouse shelves. Of course it wasn't just management who worried about these strangely good business conditions. When the buying stopped at the trade exchanges, sellers continued to sell off in response. As a result, the market in cotton cloth began to collapse. Indian merchants were running wild trying to corner the market. It became impossible to make up for cotton products that were increasingly scarce in the port. The losses to the textile companies began to mount as the strike continued. To top it off, because the companies did not acquiesce in the workers' demands for backpay to cover the period of the strike, the situation was doomed to continue on and on.

Those who made the biggest profits from the scarcity of cotton goods, which was the main effect of the strike, were Indian speculators and Japanese textile groups. Japanese-owned textile mills in Shanghai had for some time been under pressure from textile companies in Japan. As soon as the strike broke out in the Japanese mills in Shanghai, mills in Japan that had been idle began operating their machinery at full capacity. The skilled laborers of the mills being struck were soon hired away, one after another, by the firms in Japan. In response, advocacy of domestic products gained steam and a boycott of Japanese goods was organized. For the first time Chinese textile companies had a chance to plan for an increase in capital, a turning point in their development. For that reason, in order to promote their country's domestic productivity they had to nurture Russian radicals until their own capital was on an equal footing with foreign capital. If the Chinese did not make use of Russian agents, they would never be able to get out from under the control of the foreign economic powers that pressured them. Using the strike as an opportunity, Chinese capitalism chose to follow behind the uphill charge of the Communists.

Oryū's husband, Qian Shi-shan, was involved with a group of Chinese capitalists as a member of a general trading firm. When the strike against the Japanese-owned mills began, he schemed with others in the group. They increased their capital holdings in Chinese textile mills. They paid propagandists to help spread the boycott of Japan. And they did not shy away from cozying up to the trade unions, who planned strategy for the strike. This strike was unprecedented in China, and it spread its mysterious wings moment by moment like some endemic disease that has surged in from somewhere. Now the port began to fill with the unemployed. Gangs of ruffians infiltrated the city, donning the mask of the Communist Party. Secret societies were active.

"Kill the Japanese!"

"Crush the foreign capitalists!"

"For the prosperity of China!"

Walls along the streets, utility poles at intersections, and the recesses of alleyways were papered over with propaganda leaflets. Telegrams from the headquarters of the labor union began to fly out to Chinese living in other countries.

In the middle of this uproar bullets fired by Japanese working for Takashige and by the Indian police who worked for the Municipal Council wounded a number of Chinese workers. When one of the wounded workers died radical factions became increasingly violent. When they retrieved the body of the slain worker from the coroner's office, they began to assert that each of the four bullet wounds was made by Japanese guns. A group of 300 union officials and striking workers shouldered the coffin and thronged the factory demanding an investigation of the murder. However, the crowd was chased from the factory gate by the police, and in the end the coffin was delivered to the union strike headquarters.

Takashige sensed that the man they had killed was becoming the focus of the city. The group resolve of the Chinese workers hardened because of that death. Watching how skillfully things were managed, Takashige couldn't help imagining that this whole movement was the work of Fang Qiu-lan. Soon she would be acting on all fronts, bringing along thousands of Chinese workers.

But look. The more she acted, the more the crowd of workers around her would eventually die of starvation.

The funeral of the slain worker, whose body was laid out at the union headquarters, was conducted grandly in a neighboring square. Minute by minute telephone calls from observers describing the event poured into the management division of Sanki's company. These reports were posted on the bulletin board.

— Over 500 flags at funeral site.

— More than thirty participating groups, approximately 10,000 mourners.

— Angry speeches around bier. Attack on factory this evening at latest.

— Police and mourners clashing. Scores arrested.

— Student groups attack police, attempt to free the arrested.

144

These reports were mixed in with a report from partisans.

— Meeting at the home of the Russian Communist Party Secretary Cherkov. Attending were his comrade Ponomarenko, propaganda chief Kruenko, regional party members Person, Shibrovsky, and Stoyanovich. Chinese attending include Kung Tso-min and many students from the Chinese Medical School.

Telegrams arrived from markets in various countries.

— The *Washington* has sailed from Hamburg. Contains 400 tons of cotton goods.

— The *Lima* has sailed from Liverpool, 1,000 tons of cargo.

— The *Hakata* has sailed from Bombay, 2,800 tons of raw cotton.

— 300 bales of cotton cloth cannot be loaded due to interference of Niipō student group.

Mingled with these telegrams were coded messages of support from Japanese business groups that poured in one after another.

— Greater Japan Textile Manufacturers Association. Several members to Tokyo. Discussion with Foreign Ministry yesterday.

— Japan Industrial Club. Concluded there is need for warning, completed arrangements with Foreign Ministry and Ministry of Commerce and Industry.

— Kyoto Chamber of Commerce. Undertaking mutual efforts with Osaka Chamber of Commerce. Await prompt report.

— Kobe Chamber of Commerce. In line with Foreign Ministry orders, will dispatch emergency measures to General Trade Association in your region.

— Osaka Chamber of Commerce. Will petition government to take measures to aid you. Have asked for mediators to resolve current problems for trade offices in your region.

— Tokyo Chamber of Commerce. Talked with Foreign Minister, decided on resolute measures by government. Strong protest to Chinese government. Have taken other appropriate steps. China responds they will suppress strike soon.

Sanki could feel the trembling of his mother country in these telegrams. His astonishment at the progress of Fang Qiu-lan's faction redoubled.

Thirty-Four

Rumors about Japanese being attacked circulated throughout the city every day. The cargo of Japanese traders was looted and burned. Japanese businessmen fled, every man for himself, to the security of the International Settlement. The inns in the Settlement were soon filled to overflowing. Land values and rents in the Settlement skyrocketed. Chinese accused of being pro-Japanese were placed in cages and dragged through the streets like animals. Heads of unknown people hung from light poles, their noses rotting off.

Sanki was ordered to make inspections, and from time to time he would go around the city disguised as a Chinese. It became more difficult for him to suppress his desire to see Fang Qiu-lan. The closer he got to the area of danger the more severe the exhaustion he felt; and then he felt a powerful stimulation, like someone taking smelling salts for the first time.

Sanki had agreed to meet Kōya that day at the Parterre as usual. The humidity on the streets, which was approaching summertime levels, was heavily oppressive. Sanki could see the iron torso of a destroyer between buildings where the ragged clothes of beggars had been hung like tassels. A trolley bus pursued a group of rickshaws, then rammed into fruit stacked on the corner and stopped. Sanki turned a corner. Straight ahead in that section of the city, a screaming crowd gathered, flowing along with flags raised. It was clearly part of a mob that had attacked a Japanese factory and been dispersed. The front edge of the crowd, which stretched a long way back, was being squeezed into the stone gate of the police station there.

"Rescue our brothers!"

"Free the prisoners!"

The crowd advanced, its front line slowly compressing

and elongating, as it was squeezed together little by little. The stone gate, like an oven door, smoothly swallowed up the people. Then all at once the mob was spit out, pouring back toward Sanki. Water from a line of hoses sprayed out from the barrier gate. The flag bearers were swept off their feet, tumbling down the stone stairs. As the nozzles of the hoses advanced, they swept clean the human wave on the street. People spilled back out onto the area between the buildings and the trolley that had stopped on the corner. The crowd pursued by the police ran into a new crowd, swelling the ranks of the mob. A worker jumped up into a window and shouted "Brothers unite! They've murdered our comrade! Let's avenge him! Kill the British authorities who oppress us!"

As soon as he finished he fainted and fell down onto the stone pavement. The crowd stood pulsating. Harshly worded placards flew through the spaces between shoulders. Banners were brandished above the crowd. Another worker jumped up into the window and shouted, "Brothers! Think of China! How much abuse have we suffered at the hands of the British? They strangle China! They steal our bread! They take our weapons! Look on the face of 400 million Chinese! China is starving for their sake! When we try to stand up for China, the British are always there to block us!"

Some British police came over, grabbed him by the feet and pulled him down. Banners at the front of the crowd swirled around the policemen.

"Kill the British!" The crowd pushed forward on the Municipal Police as shouts rang out. Water shot out again from the hoses. It dispersed the crowd, spilling people everywhere and revealing in straight lines the pavement stones beneath the wave of humanity. Then a vortex of stones began to whiz down on the heads of the policemen. A layer of glass shards, like a glittering blue river, flew from a row of windows high over their heads.

"Kill the British!"

"Kill the foreigners!"

The crowd raised its war cry, and once more closed in on the police. The front line of the crowd and the police tumbled together in the spouting water. Soon the mob, which numbered in the tens of thousands, pushed in from all sides and swept over the groups of people fighting hand-to-hand. It seemed the large buildings around them would crumble. Because of the enormous passions aroused, the spaces in the streets now filled with the swelling crowd. The growing force of the surging throng smashed glass along the black street as it rushed the barrier gate of the police station. Then, in unison, the muzzles at the gate opened fire. A shudder, an electric current, raced over the crowd. Voices, now subdued, gave out a groan and the mob twisted in toward the walls on both sides of the street. As people were pushed back from the walls, they spun around, a torrent tracing out the trajectory of the bullets, and began to assault the gate.

"Kill the foreigners!"

"Kill the British!"

Flesh is no match for bullets, and with each successive rifle report the crowd was ripped with precision.

Sanki was forced back into the sunken entrance of a shop and could see only a pivoting transom opened horizontally above his head. The rioting crowd was reflected upside down in the transom glass. It was like being on the floor of an ocean that had lost its watery sky. Countless heads beneath shoulders, shoulders beneath feet. They described a weird, suspended canopy on the verge of falling, swaying like seaweed that drifted out, then drew back and drifted out again. As the riot continued swirling about, Sanki searched for the face of Fang Qiu-lan in the crowd suspended over him. Then he heard more shots. He felt a tremor. He tried to reach out into the crowd on the ground, as if he were springing up. He disregarded his own equilibrium, which floated up into the confusion of the external world. His desire to fight that external world, which rose irresistibly in him, was like a sudden attack of a chronic disease. Simultaneously, he began to struggle to steal back his composure. He tried to watch intently the velocity of the bullets. A river made of waves of human beings sped past in front of him. These waves collided and rose up like spray. Banners fell, covering the waves. The cloth of the banners caught on the feet of the flowing crowd and seemed to be swallowed up into the buildings. Then, at that moment, he saw Qiu-lan. A Chinese patrolman attached to the Municipal Police had grabbed her arms and restrained her near one of the banners. Sanki's line of sight was blocked suddenly, so he fought his way through the wave and ran to the side of a building. He could still see Qiu-lan in the clutches of the policeman as she silently watched the riot swirling around her. Then she saw him. She smiled. He sensed death. He sprang up and thrust his body, like the cool blade of a sword, between her and the policeman's arm. He fell down and glimpsed Qiu-lan's scampering feet. He kicked out at the mass of flesh sweeping over him and jumped to his feet. He ran smack into the butt of a gun. He jumped into the crowd that was again flowing past him and moved off with that wave of humanity.

All of this took place in a fragment of time, a vivid flash. The street resounded with gunfire, and the enormous whirlpool of the mob finally broke apart and fled between buildings like shuttles crossing each other.

Sanki forgot what he was doing. Standing there as the crowd raced around him, Qiu-lan's face pierced him like a nail. In his agitation he was struck dumb. At the same time he felt a hollowness in his numbed chest. In the distance a waterfall of glass tumbled from windows. He stepped over the head of a beggar who was picking up bullet casings at his feet. For the first time he began to feel the reality around him as its violence carried on within his field of vision. And yet the abyss-like emptiness that assailed him earlier increasingly overwhelmed his senses. He felt that now there was nothing more he should do. The glittering charm of death, which had allured him only to retreat so many times before, began to fill his heart. He looked

150

idly around. A beggar who was stealing the shoes from a dead body was struck in the eye by water from a hose and retreated. Sanki grabbed some copper coins and threw them over the bodies at a distance. The beggar hopped over the dead and wounded like an agile weasel, crawling around over the scattered coins. Sanki gauged the distance between himself and the beggar, two people who were flirting with death. He sensed a clear victory in his power to resist the external world. At the same time he felt death pressing sharply like an awl on his skin, and once more grabbing a handful of coins he flung them about randomly. The beggar kept his distance, circling around Sanki as he moved among the bodies. Sensing the circumference of his will spread out over the tumultuous street, for the first time he went numb with the pleasant feeling that he would be killed. He now felt a velocity, as if he were slipping into his final moment. Within a dazzling arc of light he was struck by an invisible shudder that danced up merrily and began to laugh. Then, unexpectedly, he was pulled into the crowd behind him. He turned around and shouted in surprise.

He had been pulled back by the arm of Fang Qiu-lan.

"Get out of here now!"

Sanki started to run after her. She led him inside a building and hurried up an elevator to the fifth floor. A young servant boy pointed to a room and they entered. Qiu-lan took Sanki in his arms and, taking a violently deep breath, kissed him on the mouth.

"Thank you for saving me again. I've been thinking since that day that I would definitely meet you again. I didn't think it would happen so soon."

Sanki could only listen, spellbound by the dizzying emotions that exploded in him. She opened the window in a busy manner and looked down on the street.

"Look how many police there are. See for yourself. That's the place where you rescued me. The person who fired at you was over there."

Sanki stood next to her and looked down. Under the smoke of gunpowder, the smell of which was rising up along the walls, the remnants of the crowd were being absorbed into the corners of the streets. A bright-red armored vehicle rumbled wearily along, smearing bloodstains and crushing shards of glass along a bullet-marked street that was now completely quiet. Sanki noticed that what he had been struggling with directly below was nothing more than a coldly indifferent district of the city. Struck by his own pathetic foolishness, he felt an unpleasant chill and shuddered.

He looked at Qiu-lan's face with eyes in which all flexibility had disappeared. Her face was like an early dawn. He thought of the gentleness of her kiss. However, the memory of that gentleness flew off, taking with it his sensation of emptiness, as though there had been some mistake. He said, "Please don't bother with me. You should go where you need to go."

"Thank you. I'm afraid that I am busy now. The place we'll gather today has already been chosen. But forget about that. Why did you come here today?"

"I just wandered by aimlessly. Even so, I can guess the kind of places where I might find you."

"You're being reckless. From now on please stay at your house as much as you can. I don't know what some of the people in my circle will do to foreigners. It may be that the shooting today by the Municipal Police will work in favor of the Japanese. It seems certain that from now on the focus of Chinese resistance will be the British. The Municipal Council has called a special ratepayers' meeting, and the proposal to raise tariffs is a life-or-death issue for Chinese merchants. We have to summon all our powers to have that meeting canceled."

"So you'll leave the problem of the Japanese mills as it is?"

"Yes. For us Britain is more of an issue than the strike. If we tacitly allow the shooting today to go unchallenged, it'll be a national humiliation for China. No matter what excuse they give for the shooting, firing into an unarmed crowd has sealed the defeat of the British. Look for yourself. You can see how much blood has been spilled. It's hard to say how many Chinese were killed here today."

Qiu-lan gave the window a push as though she were tossing all her regrets at the window itself. She paced the room. Sanki sensed a violent emotion isolated from afar in the corners of her upturned eyes. At the same time he sensed he was moving closer and closer to a realm of extreme coldness. In an instant her excited face looked beautiful again, with its clear, supple skin. He now wished that he could be infected with her fierce passion. He glanced out the window. Blood was beginning to pool up where it had flowed. *Who had killed these people?* He recalled the Chinese policemen wielding rifle barrels that had been turned on their own people. No doubt they were following the orders of the Municipal Council. Even so, was it possible to say that the thugs who showed utter contempt for China weren't Chinese?

"I have only sympathy for the Chinese today. The cunning of the Municipal Police . . ."

He fell silent. He had detected the strength of will of the authorities who had hired Chinese to kill Chinese.

"That's right. The craftiness of the British authorities isn't new. The history of the modern Orient is so filled with the crimes of that country that if you tried to add them up you'd be paralyzed. Starving millions of Indians, disabling Chinese with the opium trade. These were Britain's economic policies. It's the same as using Persia, India, Afghanistan, and Malaysia to poison China. Now we Chinese must resist completely."

He watched Qiu-lan as she worked herself up to a fever-pitch, spinning like a top. He looked off to the side, feeling an unfavorable wind brushing back against his face. In order to calm her, he had to talk about something. He spoke in soothing tones.

"The other day I heard from a reporter at a Chinese

newspaper that in order to weaken the British army hundreds of the most diseased prostitutes were being brought in from Russia. I don't know if that story is true or not, but the cunning of the Russians that lies behind all this is something we must heed. For the Chinese people to fight Britain, they must train to fight an even more cunning enemy. I'm saying this not to deflect your anger today. I'm just saying that the Chinese must be trained so that they resist the cunning of the Russians. No, that's not what I want to say. . . . What I'm getting at is that I speak up out of force of habit when there is something I ought to say. Maybe you'd better go now. I'm a little worried, since I don't know what I might say. If you have any affection for me, please go. The more I meet you, the more of a nuisance I become. And there is nothing good in that for me."

The seductive look that passed over Qiu-lan's face broke apart. A glimpse of the passion of the past could be detected at the edge of her lips, which had lost their balance and twitched slightly. She drew close to him. Concealing her anguish beneath her eyelashes, she kissed him again. But he felt more disdain than affection in her lips.

"Please go. There's no need to pity me like that," he said. "You have no choice but to love your country."

"You're a nihilist. If I thought as you do, I'd only be interested in acts that are doomed to defeat."

"You're misunderstanding. I'm not plotting to drag you down. It's just that I wonder how I came to be with you here. It may not be good for you, but to me our meeting was a stroke of luck. Even so, there is absolutely nothing you can do to stop my painful efforts to rid my life of the good fortune of meeting you. So please, go quickly."

Sanki opened the door for her.

"All right. I'll leave. But I don't think I'll be able to meet you anymore."

"Good-bye."

"Before I go, I'd like to hear your name once. You've

never told me your name."

"No, that's . . ." Sanki fell silent, his face clouding over. "I've been very rude to you, but not giving you my name has been best. It's enough that I know your name. So please, let's leave it at that."

"I can't go like this. Urban war will definitely break out tomorrow, and I don't know what our fate will be. Before I die I'd like to be able to recall your name and thank you."

Sanki could not fight the feeling of sadness that swept over him. He adjusted his stance like a folding fan that has been shut with a slap and quietly pushed her by the shoulder out the door.

"Good-bye."

"I'll come here again on the evening of the special ratepayers' meeting. Good-bye."

Standing in the middle of the room, Sanki caught himself straining his ears listening for the moment her footsteps would fade in the distance. He was tired, wondering again what he had been doing all this time.

Thirty-Five

Wild rumors began to fly throughout the city following the battle in the streets. White chalk marks were affixed to pillars on the houses of foreigners who were to be slaughtered. The Municipal Council, anticipating mass attacks in retaliation for the shootings, mobilized the Shanghai Volunteer Corps. Essential roads were guarded by the police. Armored vehicles crawled along accompanying the mounted police, who galloped back and forth with swords drawn. The wives of foreigners drove the cars carrying the militia, and messengers hurried between machine gun units. A state of martial law was declared in the city. The police would remove their holsters and wade into the boisterous crowds to drag out Russian Communists, as if they were pulling out the core of the insurrection. Speakers calling for the expulsion of foreigners cropped up one after another at the intersection of every street. Crowds squeezed in among the drawn swords of the police and surrounded them. The police brandished whips and tried to disperse them, but the crowds simply jeered and continued to swell.

Sanki had hardly been able to sleep since the previous night. He wandered the streets and alleys dressed in Chinese clothing. He no longer considered what might happen to him in the city. Occasionally he would try to calibrate the position of his own heart, as if trying to bring a hazy film into focus. Suddenly his surroundings began to reverberate, and a trolley, its windows smashed by flying rocks, came skidding across the street smeared in blood. It passed by as evidence of a battle that had taken place on some street nearby. He became aware again of the fact that he was Japanese. How many times had he been informed of that fact? Because of the danger posed by his being a flesh-and-blood embodiment of Japan, he felt that the crowd pressing in on him was a beast with fangs. He pictured simultaneously in his mind the spectacle before him now and the spectacle of his own body flowing from his mother's flesh. His own time, the flow marked by the interval between these two spectacles, was undoubtedly also the time of Japan's flesh and blood. And perhaps from this point on as well they would be one. So what could he do to liberate his heart from his body and freely forget his mother country? His flesh could not resist the simple fact that the external world forced him to be Japanese. It wasn't his heart that resisted. It was his skin that had to take on the world. And so his heart, in obedience to his skin, also began to resist. As Sanki walked through streets where weapons flashed at every corner, he became conscious of the faces in the crowds, which, because of the presence of the weapons, increasingly agitated him. People lost their individuality in the metal stream of bayonets and machine guns; and once they lost their individuality, they became more and more audacious as the throngs grew larger. In the midst of this people's movement, however, Sanki was still aware of his self, which had instinctively resolved to commit suicide. At the same time he felt the dynamic power of responsibility to his mother country, for which he was performing his suicidal actions, and wondered whether he would die of his own volition, or be forced to die. *Why is it that wherever I go my life is so dark?* He got the sense that the ideas he held about himself were not really his, but ideas he was made to think for the sake of Japan. Now he wanted to think for himself. But that would be to think of nothing at all. It would the same as killing himself. *Right, so everything is empty.* Recognizing his isolation, he felt depressed right to the very pit of his belly.

Guns filled with powder were concealed about the city in the face of hopes that were no longer visible to him. Crowds agitated for the expulsion of foreigners and moved on government offices. Water shot at the crowd from the nozzles of Fire Department hoses, which looked like hornet's nests arrayed on both sides of the street. Torrents of water shot into openings in the crowd, and stones fell with a clatter between people who had been knocked over. At each intersection police surveyed the crowd. When people heard a disturbance they headed in the direction of the noise. Sanki escaped from the swelling throngs and caught himself again looking for the figure of Qiu-lan as he had the day before. He stared into cracks in the crowd, which split apart because of the water and then regrouped. He saw leaning flags that had been knocked over. He craned his neck looking for shining earrings amid flying stones. He sensed in his heart a rise and fall in the crowd identical to the time just before he saw Qiu-lan yesterday. He anticipated the bullets that would soon come shooting out along with the water from the hoses. If a gun were fired once, no one, regardless of who they were, could predict the unrest in and around the port. At that moment the outer contour of the crowd was pushed forward by the force of the crowd's growth behind, and as it moved forward it obliterated the phalanx of hoses. The order to fire was given. The crack of rifles continued in succession. Sanki felt the pressure of the broken, surging crowd on his body. The human wave, which had been moving forward, now reversed its course and swirled over him. The stream of people blocked the trolley and threw rocks at the foreign shops on both sides of the street. When looting started, the crowds became violent and a riot spread over the streets in all directions. The mob directly in front of Sanki stopped suddenly and surrounded a Chinese man. They started to beat him, shouting that he was a dog. Then this "dog" was torn apart. His arms were raised high in the vanguard of the mob, which carried them off. His legs, looking like the horns of a large beast, moved off with the rest of the mob in the opposite direction. On the second floor of a building above the legs, which wobbled as they passed, the figures of Japanese dancers moved around together inside the windows. A shower of stones aimed at the windows skittered about. The mounted police turned on the mob and charged. A new armored vehicle followed the horses, shaking its antennae-guns, apparently eager to test its firepower. The crowds on the street retreated to the alleys, popping up again at the entrances of alleys farther along like water under pressure. As the alleys filled up, jeering laughter began to wash over the police.

The crowds mocked the mounted police right under their noses, as they slowly neared the hall of the General Labor Union. Labor associations and student groups had gathered there earlier and were holding a conference. On the streets surrounding the hall tens of thousands of students, men and women, were amassed waiting for the results of the meeting. The conference was called to discuss a proposal put forward by student groups to have merchants join the strike of the workers and students against foreigners. If this proposal passed, then all activity in the city would grind to a halt. And that would likely happen quickly.

Sanki realized that the cooperation between the Communists and the capitalists would pose a menace to the special ratepayers' conference scheduled to open two days from now. In spite of that, it occurred to Sanki that if on the day of the conference foreigners passed a plan to raise tariffs—a plan that would surely strangle Chinese merchants—the unrest in this city would begin to spread around the world. As the crowd that had been shot at flowed toward the hall, venting its violent anger at having been fired on again, it crashed into the crowd already surrounding the hall. There was a shudder as the mob flooded into the meeting. At the impetus of the wave of people who came crashing in, a strike resolution was presented, demonstrating the rapid progress of events inside the meeting.

Sanki believed that Fang Qiu-lan was hidden at the center of the vortex of this crowd. In order to find her he looked into the hues of the shaking whirlpool. His skin felt the layers of body heat maintain their equilibrium in the packed crowd. Then he tensed up at the uneasy feeling that he was the lone outsider. He could feel the countless fangs of the mob assembled between Qiu-lan and him, and he saw himself being gradually excluded by the common temperature that flowed through that crowd.

Thirty-Six

When Sanki finally broke away from the mob scene and went home, he found that Kōya had arrived and was waiting for him.

"I can't stay here any longer. In four or five days the lumber will arrive. When it gets here I'm going to take Miyako and run off to Singapore."

"Does Miyako know your plans?"

"Not yet. I don't know if I can get my money, or if Miyako will refuse me, but either way if things don't turn out right, then it's suicide."

"Well, they're both ruined for you. Starting tomorrow the banks will come under real pressure."

"In that case I can't even afford to commit suicide."

Sanki gazed silently at the perplexed expression on Kōya's face that revealed itself after his laughter died away. It was impossible for him to step into the cold mental state that flowed inside Sanki. And Sanki, for his part, could feel from the undulations of Kōya's healthy desires the warm sun of a phantom past he had forgotten long ago. Kyōko's face appeared in every corner of the room.

"We can't go on like this. We have to do something," said Kōya.

"What are you going to do?"

"If I knew that I wouldn't be in trouble, would I?"

"Aren't you better off convincing Miyako to marry you?"

"And what will you do?"

"Me?"

Sanki only wanted to meet Qiu-lan one more time. The one possibility was limited to his sneaking a glance at her when the ratepayers' conference opened in two days. Sanki became

161

aware of the sharp reality that for both of them their last desire in all this turmoil was to see a woman. He laughed and said, "You can't get Miyako off your mind, can you?"

"I can't, even though she treats me so coldly. To her I'm no good unless I sell off all the lumber in Singapore."

"When you got here you said that you wouldn't go back until you had defeated the Philippine competition. But maybe I shouldn't make sarcastic remarks. I don't think you should see her anymore. She's got you turned completely inside out."

"I'm not the only one who's messed up. The whole city is topsy-turvy. But it doesn't matter if I get back on my feet or not, since I'll just get turned inside out again."

Kōya stood up. He looked like he was carrying the weight of the world. He pulled a letter from Kyōko out of his pocket and left. In the letter she wrote that all the unrest in the city kept her from returning to Shanghai.

Sanki thought, who is it that prevents Kyōko from coming back? From the depths of his memory of the wide black wings of violence he had witnessed day after day, the face of Qiu-lan appeared in its various manifestations.

Thirty-Seven

Miyako got onto the rickshaw. She had been invited out by Kōya and wanted to go see the figures of her foreign suitors, who had joined the militias and were performing their duties in the city. In contrast Kōya, whose self-esteem had been laid low by the repeated blows of Miyako, could only steel himself against further assaults. The two got off the rickshaw that evening at a riverside park. As always prostitutes were lined up on benches with their heads drooping. A fountain sent up tongues of water visible in the gaps between the chilled, poisoned skin of the women. The light of a gas lamp filtered through the shade of the linden trees after a rain. Kōya continued to press his talk of marriage, all the while trying to gauge the meaning of Miyako's expressions.

"There's nothing left for me to say. Would it be wrong of me to ask you one more time?"

"You really are tiresome. Pressing me like this all the time. Enough already."

"I've confessed everything to you. But I still have one request."

Miyako leaned on his shoulder and laughed. "I don't dislike you. It's just that when someone says the same thing over and over, it makes me a little crazy."

When Kōya sat down on a bench, Miyako followed suit. He kicked at the lights of the junks with the tip of his shoe and began to squirm as if he were trying to slip out from between the words they had spoken in the past. Then, from the forest of masts on the opposite shore a rioting crowd suddenly appeared and ran inside a factory. Glass shattered at a power station. Guns spit forth fire inside the windows. The darkened shadows of the

163

riot moved to a tobacco factory next door. From the sea a group of blue lamps on motorboats began to race around, aiming for the masts on the far shore as though to close them in.

Kōya shook Miyako to pull her distracted mind away from the uproar in the distance.

"That's there, this is here. Listen. I sit here and talk with you like this, but it doesn't do any good. Why can't you just say yes, to set me at ease once and for all? Let's go to my place right away."

"Look at all the smoke over there. That's English and American tobacco. This area is finished."

"I don't care what happens to this area. It was broken down to begin with. Run away with me to Singapore."

"There's no place as important to me as this city. If I left I'd be a fish out of water. If I couldn't do anything, I'd die. I've always resigned myself to this life, but when it comes right down to it I like living in this city."

The mood he had tried to create had been shattered. Kōya grabbed the back of the bench, as though he were seeking refuge, and said in a flustered voice, "Don't think about that kind of thing. If you marry me, I'll make things right. That's enough isn't it? If I do that, I . . ."

"I never thought I wanted to get married in the first place. If I had wanted to get married I would have said yes right away when you first brought it up. A woman like me can't put on airs like you do when it comes to marriage."

Kōya burst out laughing, as if embarrassed.

"Look, you can criticize me all you want, but I don't have time to put on airs. Anyway, no matter how much I chase around after you, I'm just running round and round. It's no big deal."

"Listen to me carefully. I'm not right for you. I can't imagine a life with only one man. Whenever I look at a man, they all look the same to me. If we married, you'd be sure to run around on me. Beyond that, in my own fashion I've cajoled

164

and fooled a lot of men, and some got really angry about it. The ones who think they were deceived by me are fools. I mean, nowadays, there aren't many men who get annoyed, thinking they've been deceived. Not even in Japan. What kind of woman am I to you? I'm sure you can tell at a glance. When you talk to me about becoming your bride, I take it as a joke. That's just the way I am. I can't go for an ordinary life."

As the tide came in, the air dropped like a cold curtain and seeped into Kōya's body. He released her from his arm. Shadows of women he did not even know yet mingled in a corner of his heart, which was sinking like a broken chain. Out of all those shadows, only Miyako's floated up distinctly.

"I can't give you up." Kōya tried to embrace her. Several prostitutes, clumped together on a bench behind them like a bunch of mushrooms, stared at them. He let out a sigh, pulled away from her, and straightened his back. In response Miyako's body leaned into him. As he pulled her near him again, he was astounded by the sudden change in her attitude. She said, "Please let me stay with you like this for a while. If I don't do this with someone once in a while, then I fall into bad habits. I understand how you feel. But I'm not right for you. You should find a beautiful woman and go back to Singapore. It's my disposition. I'd do this sort of thing with anyone. I'm sorry to treat you like this, but I can't help it."

Each time the tips of her imitation leather shoes lightly touched his shoes, his arms went slack. He knew very well that this was simply a new tactic to comfort him.

"I knew all along that you were kind, so please stop leading me on. I can't help it if I love you."

"You're not yourself tonight, talking about such tedious matters. Look at that bridge over there. The militia charging about. And you? Here you are talking childishly. At a time like this you should do something more. Do something."

Kōya pushed her onto the grass and stood up. But then he knew he had played into the hands of a woman who had schemed to make him angry. So he sat down in front of her and said, "Stop tormenting me. I'll always be inferior to you. My only fault is that I've fallen in love with you. Why do you tease me like this?"

Miyako shook her hair and got up.

"Let's go home. I know you love me, and that makes me more selfish. Please don't say anything more to me."

Kōya realized he had just been brushed off and was unable to move. Miyako walked on alone toward the park entrance, glancing back from time to time. Kōya had slumped onto the grass. In the scene over his head, in the distance, shots continued to be fired from the tobacco factory, which was now ablaze.

Thirty-Eight

The strategy of the Chinese in Shanghai changed. All of the Chinese trade associations—the Federation of Street Unions, the Chinese Ratepayers' Union, and the Shanghai General Labor Union—united and agreed to begin a merchants' strike. Student groups went around to every shop and advised them to cease operations. Notices announcing the merchants' strike formed a new layer on walls everywhere. Trolleys stopped, telephones stopped. Schools announced they were closing without setting a date for reopening. Throughout the city, shops shut their doors and markets were locked up. The Municipal Council went ahead with its plans to convene the special ratepayers' meeting. The district around the meeting hall was placed under martial law. Police and militia units circled the area, bayonets drawn every few yards. As the time of the meeting neared the district grew eerily quiet as portentous rumors flooded the city. Eyes of militiamen flashed. Police moved in and out of the buildings in the neighborhood, working continually to ferret out hidden bombs. Armored cars slipped noiselessly between rows of hoses hooked up to fire hydrants. Presently armed foreign delegates began to arrive one after another.

Sanki also arrived precisely at that moment. Beyond the line where traffic had been suspended on the streets adjacent to the hall, crowds of people streaming in from various sections of the city massed in the squares and looked at each other's faces as if they were waiting for something to occur. Slipping through the mass of humanity, Sanki searched for Qiu-lan's face, which he was certain would be hidden somewhere in the throng. If she had not forgotten her words, her tacit promise to him, he expected she would not forget that he would look for her in this area. However, as he walked along he began to have a premonition, like the crowd around him, that something unforeseen was about to happen. The crowd inched forward little by little until it transgressed the traffic barriers and pressed toward the hall. The mounted police followed the contours of the roiling crowd and made their horses prance. A vehicle carrying members of the Scottish militia, their weapons bristling, raced by at full speed. Part of the crowd fell silent. Then the silence spread through the crowd, which had just now been so raucous, as though every sound was being sucked up by a mysterious breeze. At the moment when all noise stopped completely, only the footsteps of the Chinese reverberated faintly in Sanki's ears from the depths of that silence. He realized that that sound, which indicated nothing meaningful, was merely the silence itself. Then the crowd began to make noise again. A ripple of words spreading through the uproar announced the adjournment of the meeting. If that were true, then the aim of the Chinese business and labor groups had been achieved. Sanki learned from the murmuring that the reason for the postponement was the lack of a quorum. He could imagine Qiu-lan's smiling face announcing that the meeting had been canceled. She was no doubt somewhere in a building nearby absorbed in her next scheme. Of course, if the merchants' strike continued, eventually it would have a deleterious effect on the Chinese merchants as well. And if they were adversely affected, they would eventually come into conflict with the activities of Qiu-lan's faction, for whom the continuation of the strike was a necessity.

The more Sanki thought about it, he was sure that some scheme would be hatched tonight. And he understood that such a scheme would be aimed at uniting the business groups and the masses. But how would they do it? If they could somehow force the foreigners to fire their weapons, that would be sufficient.

Sanki was aware that the gyrations of his mind were an extension of that futile part of himself. If he died now it would be all right. If he died, that is. Regardless, the desire to see Qiu-lan followed after him relentlessly; and he continued to kick at the shadow of the man who dominated his interior. He sensed the color of earrings flashing from a crowded street corner that was merging at dusk into the rainy-season sky. Staring at that point of light, he moved like a fish through the crowd, which formed a tunnel around him. Before he got to the corner he stopped. Even if those were Qiu-lan's earrings, deep in his heart he considered what would happen once he met her. Even if he found her, there was absolutely nothing for them to do. *In that case . . . But no. Why would she come looking for me right in the midst of this disturbance?* He pressed his back against a wall and suppressed his feelings, his desire to imagine that she would come looking for him. *And yet if she had not forgotten her own words?* At this he laughed, making light of the feelings of love that sprang up and would not be denied, despite his best efforts.

An American cavalry unit came galloping in Sanki's direction through the crowded alley in front of him. Suddenly gunfire erupted from the buildings on both sides of the alley. The lead horse reared up. In the uproar another horse fell limply to the ground. A third horse threw its rider, leaped over him, and galloped off. Several other horses tried to follow, their heads drawn up as they ran around in circles. One horse pranced into an alley. Rifle barrels gleamed over the heads of the confused horses. The cavalrymen turned their rifles on the buildings and started to shoot. Again the horses began to run around in the crowd. People poured out from alleys on all sides and whooped loudly at the prancing animals. A shower of rocks were aimed at the horses' eyes. One horse jumped over another that had fallen, kicked at the surging crowd and escaped.

The crowd closed in on Sanki, swelling and contracting at the advance and retreat of the horses like some liquid solution. With each oscillation he was knocked about by the undulating motion in a strange version of battledore and shuttlecock. Twisted around by the movement, he eventually slapped against a wall near the entrance to an alley.

When the horses fled, the crowd filled the street, frolicking and imitating the bewildered cavalrymen. Gunsmoke was seeping from the buildings where the shooting had started. All at once a machine gun brigade from the Municipal Police pulled up and took revenge by firing into the crowd. The crowd sprang up. People lost their voices and began to shake like a violent wind. A whirlwind of bullets, centered on the bodies that had fallen, split the wave of humanity exactly in two. The entrance of the alley filled with crawling bodies. The gate at the entrance, which had been shut, now had a hole in it that shined forth like an eye. The crowd, which had fled too late, cowered under the gate and groaned.

Sanki, alone of all the bodies huddled there, looked back around over the road. He strained to spot the body of Qiu-lan among those who had fallen and were not moving. Someone had stumbled and was writhing beside the neck of a fallen horse.

A hazy smoke crept over the bodies from the houses where the first shots had been fired. The smoke shimmered each time the patrol passed. Because he had been forced to witness day after day the sound of falling corpses and the confusion, Sanki viewed the dynamic scene before him as a common, everyday event. Nonetheless, though his heart had grown indifferent to the turmoil around him, he clearly sensed the vivid extension of his feelings of love, which roamed freely over the confusion of the external world.

The number of people on the street dwindled and the municipal police surrounded the houses where the shots had been fired. A machine gun was set up. Then, as if they were disinfecting a house, they sprayed bullets into the pitch-black interior. The sound of crashing objects and moaning voices arose together with the rhythmic clatter of bullets ricocheting off stone. The door spewed out white powder, and, as he watched, a hole opened in it. The machine gun stopped and the door was kicked in and knocked off its hinges. A squad of policemen, pistols raised, slipped in under the characters on a sign that was still swaying as it dangled from a rail. A group of young Chinese and three Russians were hauled out at gunpoint.

Sanki stared at the Chinese, who were dragged off to a corner of the alley, and wondered if Qiu-lan had been in there. The group that had been arrested was forced into a vehicle and escorted away by the machine gun brigade. As soon as they knew the guns were gone, the crowd trickled out from the alleys. They pulled corpses from the darkened street back into the alleyways. The heads of the corpses, stretched out at full length, were dragged along like writing brushes, tracing out black lines on the asphalt with blood-soaked hair. A foreign car came sliding by, riding over the corpses. The faces of a man and woman who had been kissing inside that car appeared disheveled, out of fear of being discovered, and were obscured by bouquets of jasmine. Stones came flying at their heads. The vehicle ran over the line of corpses and sped off, jostling those two tired, limp faces.

Sanki slipped through the crowd and came to the front of the building where he had met Qiu-lan previously. He could feel in his searching eyes the exhaustion of his whole body. As he grew weary, the phantoms he was seeking—those things he thought were there that were not—began to dissipate. As he trudged aimlessly between the buildings, his body, bearing his heavy heart, came back to him. He lingered awhile, walking back and forth beneath a gate. He thought that if Qiu-lan were here she would definitely have to pass this spot. He looked up at the top of some tall buildings and stood with his back pressed flat against the frame of the gate as though he were napping. Then he saw three young Chinese approach from the other side of the road. One of the men, who had a short bristling mustache, brushed Sanki's right hand as he passed. Sanki felt a hard scrap of paper from the young man's cold hand. Caught off guard, he realized now that it was Qiu-lan disguised as a man. By the time he recognized her she had walked on shoulder to shoulder with the other two. Gripping the scrap of paper, Sanki followed

171

her a short distance. But then it occurred to him that he was putting her in serious danger. Her graceful shoulders gave a feeling of gentleness, and she glanced back at him once. Sanki felt in the soft light of her eyes a lament at parting, at having chosen not to come to him. He stopped in his tracks and did not follow her any further. His heart was violently agitated by the anticipation of reading her note.

Seeing her figure swallowed up in the crush of people, Sanki hurriedly turned round and went back. He brightened up as though all his hopes had just been thrust into his hand. He walked on, oblivious to the road he had been trudging along just moments earlier in a melancholy mood. He saw a bridge to the safe side of the river. He opened the letter when he crossed over and glanced at it. A note had been scribbled in pencil, apparently in haste.

"We will be in terrible danger tonight. Thank you for all you have done for me. Please take care of yourself. If we survive this, please call on a messenger named Chen who works at the Jordan Madison Company. Farewell."

Sanki moved through the proudly blooming canna flowers in the middle of a park. There was a lawn there. Scraps of paper rustled in the wind and blew at his feet. Grabbing hold of an iron railing, damp in the blowing mist, he looked down at the waves at his feet.

It's all over.

The more he thought about it, his face leaning forward over the waves, the more Sanki was aware of a profound emptiness.

Thirty-Nine

Late that night Sanki knocked at Miyako's door. Miyako appeared in her pajamas, pulling on a housecoat. Without a word she had Sanki sit on the divan. He motioned an apology with his hand, and then collapsed, his eyes closed. She brought him a whiskey and sat down next to him, silently staring at his pale face. A candle flame passing through the hall of the house next door slid through the pomegranate leaves in the window glass and disappeared. Sanki finally opened his eyes.

"Please forgive me for acting this way tonight."

Staring at the bottom of the cup she was pressing to his mouth, he strongly grasped Miyako's hand. She said, "You're acting very odd tonight. I was startled just now, you going on so, but I didn't know what was wrong."

Miyako suddenly became more animated. She looked into the mirror and patted her face. The housecoat she had pulled on slipped down off her shoulder.

"Just before you arrived I was having a dream about you. And then you showed up. Just imagine what I was doing with you up to then."

She came back over from the mirror and cradled Sanki's head on her knees. Her face was close to his. "Cheer up. I hate looking at your tired face."

He got up and clasped her hand. "This is really tedious."

"What is?"

"Will you let me sleep here quietly?" He sank back and closed his eyes. Miyako shook his body violently.

"This won't do at all. You wake me up then go to sleep yourself? I'm not your wife yet, you know!"

Sanki drank another glass of whiskey.

"That's it. Good boy. Well, I never accepted your self-ishness from the beginning. I could never once sympathize with someone like you. Every time you look at someone you're frowning. You only think about the most boring things. Stop acting like that. If I ever fell in love with someone like you, it'd be the end of the world."

As she berated him Sanki could feel the intoxication from his drink circulating through his body. "Please forgive me. I understand why you're scolding me this way."

"It's only reasonable to scold you. Why should I have to look at your melancholy appearance. I can see a lot of people like you moping around on the streets. I may be a really stupid person, but at least I know what's interesting."

Miyako turned away, apparently in a foul mood. She took a cigarette. Observing her appearance, her sudden anger was unexpected. Exhausted, he slumped back on the divan. Miyako swept up the housecoat that she had dropped on the floor and went to her bedroom.

"Why don't you stay up with me a little longer? I'll perk up eventually."

"No thanks. I wouldn't be your companion for anything."

"It's not so bad having a man like me around some-times. It's certainly not something to get mad about. I don't know how many times I've had a brush with death today. I seldom come here really tired. When people are tired they tend to go to the closest place they know. So don't be like that. Stay with me for a while."

Miyako stood in front of the door and turned to face Sanki.

"What has happened to you? You aren't a ghost, are you?"

"I don't think I am. The truth is that I came here to make a small confession. But now I don't feel like talking. If I act any more foolishly I'll end up having to make an apology to the gods."

"That's right. But you don't just owe the gods an apology. You owe me one too. It's OK for you to think about Kyōko all the time, but what about me?"

"Kyōko is Kyōko and you're you. If I'm going to be a frivolous man I may as well go all the way. That's why I was thinking I should be reckless tonight, come what may. But in the end I failed. Somehow, once I start talking, I end up talking like this."

"So talk. Tell me what you were doing before you came here."

Miyako flopped down next to him, cradled his head again, and began to rock. Sanki went over in his mind all the things that had happened that day. He began to feel heavy as his heart collided more and more with his body. He started to speak as though he were liberating his suffocating emotions.

"Recently I've been attracted to a Chinese woman I admire. I've been struggling with my self-respect for a month. Tonight was the final straw for me. I thought I would be killed and that if I were to die that it would be better to be killed by the Chinese. If just one Japanese were killed, it would strengthen Japan's position. At least I thought so. I'm a patriot, so if I'm going to die then I figured it should be for my country. But I can't get the Chinese to kill me. All this time I'm thinking if I die but I'm not killed it won't do any good for my country. And so if I am going to die, then I should try to be killed. Always this dilemma. Now it looks like I won't even be killed."

"What a fine station in life. I hate stories like yours."

"I wondered why I hadn't been killed. It was because I was wandering about dressed up as a Chinese. So why did I dress up like a Chinese? If I hadn't and I somehow managed to meet the woman, it wouldn't have done any good. That's my new torment. See? These clothes are new, right?"

"You're such an idiot. I've heard all this before. Just a little while ago I was dreaming about you. It wouldn't hurt you in the least to think about that."

"But look at it from my point of view. Maybe all this is nothing more than an absurd dream, and I may be a little crazy

175

to take it seriously. If you chase after foolish things all the time, sooner or later it affects your mind and you become good at being a fool. In your case you're getting sulky and acting silly about Kōya's proposal. You understand, don't you?"

"Of course. Distracted by someone like you, I'm ready to become a bride. If it's you. You can tell Kōya that. The fact that he introduced me to you makes it all the more ridiculous. I won't marry him, because I want to marry you. That's my revenge on you. You only care about Kōya's feelings, and you're scheming to get away from me. If you weren't, you wouldn't be telling me these things about your Chinese woman. You're pretty pathetic. After all, being a patriot is no big deal."

Miyako stood up and began to tap the round table with a white orchid flower she had pulled from the vase. Aware there was another fool in the room, his spirits rose pleasantly over his liquor.

"Come here. A patriot is an extraordinary person. I sympathize with you. I am definitely the one who understands you the best. Without understanding there can't be love. So come here. I love you."

Miyako pushed him away when he tried to move close to her. He stumbled into the wall behind her, and put his hand on her shoulder.

"Stop it! I'm not Chinese!"

"It doesn't matter whether you're Chinese or codfish. Once a person says they're a patriot, then no matter who they are they're my benefactor. Is there anything else except patriotism for those of us in the lower levels of society?"

Sanki picked her up by her legs, as though he would trip her, and spun faster and faster in the middle of the rug. Then his legs buckled. The two of them collapsed in a heap. Miyako was thrown away from his chest as she fell and lay there not moving. Sanki was face up. Gazing happily at the flowers of the wallpaper, which continued to spin around him, he saw the face of his mother emerge from the floral pattern. He started laughing and couldn't stop.

Forty

Although the special ratepayers' meeting had been canceled, the merchants' strike deepened. Chinese banks closed the day after the meeting was canceled. Cheques from the Qian Zhuang were suspended. The gold market was closed. Foreign banks were powerless in the face of the chaos in the currency markets. The port's financial functions had been utterly disrupted, and only the faint sound of foreign exchange could be heard, like a pulse, in the recesses of the foreign banks.

Banks weren't the only things to have collapsed. Nearly all the factories in the city were locked up. The coolies on the piers went on strike. Hotel workers began to run away. Chinese patrolmen on the police force quit, followed by rickshawmen, drivers, postal deliverers, ship crews, and all others employed by foreigners.

Ships floated idly in the harbor loaded down with cargo. The printing of newspapers became impossible. Musicians carried food to the guests at hotels. Bakers disappeared. Meat and vegetables were no longer available. Foreigners were gradually besieged in the seaport, struck by the new power of the Chinese.

Sanki enjoyed walking along streets that held almost no pedestrians. The city, usually crowded and bustling, was suddenly like a forest. But it felt to him that the streets were bustling in a very different way. The militia frequently chased after trucks on which rioters had placed bombs. Sometimes groups of Chinese cyclists, wearing white gloves, would slip like a breeze between buildings under the cover of evening shadows as they secretly conspired. Foreign wives carried food to the exhausted volunteer militia. Eyes sparkled, spying on the outside from cracks in the closed doors that lined the streets.

Sanki heard rumors about the Japanese section of the city, which was assaulted frequently by rioters. So he headed toward that part of town. Wives and children there had been sent to a haven, while a volunteer garrison organized by the community bravely defended the streets and kept all-night vigils. Then, fragments of the memory of his affection for Qiu-lan came to him, affecting his equilibrium. He left the road as though he were covered by smoke. He went out when he learned that food supplies had been cut off from the Japanese settlement, when he heard rumors of Japanese being assassinated, and when he had evidence that rioters had appeared in the streets somewhere. Before long he began to feel as though he was a scout moving around the perimeter of the Japanese settlement. Each time he went out he was overwhelmed by stories of the increasing number of Japanese who had been hurt. These stories seemed to suffocate him.

One day, when Sanki and Kōya went out to their usual place to get a meal, they were refused and told there was no food. It was said that Chinese who smuggled in rice were executed if they were caught. There were no eggs or meat. Even shortages of vegetables became commonplace.

As Kōya accompanied Sanki he said, "There's nothing left to do except starve to death. The banks may still be here, but they're just a pile of stone. My lumber has arrived, and there's no one to unload it. I've been dumped by Miyako, and there's no food to eat. Do the gods know about these cruel tricks? Do they?"

Sanki could feel his stomach, which had been empty since the previous night, climbing up and complaining to his head. He was vaguely conscious that the party responsible for his hunger was his Japanese body. If his body were Chinese, then all he'd have to do was lift his hand to be able to eat. Not unreasonably he felt that this territory, Shanghai, had penetrated his flesh and bones more solidly than iron.

Kōya asked, "Do you get a per diem during the layoff?

178

I'm already out of money. I'll be relying on your per diem for a while, so don't forget it."

"That's right. I'd forgotten all about the per diem. Things turn out one way or another. If they don't pay it, then I'm going on strike next."

"And what will happen to your strike? You were beaten to it by the Chinese, so nothing would come of it."

"In that case I'd cooperate with the Chinese."

"You'd only make it more and more impossible for us to get food."

"Let's stop talking about food. I'm so hungry I can't stand it."

"But if they pay a per diem to the Japanese during the strike, and don't pay it to the Chinese, then there will be an even bigger strike. If things go on like this, I'll never eat again."

The two walked along, reading the scraps of paper pasted above the doors on the houses on both sides of the street. The scraps read "Assassinate foreigners!"

"Look on the bright side. We have to eat first in order to be killed," said Sanki.

"If I get killed any more than this, it'll be the end of me."

They laughed, but Sanki couldn't help thinking that his existence was a hindrance to Kōya and Miyako. Even with them he couldn't escape the fact that his existence was somehow unnecessary.

Sanki looked at Kōya. "Do you really love Miyako?"

"Yes, I do."

"How much do you love her?"

"For some reason the more she puts me down, the more I like her. It's as if I like being kicked."

"If you get married and things don't go well, what will you do?"

"Hey, things aren't going well for me now. How could I stand it if they got any worse?"

179

Sanki thought of himself in the past, of his secret love for Kyōko. Back then Kōya had the rights of an older brother, and so he always had Sanki by the throat. Now he was turning the tables and choking Kōya.

"So what do you think of Osugi?" asked Sanki.

"Her? To me she's the kind of woman who gets sacrificed on the way."

"She may be a sacrifice to you, but I was thinking about marrying her. You took her, didn't you."

For a moment Kōya blushed scarlet. Still red, he nevertheless thrust out his chest and said, "Maybe I did, but hasn't she been sacrificed by everyone now?"

Sanki thought of Miyako, who was becoming his sacrifice. He now looked at Kōya, who was becoming Miyako's sacrifice, in a different light.

"Anyway, I won't find a more suitable woman than Osugi. If you've tossed her aside, then you won't object, will you?" said Sanki.

"Stop joking about those things. Right now we can't get anything to eat. Pretty soon you'll be scrambling around for food."

Sanki fell quiet. His stomach, which he had forgotten momentarily, reared up again. He knew what a beggar's stomach felt like. His head, following his stomach, was restless, and he naturally thought of Fang Qiu-lan again. This strike was the thing she most wanted. As if he were staring at Qui-lan's sharp fangs, he took off in the direction of some streets where they might have an abundance of food, calculating the condition of his empty stomach, which stabbed at his side.

Everywhere they went was hard up for rice and vegetables. Someone said that foodstuffs would arrive from Nagasaki by tomorrow. To fill their bellies before then they would have to go through dangerous areas where mobs frequently appeared. And even then they still did not know if their destinations had food or not. Sanki promised to meet Kōya at the Turkish Bath, and, after seeing him back to a safe street corner, he set out on his own to find something to eat.

180

Forty-One

After Kōya left Sanki he found it increasingly difficult to deal with his hunger. To make matters worse, there was a shortage of tobacco to go along with the shortage of bread. He was the only person walking along the empty street, even though it was still early evening. It seemed that people were peeping out at him behind cracks in closed doors. When all was said and done, his brother Takashige had done a terrible thing. His bullets, and those of the Indians, were the cause of all the turmoil in the city. He considered the lumber on the ships floating in the harbor with no one to unload it. *That damn brother of mine!*

A rickshaw, apparently oblivious to the revolution rocking the city, came up to Kōya and encouraged him to get on. If a rickshawman were discovered pulling a Japanese now, he would certainly be killed. In spite of that, Kōya felt lucky to be offered a ride and hopped on. He had no idea where to tell the rickshawman to take him. After several minutes of traveling in the direction the rickshaw was facing when he got on, he looked at the runner's back. He was intrigued by this man who had given him a ride. The runner was pulling along someone who, for all intents and purposes, was the equivalent of the god of death. *Why not try following after him here and there, like a god of death, until the man was discovered and killed.* As Kōya mulled over such thoughts, he felt like creating mischief for his own satisfaction as recompense for the series of blows he had suffered the past two days. He raised his walking stick and struck the shafts of the rickshaw, shouting "Run! Run!" The runner hunched his back a little lower and began to increase his speed.

But where were they going? He conjured up a map in his head. Yamaguchi's house was the nearest place. Kōya had heard stories that discarded women loitered about there. What would they be doing living together with those corpses during this revolution? In any case Yamaguchi had said that he would give one of his women to Kōya. *All right. I'll go to Yamaguchi's house.* With no sign of anyone around, the early evening had a pleasant feel for Kōya as if it were giving off a mysterious light. He remembered the second line of work Yamaguchi had disclosed to him: the purchase of dead bodies from the Chinese to make and export skeletons for medical use.

Yamaguchi had proudly told him, "That's right. For the price of one body I can keep seven Russian mistresses. Seven." *Now he must be really happy. The number of dead would surely rise because of this uprising. Even this runner in front of me. If he were caught and killed, Yamaguchi would purchase him. . . . That's it! It would be the same as selling him. I'll tell him in a haughty manner, Hand over the money!*

"Run! Run!"

At each intersection the runner turned his pockmarked face, sweat pooling on his skin, and looked up at Kōya. Then he would head off in the direction Kōya pointed with his stick, raising a patter of bare feet over the deserted pavement.

Kōya thought that if Yamaguchi wasn't home he would try Oryū's place. Her husband would be managing the General Chamber of Commerce. He had no doubt that Fang Qiu-lan of the Communists was conspiring with Qian Shi-shan. According to Oryū, Fang Qiu-lan used to visit the secret room on the second floor. *If I killed Fang Qiu-lan. That's it. She's the bitch responsible for my lumber rotting away. But if I killed her, that's all I'd accomplish. It wouldn't amount to anymore than another murder.*

As he sat on the rickshaw he considered whether his thoughts were whimsical or sincere. Because of despair and hunger, he couldn't tell at what point his dream-like thoughts passed by without connecting to reality.

He noticed that the colors around him were gradually shifting to a pale gray. And before he knew it he sensed that he had come into a dangerous area outside the International Settlement. However, the insistence of his hunger overwhelmed any sound judgment concerning the conditions converging upon him, and so he continued to glide along in the rickshaw. He wondered what Miyako was up to now. *She might be waiting for me to go help her, regretting that she refused me outright last night. Or perhaps she was being assisted by that Scottish military officer who loved her. Or maybe by that guy Pfilzer. Let them die, the sons-of-bitches! Die!*

On the surface of the road in the distance the cottony ament of late-blooming willows was like blowing snow. He pulled out the handkerchief he had secretly taken from Miyako and brought it to his nose. The bluish grasses along the road were covered by the scent of Miyako's breast and faded away. He could feel the laughter of her torso in his arm. He calculated the amount of lumber on the ship he had used for her sake. Now, however, everything lay in ruins.

Just then the rickshaw passed under an arched brick gate, and he could see a rectangular space glittering ahead of him. An ice truck belonging to a Japanese company was being attacked by sixty or seventy rioters. The ice had been pulled off the truck and the company workers had been captured. The ice had split on the asphalt, and the Chinese and Japanese were fighting in among the shards. Kōya jerked back as though something had been stuffed into his open mouth. But the runner, in opposition to Kōya's wishes, continued to move ahead. Kōya jumped off and some of the rioters, their attention drawn by his sudden movements, came running after him. He flew into an alley, following along the wall until he came out onto a riverbank. Alone now, he knew that to move on would invite discovery by the mob. If he wanted to get away he could either jump into the river or double back out onto the street again and duck into an alley on the other side. As he crawled along, he looked toward an alley and the base of a building from where he could see the arched gate. The fight had continued there in the middle of a flurry of ament, which swept violently over the scene like a blizzard. Torn shirts whirled around on the truck amid the ament. Every time the tip of an iron rod hit the ice the surface would glisten, sparkling among the tattered clothes. The rickshaw he had been riding just a few minutes ago was overturned beside the arched gate, its pale yellow wheels pointed to the sky. Two legs were sticking out from under the rickshaw. Kōya knew for certain that those were the legs of his runner, who had been alive a few moments earlier. Blood was trickling down in a stream from the top of the board of ice that was now leaning to one side. Coolies, smeared in blood, picked up hunks of the ice and ran off.

Kōya reckoned that Yamaguchi's house was very close by. It would be far more dangerous to turn back now, having come this far. He would have to remain hidden there until the rioters moved from the chunks of ice to another spot.

At that moment the glow of a multi-rayed sunset was flowing over the top of a complex of buildings. Each time hunks of ice were picked off the asphalt and thrown their shattering facets would glitter in the light. A Japanese man who had suffered wounds from his shoulder down his back abandoned the truck and ran off with blood sticking to his shirt. He looked like he had wrapped himself in a bright red flag. The mob started chasing him.

Once the mob moved on, vacating the area in front of him, Kōya went out onto the street and took off running away from the mob in the direction of Yamaguchi's house. However, the moment he did that several of the rioters who had gone into the alley in pursuit spotted him and gave chase. Kōya was running like a gust of wind. He slashed through the whirling willow ament. Behind him he could hear fragments of ice and cursing voices speeding up their pursuit. He thought that he would dash into an alley again so that he wouldn't be overtaken. But then he spotted the barracks of an American garrison up ahead on the right side of the street. He abruptly plunged in among a line of uniformed soldiers standing there.

"Please, gentlemen! I beg you. I'm in danger. Over there . . ."

The soldiers merely laughed and made no effort to move, as though they were welcoming the mob that pursued him. It did not matter that he had stopped among soldiers. They did not move, and the danger was closing in on him moment by moment. Circling once around one of the soldiers, he pushed through to the rear as if squeezing through a picket fence, and took off running again. There was a bridge. Kōya looked back from the bridge to see if the soldiers had intercepted the mob chasing him. But the rioters had already passed the soldiers, who stood there laughing, and were now almost on him. Kōya was out of breath. He couldn't tell if the joints in his legs were moving. He seemed at times to be swimming through space, and from time to time he stumbled forward. He would catch himself with both hands, and then run some more. Reaching the other end of the bridge, he could see at the next corner British soldiers dressed in new grass-green uniforms. When the British soldiers saw Kōya running toward them, they immediately formed ranks and aimed their rifles. But they weren't aiming at Kōya. They were aiming at the Chinese rioters chasing him. Kōya raised both arms and, like a runner breaking the tape at the finish line, he dashed in among the soldiers' rifles, putting all his feelings of gratitude into lips that would not move.

When he arrived at Yamaguchi's doorstep he stood there in a daze and was unable to tell Yamaguchi anything.

"What happened to you?" Yamaguchi asked as he came out the door. Kōya remained silent. Yamaguchi slapped him hard on the back, led him up a flight of stairs, and gave him a drink of water.

"You want to sleep?"

"I'll sleep."

Kōya lay down on the bed there.

"Give me some bread. Bread! No, water . . . water."

Forty-Two

Once the sun had set and he had had a good meal at last, Kōya perked up. He told Yamaguchi about all the things that had happened to him since morning. "That's why as soon as I entered your house I underwent a sudden, sharp conversion. I've become a patriot like you now, except that maybe I'm even more patriotic. So get used to it."

"Fine."

Yamaguchi, the architect who supported Asia for Asians, pulled a knife from his pocket and thrust it forward, telling Kōya that they would make a blood oath. Seeing the black finger marks that had accumulated on the groove of the knife, Kōya drew in his chin thinking that the skin of the bodies Yamaguchi touched these days had no doubt accumulated there.

"That reminds me. I have to get some money from you," Kōya said. "The runner of the rickshaw that brought me here today was killed under the gate. So what do you think? It's the same as if I killed him, so it's natural that I should get the money for my labors. I haven't a cent and I'm in a real bind. It's not a joke."

"No, that's not right. You're not the one who killed him."

"But if I hadn't gotten on the rickshaw would that guy be dead now? And just who do you think it was who went to the trouble of being chased all the way to your house?"

Yamaguchi waved his hand to brush away Kōya's resourcefulness, which annoyed him. "No, no, if you're going to talk like that, then I'd always have to pay you in advance for bones, wouldn't I?"

"But I need it now. I don't have any prospects of getting my lumber off the ships. This is all the money I have." Kōya shook his pocket and jingled some coppers. "If you don't give me something, then I'll have no choice but scrounge off you here until I die. Do you want that?"

"No, that would be a bother too,"Yamaguchi conceded, flipping the knife onto a desk.

"If it's so much trouble, then it's better to help me out of my bind. I almost gave up my life today just to bring in that driver."

"Oh, all right. I suppose there's nothing I can do about it. Under the circumstances I can sympathize with you this time. I'll work something out."

"Thank you. You're a true patriot. I'm counting on you."

Yamaguchi stood up and took a candle out of the desk drawer. "Let's go to the basement. I'll show you my workshop. I'm in the process of making three skeletons. I've never shown this place to anyone, so keep that in mind when you come with me."

Kōya followed Yamaguchi and descended through an opening in the floor. He climbed down a ladder into the basement through a pitch-black square opening that reeked of mold. Yamaguchi turned around and looked at Kōya. Fixing his eyes on the depths of the candle's light, which made him look like one of those pictures in a detective story, he said, "Once you enter here there's no turning back. So prepare yourself."

"What are you talking about? Are you going to take my life too?"

"Of course. After all, if I spare you my own food will start to run out."

They pushed open an interior door and moved further in. Kōya's legs froze. Under white bones dangling from the wall a Chinese assistant was washing a severed leg with a brush and alcohol. Kōya had anticipated that such work was needed to prepare the bones. But when he took a closer look at the edge of a bucket filled with bones, lying in a sparkling, pure-white mound, he noticed something slithering. It was a swarm of insects trying to crawl out. He felt the cold shells of the bugs as they came creeping one by one at his feet. He could no longer stand there.

"I'm getting out of here. This is more than enough for me." Just then he glanced at the wall. Rats were scurrying around some of the white ribcages hanging there. Two, then three, then a lot more than three. Gradually he made out a swarm of rats crossing from one of the pitch-black corners, crawling in and out of the openings in the ribcages as they followed along the wall and descended.

"Do you feed them?"

"Of course I do. If they beat us to the bodies it saves us a lot of work. Rats have subsisted since ancient times by scavenging." Yamaguchi's face cast an enormous shadow in the flame of the candle. He resembled a savage tribesman. Kōya was frightened.

"There's a revolution going on over our heads, and you spend time down here thinking about such things?"

"There may be a revolution up there, but it's a Chinese revolution, isn't it? The only ones who will come out weaker are the whites. If we don't stick it to the Europeans at least once, we'll always play the fool for them. So I'm all for Asia."

Yamaguchi went over to the rats and stuck out his hand. A large number of rats clambered over him from his knees to his shoulders, gathering, climbing, rolling and falling, tumbling and crawling back up to his head. He turned to Kōya, rats stuck to his body like a suit of armor.

"What do you say? Want to give it a try?"

Kōya closed the door and started back to the ladder alone.

"Hey! Don't run away, Kōya! There's more inside! In here!"

But Kōya had seen plenty. Nauseous from the stench and filth, he climbed back up the ladder, his hand on his chest. He tried imagining Yamaguchi's Russian women, who were in effect supported by the bones he had seen just now. Those women, of course, had been driven from their mother country by revolution. *What did they look like?* He could hardly wait to see them.

Forty-Three

Yamaguchi introduced Kōya to the young, stout-hipped, Teutonic Olga. At first she was sullen and quiet. But as soon as she learned that Kōya was Sanki's friend, she began to chatter away in English as though someone had thrown a switch.

"Oh, you're a friend of Sanki? I wonder what he's up to? I spent a week playing with him here."

"That's right. He was here for a week, but in the end Olga was too much for him and he ran away." Yamaguchi was standing in front of a mirror wiping off the shaving soap that had built up on his razor.

"He was here? I didn't know that. Is that right? Him?" Kōya looked at Olga differently now. "So tell me, Olga, what do you think of this Chinese revolution. Is it different from Russia's?"

"Let's not talk about revolutions. Olga here will just end up crying. Once she gets started talking about the revolution, she gets like a crazy person."

"I'd like to hear about that more than anything else. C'mon, ask her to talk about it a little."

"If you really want to hear about that do it later on your own time. If I don't do a little work now I won't be able to sleep."

Was Yamaguchi planning to turn Olga over to him, as he had mentioned once? Kōya searched Yamaguchi's face, concerned that he might use her as payment for the rickshaw driver in place of money.

Yamaguchi put his razor down. He stared into the mirror and stroked his chin over and over. "Of course, it's OK if I leave you here alone, isn't it?"

"What do mean, OK?" Kōya looked up at Yamaguchi suspiciously.

189

"Because there are a lot of rats around. You don't get it, do you?"

"No, I'm afraid I don't understand. If you don't want me to attract your rats, you don't have to go out, do you?"

"You have to understand. Given what's going on out there, your rickshawman will likely be picked up if I don't hurry. After that I have to go over to Osugi's place."

Kōya was caught off guard by the mention of Osugi, and there was an unconscious catch in his breathing. His words stuck in his throat. *So this man as well . . . ?*

Kōya drew Osugi's face in his mind. It occurred to him that both Sanki and Yamaguchi knew what he had done to her, and deep within his heart he felt that they were stabbing at him. However, he secretly grew haughty, and an absent-minded laugh came to his lips. He said, feigning innocence, "Osugi? Isn't she at Kita Shisenro in Minagawa? 13-8?"

"Oh, so you've been there?" For an instant a frown flickered over Yamaguchi's face as he returned Kōya's stare.

Thinking that Yamaguchi might be sincerely in love with Osugi, Kōya was again caught off guard and corrected himself. "No, I heard that from Oryū. It was her doing that forced Osugi into that. It's pathetic, really, but there's one other person who should be pitied."

"Do you mean me?" Yamaguchi clenched his fist as if he meant to strike Kōya.

"Don't be ridiculous. Why should anyone pity you? Olga is the one I feel sorry for. Do you really expect her to tolerate spending the evening alone?"

Yamaguchi snickered and calmly put his hat on. "Tonight might be a little risky. If I'm killed I have a favor to ask of you. Apparently Fang Qiu-lan was shot and killed by her comrades. They suspected her of spying. Didn't you chase after her once?"

"Killed? Fang Qiu-lan?" Kōya blurted out.

"I don't know if it's true or not. She was suspected of

carrying on secret communications with some Japanese man. I was thinking that I might get her bones."

Yamaguchi pulled out a notebook and a letter from his pocket. He showed them to Kōya. "If I die I want you to meet two people for me. A Chinese man named Li Ying-pu and an Indian named Panjit Amuli. The Indian runs a jewelry business, but in fact he's a member of India's Congress faction, a top disciple of one of its leaders, Chittaranjan Das. When you meet them they'll tell you what to do."

"Then you're going to become a corpse yourself tonight?"

Yamaguchi studied Kōya for a minute, then burst out in a high-pitched laugh. "That's right. If I end up a corpse, feed me to my rats. I'm sure that's what they really want."

"Maybe it is. After all, there are probably a few Marxists among the rats these days."

Yamaguchi sensed a gentle friendship in Kōya's making light of a such a situation. He patted Olga on the shoulder and said to her in English, "You be nice to Kōya here. There's no one else besides him who can help you find your beloved Sanki." He turned to Kōya. "Sorry for the bother, but I'm counting on you. Please go ahead and read this letter from Li. It's rather well-written."

Kōya saw Yamaguchi off. He was sure Yamaguchi had lied when he said he would go to pick up the body. Instead he was probably undertaking something else, perhaps some task for his pro-Asianist faction. Kōya looked at Li's letter. It had been delivered by messenger, with no return address, three days earlier.

My Dear Yamaguchi,
Who has devised this tragic scheme in our city today? If people who possess the right to fair and impartial debate have no universal, inalienable right to life, then the world will without question enter an age of dissolution. The incident this time is not an interna-

tional dispute. It is not between China and Britain. It is in fact a crucial point in the ebb and flow of yellow and white. In short, it is nothing less than the first sign that the yellow race will be destroyed by the white. Consider this, my friend. The main races in the world today are the yellow and the white. Black and red have already been subjugated by the white. American Indians, the Malay of Southeast Asia, the African Negro. Within a few decades all will be extinct. The white man strictly enforces his plan for racial extermination, and the aims of his imperialism will be achieved only after he controls the entire world. The wickedness of his heart and the extremism of his aims are plain to see. We yellow people are on the verge of a crisis. The white race has subjugated four of the five continents. The only unspoiled paradises left are the nations of Asia, the home of the yellow peoples. Yet try examining a map of Asia, my friend. The southernmost Pacific islands, the Philippines, western India, Annam, Burma, Hong Kong, and Macao. The white man dominates them all, and yet his ambition is not quenched. Japan and China share the same race, the same culture. They are neighbors, and closely related. If China collapses it will do Japan no good. So why raise high the national flag and put your trust in it? My friend, we are now being lulled by mellifluous voices that distract us from the white man's plan of racial extinction. When we look closely at our two nations, they seem to be asleep, in a daze, hoping for some great happiness, unaware of the impending tragedy of the death of a race. I pray that you agree with my assessment, and that we will rise and work together. And I beg to discuss with you our efforts to help our peoples.

Li Ying-pu

To Master Yamaguchi Takumoto

Olga came over next to Kōya, jangling the kind of gold bracelets that Chinese wives wear on their wrists. "Mr. Kōya? If you know anything about Sanki, please tell me. I want to meet him."

"Sanki? I was with him just a little while ago. I have no idea where he went after we split up to look for food. He may have been killed along the way."

"So he's dead already?"

"I don't know. I was nearly killed myself coming here. Anyway, there's a revolution going on outside, so it's hard to predict what will happen. Did things like this happen during the Russian revolution?"

"Yes, they did. No one knew what would happen in the streets. Sometimes there was gunfire and that's all. People passing along would talk excitedly about it without anyone knowing what had actually happened. At that time my father told me that it was a revolution, but no one really understood what that meant. So whenever someone explained that what's happening is a revolution, I'd go blank, thinking it would soon be over. Now it's completely different. If people really understood what a revolution involves, it would never happen."

"What happened to you after that?" Kōya was now curious.

"My father said we'd be in danger if we didn't run away. So he took my mother and me and fled from Moscow while there were still places that didn't know about the revolution. We aristocrats may be aristocrats, but we're like anyone else when it comes to money. If you don't have it in an emergency, you're stuck. We had simply fled without taking much of anything, and soon our money ran out. There was nothing else for us to do but stop along the way and go to a local newspaper. My father's idea was that rural newspapers knew nothing of events in Moscow, so we could sell them our reports of the unrest we witnessed. My father was able to get money by giving the newspapers a scoop. He was clever, don't you agree? We took the money

193

for our reports and headed to the next town when the money ran out and sold our stories about Moscow and the other places we had been in the same way. We did this over and over, competing to stay ahead of the spreading wave of revolution. When it finally caught up with us, my father was taken captive and he almost died. I still remember those days vividly."

Lost in her memories Olga clasped her hands to her breast and looked up at the sky as she must have done back then. She seemed to be trembling as she stared ahead quietly for a few minutes. *What's wrong with her?* Olga was trying to speak, but she couldn't.

"What is it? What happened next?" Kōya prodded her.

"Whenever I tell this story, I get an epileptic seizure. Please hold me so that my body won't arch backward." She sat on his lap. "If I start to convulse, please hold me tight. If you do that I'll be all right."

Kōya held Olga, wondering what he should do if a seizure occurred. He also wondered if this weren't some trick of hers, and he was no longer sure if what she was telling him was the truth. Like a conjurer rehearsing before employing some sleight-of-hand, Olga stared for a few moments at her ring, which gleamed a flaming red, and flipped at her earring with the tip of her fingernail. She quietly took a number of deep breaths. Kōya looked at her as she seemed to be mumbling a spell, and he felt that perhaps she was taking precautions against the seizures that overcame her so often. Yet if she really did have convulsions in this state, he decided that he would hold her tightly so that she would not hurt herself.

"Are you sure you're all right? If you scare me, I'll run away. I have no idea what to do if you have a seizure. It'll be the same as a revolution to me."

"I'll be fine. Just hold me tight. That's it, that's it. If I start shaking, just gradually tighten your grip. My father always held me like this."

"Your father is still alive?"

194

"No, he died in Harbin. It's amazing he made it that far, since he was almost killed in Tomsk during the revolution."

"So you fled as far as Tomsk?"

"Yes. It's a place I'll never forget."

"But they have telephone and telegraph there. It's a little surprising you could continue on that far with your newspaper trick."

"We didn't know anything about the place. As the revolution spread, phone and telegraph offices became the targets of the struggle between the imperial and revolutionary armies. So the equipment was apparently destroyed there pretty quickly. If the phones and all had been working, then of course people like us wouldn't have fled to a place like Tomsk."

"That's too bad. Tonight the forces in the Settlement have given priority to protecting the phones and telegraph. They say that the water supply is in danger. The electricity is still on, but that may be cut soon. You had steam trains, right? At that time?"

"Yes, steam trains. But they only went as far as Tomsk. When we got there the revolution had arrived ahead of us, and they put people who were under suspicion on a tall platform in the square. The people were gathered there in the street and a committee chairman questioned them about those who were on the platform. Did this man ever engage in any counter-revolutionary activities in the past? And people in the crowd would attest to the fact that the man was so-and-so who did such-and-such, that he was very religious, or that he was charitable, or that he hadn't done anything bad. When everyone's testimony was finished, the man was pronounced innocent and let go. In the case of my father, no one knew anything about him. They glared at him suspiciously, but it looked like that would be all there was to it. You see, they had been executing people nearby, and so my father left us and went to buy bread alone. That was when he was arrested, and before we knew it he was forced to stand there on that tall platform. I was sure my father's life was

195

over. All I could do was look up to heaven and cross myself over and over. Then a woman's voice could be heard in the crowd, repeatedly vouching for my father. I wondered who that was, then saw my mother there. She was the only one raising a clamor from below, saying that my father was on the staff of a branch office of a company in Omsk that exported refrigerated goods, and that when the British Union Meat Company Trust had tried to buy up the rights of a northern Russian fishery he had opposed it and worked to preserve fishing rights for Russia, and that he had planned the construction of crab-canning boats in the north Pacific for the sake of the people. As she spoke she grew more and more desperate, rambling on about all sorts of complicated matters. The chairman just listened impassively to what she was saying. She grew red in the face waving her hands and stamping her feet, and I don't know how, but she came up with an idea. She told them that if they would send a telegram to a fishery in Azerbaijan and ask there they would learn the truth, that this man had worked with his older brother to form a fisherman's union in Azerbaijan in order to weaken the power of the fishing companies. The chairman, who had been silent up to that time, simply said, "All right" and let my father come down from the platform. My mother almost forgot herself and started to run up to him, but right away she looked off in the other direction and pretended not to know him. I was blinded with gratitude, and as I crossed myself I was shaking. The next time I . . ."

Olga stopped in mid-sentence and began to shake more violently on Kōya's lap. He held her more securely so that she would not bend back. "Are you OK? Hey!"

She stretched her neck as if she were swallowing hard. "I'm fine. I'm just shaking a little. Whenever I think of that time I get frightened. It was back then, when I came to after my seizure, that my father was holding me like this. We followed the railroad until we finally reached Harbin. But once we got there we didn't know what to do. We sold some jewelry to a

Chinese person and were able to get by for a while. But as it turned out we couldn't stay there very long. Harbin fell into Soviet hands and the situation was uncomfortable. There was nothing we could do, so we came to Shanghai. We still couldn't figure out how to make a living. Because we were at a loss, it was hard to get food day after day. We had never been in such a tight spot. Up to that point I had always been considerate toward my mother and father, but in the end I debased myself. I put myself ahead of father, mother, everything. I figured that as long as I had something to eat, I didn't care about the consequences. I was once a truly devoted child, but when I got here I became a beast. It's all so pathetic. Then I was sold to a Japanese man named Kimura who was wild about horse racing. Never once did he think of me as a human being. I couldn't understand a single word he said, and when we met he would abruptly seize my body and slap me around. At first I thought it might just be some Japanese custom. After some time had passed, he took me to the race track one day. When he lost his money gambling he sold me on the spot. Yamaguchi was the one who bought me. It was the first time I had ever known a man as terrible as Kimura. I found out later from Yamaguchi that he had always been that way. He'd accumulate mistresses like a savings account and then sell them off when it came time for the races."

"Yeah, I've heard the man is crazy," Kōya said, pushing with the tip of his tongue the ends of Olga's dewdrop earrings, which were coldly touching his dry lips.

"Since then I've met a lot of Japanese people here. But there's only one person like Sanki. I've never met such a high-minded person even among the Russians and Chinese. I wonder if he's really been killed?"

She gazed through the window at the leaning supports of a bridge and at a boat stopped dead in the mud.

"If he's been killed, then I want to die too."

Kōya thought that if she was going to talk about Sanki

197

like that and grieve in front of him, then he would tell her that his younger sister Kyōko was the love of Sanki's life. But if he said that and Olga disliked him for it, things would not be pleasant while he was here. And so he kept his peace.

"What do you think, Mr. Kōya?" Olga turned to him and suddenly put her arms around his neck. "Do you think that the old Czarist government will ever return to Russia?"

"That's finished. Even if it came back it would be overthrown again."

Olga shuddered, as though she felt a chill. "If that's true, then Russia will never be the way it was, no matter how long we wait."

"It's hopeless. If a city like this can undergo revolution, then pretty soon disturbances are going to break out in every nation."

"Still, we're all waiting for the old days to return. If things are going to stay as they are, no matter how long we wait, then it's better to die."

Feeling her body start to shake as before, Kōya said "Are you all right. This is weird. Hey!"

He tried shaking her. She took out a handkerchief and put it between her teeth.

"I'll be fine. Please hold me tighter."

"What's with the handkerchief?"

"My father gave it to me. Whenever I feel sad I bite on it. Then my father appears and always asks me, 'Are you still living?' He bought some gemstones cheaply in Harbin and wrapped them in this handkerchief. He was going to slip through Russia and go to Germany to sell them. If you do that you can make a huge profit. However, he always said that he would come under suspicion if he had no business in Moscow and didn't get off the train. It was so frightening for him to get off there. He told me that he would take me to America, but . . . I want to see my father again. I want to see him. Go to America and live there with him. Live there . . . ahh!"

Olga abruptly bit on the handkerchief and seized Kōya as though she were biting into his shoulders. Kōya knew this was not normal, and he peered into her face. It was drained of color. Then the convulsions started. He didn't know what to do. All at once Yamaguchi's intention, which was to fob off Olga on someone as quickly as he could, looked despicable to Kōya. But for now he couldn't do anything but hold her tightly.

"What's wrong? Come on now, snap out of it!"

It didn't matter what Kōya said. Olga, her cheek firmly pressed against Kōya's neck, continued to twitch and tremble silently. Her hands, fingers tightly curled under, turned blue. Her head began to bend back. Her eyes were open, unfocused. Her teeth were grinding, and one of her arms clutched his neck tightly. She screamed "Ahh" again and began to shake more and more violently on his lap.

He laid her on the bed and held her without taking his arms away. They were both sweating profusely. Her face, which shook as she pressed it against his neck, was deathly pale. Then it flushed red, twitching from her eyes to her mouth. Not knowing what to do, Kōya thought that if her convulsing body was going to seize up like that then he should try to massage it. As he held on to her he began to rub her arms, legs, and body, all of which continued to convulse.

The flexibility and rhythmic movements that appeared in her writhing body soon made him aware that what he was struggling with was not her sick body, but himself. He was aware of his feeling that Olga's unconscious body had become, in its wild beauty, the ideal form of a woman's movements. The fear of her he had felt disappeared, and he wanted to care for her tenderly.

His massage soon took effect, and when Olga let out a huge sigh, she immediately stopped convulsing. Her complexion softened and went back to its normal color. As she slowly recovered her normal breathing, she fell asleep.

He let go of her and opened the window for some fresh

air. The surface of the river with its countless black bubbles was tucked in among the roofs of darkened houses. A single vehicle, carrying members of the Scottish militia, ran along the river and out of sight. All he could hear then was Olga's breathing.

Yes, this will do.

Kōya looked on Olga, lying there soaked in sweat, as if he were looking at a bride. He took off his jacket and hung it on a hook. Working up a lather in the soap jar, he brushed it on his face, opened the razor Yamaguchi had tossed aside, and started to shave.

Forty-Four

Sanki arrived at Miyako's place at dusk. The minute she saw him she blurted out, "There was a riot nearby today. Some Japanese had their shirts torn. They had to run away. Yesterday a Japanese covered in blood was carried out of the area by car. And I hear our water system is in danger tonight. I'm really glad you came here. Please don't go home for a while. No matter what, I won't let you go home tonight."

He sat down on the divan. "Could you give me something to eat. I haven't had anything since last night. Everywhere I've gone there's no food, and there's nothing I can do. I came here thinking that maybe if you had a little something you could spare some. Please."

"You mean you didn't come here for me?"

"Never mind about that. Maybe next time. Today I'm here as a beggar, so let's save the silly thoughts for another time."

"Well, I'm so happy." Miyako spoke teasingly as she brought some bread from the pantry. "Excuse me for saying so, but an Englishman in the militia brought this bread especially for me. And now you've come to take it away."

"I know what you're getting at. Just let me know whether I'll get any or not. If not, then I'm going somewhere else. I hate your insinuations."

"Oh, I'll give you some. I don't care if I don't eat. It's just that it's going to be a hand-to-mouth existence for me for a while. If you take it thinking that it's just bread, then all my struggles up to this point will mean nothing."

"What should I do then?"

"Just think about it and you'll figure it out. I'm bullying you now. And why are you being bullied? You can't say you don't know. How long have I been waiting for you since we met

201

the other day? Then you come here, and just when I feel really happy you ask for food. That's fine for you, but if you look at it from my point of view, would you want to give up your bread?"

"Then it can't be helped," Sanki said, and stood up looking for his hat.

Miyako set the bread on the table. "So you intend to go home, just like that?"

"I'll go home. I was hungry, and I came here thinking this was the one place where I wouldn't have to talk about how hungry I am. Now you tell me about your English soldier and ask me to think about things beyond my comprehension. If I have to think about that stuff, why come here?"

"OK. You've had your say. I don't owe you anything, least of all bread. Go on home."

He headed toward the door. But it occurred to him, had he come here to talk with her? He should simply take the bread from her. . . . Still, the inertia created by their argument was too strong to allow him to reverse his steps. He went down the stairs and out the front door. Throwing her slippers on, Miyako came running after him.

"I'm no match for you, Sanki. You really are a fool. I don't care what you do to me, so go ahead. Eat the bread and go home. I hate you." She took Sanki's arm and they went back.

"All right. But I'll only take some bread."

"Bread, anything. Go ahead and plunder what you like. I've decided I have no more to say to oddballs like you."

Back in her rooms, Sanki loaded up his arms with bread. He laughed, "This will keep me alive? It's absurdly light."

"Hurry up and eat it. To think that I'm jealous of loaf of bread. I can't stand to even look at it."

Sanki unexpectedly felt his face smiling, and soon, as he picked up the bread, he was laughing out loud. "Is this a tragedy or a comedy? When I have food to eat, I'm a pessimist. And when I don't, I'll go so far as to steal someone else's. Then, when my stomach's full again, I'll go back to being a pessimist.

My stomach is apparently a factory for pessimists. Anyway, a strike has hit that factory, and it'll fall to pieces soon. So please be patient and wait."

Miyako was busily setting out sausage and butter. "Don't make excuses. I understand. It's enough for me that you're still alive. I've never felt kindness toward anyone else like this before, so please don't hold back. Go ahead and eat it all."

Sanki set the bread down and stood up. Out of the blue he went over to Miyako and embraced her from behind. She stopped and twisted around. A silver cup filled with liqueur slid on a silver tray she was holding and fell over. He recalled the look in Qiu-lan's eyes, which were filled with disdain after she had kissed him. He released Miyako and took the bread. She stood there, her back turned to him, like some country lass.

"Please, go ahead and have your drink," Sanki said.

She spun around and glared at him. "Did you come here to mock me?"

He remained silent, holding his bread and taking a bite.

"Did you come here just to make me angry?" Miyako slowly went pale. "I hate you. Go home. Go home!"

"You've been thinking silly things for some time. I just wanted to thank you, but you wouldn't let me."

Miyako rushed over to Sanki and swept the bread out of his arms. It fell to the rug and rolled to a stop by the wall. He stared at it and sighed. "I guess I'd better give up on the bread." He went back to the divan, threw his legs up and closed his eyes.

"Go home! Go home!"

Miyako shook him violently and he imagined being married and living with her every day. No doubt their time would be consumed in a constant collision of alarming emotions. His body gradually shifted and he fell on the floor. Now it was too much trouble to move. He remained on the floor and opened his eyes. Soon he was staring at the bread. He wondered how many hours would pass before he could eat that bread. If he remained like this until Miyako's mood improved, the bread was not likely to go anywhere. Yet if he remained like this, Miyako would make no effort to move first. *Why wouldn't his body move toward Miyako?* He continued to feel the phantom of Qiu-lan drifting up between Miyako's body and his, and so he made no effort to move toward her. At the same time he was getting no closer to the bread. He stood up in front of Miyako, who was now pale with anger, and left without another word.

Forty-Five

It was completely dark outside. Clusters of rickshawmen, cleaning themselves of lice, stretched their legs out onto the streets, which were empty of pedestrians. Sanki chewed the single morsel of bread he had snatched from Miyako's house and considered his plans. Winding along the road, a vehicle carrying some volunteer militia sprouted flowers of drawn swords as it slipped past the spikes of barbed wire, entwined like withered vines in winter. Locks of hair that had been shorn somewhere tumbled gently on the road at the mercy of the breeze stirred up by passing cars. A child crawled along licking at the white powder of peanuts that had been dropped and ground up finely on the asphalt.

Sanki walked along a canal. He was facing in the direction of Osugi's house. He realized that he had not thought about her for a long time. Osugi, who had been fired because of him. Osugi, who loved Sanki and had forgotten that she had been loved by him. Thinking this way about her, he wondered what she had been doing recently.

He cut short his sentimental feelings and they faded by degrees as he walked along the banks of a canal. Soon his empty stomach, which had not had anything since morning except that bite of bread, assaulted him again and replaced Osugi in his thoughts. His body lost all heaviness and he felt he was turning transparent. The scenes all around him were jumbled together as in a body without bones. He stopped on a bridge and looked vacantly at the surface of the water in the canal. Because of the sluggish tide that pushed up from the ocean, the edges of the small boats rubbed together squeakily as they bobbed in the muddy water. The effluence of the city, looking as though it had not been treated at all, filled up the spaces between the boats and spread out in waves, bending with the river in the depths of the pale blue light from the stars. Whenever Sanki passed this spot, he thought of the rusty cranes thrusting out over the water downstream from here, mud in the teeth of their gears. On peaceful days young girls put jasmine flowers in their hair and sold glass lamp chimneys beneath those cranes. A sampan smuggling contraband raised its black sail and slid past warehouses on the banks. Like a demon spirit, it darkened the area all around it as it continued silently, steadily upstream.

At the mouth of the river, where sails had massed, Sanki recalled the rainy evening when he ran to the hospital supporting the injured Qiu-lan. And then on to the Chinese street where she lived . . .

Just then he sensed two or three shadowy figures flickering, entangled, coming toward him around a corner by the canal bank. A knot of people quickly lowered their voices and stopped behind him. Sanki stared at the water, calming himself, fighting the urge to look behind as though he were trying to suppress the perilous atmosphere swirling about him. The people behind made no effort to move. He glanced back casually, and vaguely saw in the starlight the pockmarked, irregular faces of several men standing around him. He put his elbows on the railing again, and turned his back on them. Two arms slipped quietly around his waist from behind as if they were going to test Sanki's strength. Then his body was on top of the railing, and he felt the chill of its dampness on his hips. He did nothing. He put his hands on the shoulders of the man who had grabbed him and looked at the faces around him. Then that knot of people, which had been motionless, fell on him. In an instant he felt the sky breaking in two as he dropped headlong into a hard gust of wind.

He noticed that once his body had stopped falling he was stuck tightly to the edge of a plank. He tried stretching his legs and found that he had fallen between the boats he had been looking at just a minute ago. He glanced around. The sludgy surface of the water formed by the sewage was up to his neck. He tried to get up. But what would he do once he got up? The heavy band of the air of the past came alive, passing before him in black spots here and there. He had fallen face up into the waste, his eyes closed. He began to feel his head moving freely again. He pursued that, seeing how far he could move his head. Then, aware at last that he had fallen into raw sewage, he started to laugh to himself, as though he were measuring his own specific gravity.

How long am I going to stay here? His clothing was becoming water-logged. Sanki looked up from between the boats at the bridge. The row of dark Chinese faces was still there, staring down at him from the railing. He stared back at them without moving, since he had to wait for them to leave the bridge. *That fertilizer smell of the sewage filling the spaces between the boats! It was the smell of a Japanese village. Right about now mother, wearing those glasses with their patina of age, is probably winding thread and darning the soles of socks. She has no idea that I've fallen in among these boats here and now.* His mother was quickly replaced in his thoughts by Qiu-lan. *Damn you Qiu-lan, pull me out of here! I have to meet you one more time. I'll go on from here to the Madison Company you told me about. But what would I do if I met Qiu-lan?* When he did meet her he wanted, more than anything else, the recompense of scolding her violently.

Sanki looked up at that moment, and as if in a feverish dream he sensed Qiu-lan's sticky lips pressing down on his head. The stars, which he had forgotten briefly, began to sparkle even more brightly in the sky directly overhead. He looked up at the bridge. The Chinese men had disappeared. The crumbling mortar of the warped railing drifted up among the stars. He crawled out from between the boats and followed a rough stone wall, which was crumbling into the mud, until he came out onto a road. He stripped off his jacket and trousers and threw them away. Wearing just a shirt, he walked off to the nearest place he could think of, which was Osugi's. When he left Kōya that morning he had heard him say her address, but he wasn't exactly sure if Osugi would still be there. If she weren't there, he'd have to cross back over that bridge to go to his house, where there wasn't a scrap of food. Even so, it did not matter whether or not Osugi was at home. He had no other option.

Walking on, he felt that the dangerous part of town was now far behind him, and the fatigue and hunger he had forgotten for a while came back all the more violently. The road into the section of the city where Osugi lived was gradually narrowed by the walls of the rowhouses. He followed it and soon saw, glistening one after another before his eyes, pork swollen with fat and the skins of ducks—the sorts of things he had seen when he had passed by here on other occasions. At that moment he could hear the cough of a patient with some lung disease, sharp and raspy in the stagnant dust that blanketed like a fog everything on this road and the alleys connected to it. The sooty lamp of a dumpling vendor flickered and distorted the insides of the walls. The frames of several ladders twisted high toward the sky. Rickshawmen, riding their own rickshaws, stealthily imitated the faces of their customers in the dark night. Some whitefish had fallen into the cracks between the paving stones on the uneven road. To the side of a used metal fittings shop, where rusty keys were jammed tightly in a pile, he saw a line of blind people and opium addicts crouching exhausted beneath a crumbling bluish wall.

Sanki finally found Osugi's house, just where Kōya had told him, and knocked on the door. A long silence passed and no one came to open up. He worried that some Chinese person might hear him if he called out in a loud voice, so he rapped on the door again with the metal handle. A few more moments passed, and then the peephole in the darkened house opened a crack.

"My name is Sanki. Is there a person named Osugi here?"

The peephole slapped shut, and a side door opened up. A heavily perfumed woman inside abruptly grabbed Sanki's hand.

He passed through the door in silence. Guided by the woman, whose face he did not immediately recognize, he groped his way behind her up a narrow ladder. Her feet lightly kicked his chest a few times and his cheek bumped into her waist. At last they emerged into a second-floor tatami room. Thinking that this woman must be Osugi, Sanki spoke to her for the first time.

"Is it really you, Osugi?"

"Yes."

She answered meekly. Sanki was touched and gently stroked her shoulder and cheek as she stood there sticky with sweat.

"I know it's been many days. I came crawling here after I was tossed in the river. I'd like to borrow a robe. Anything will do."

Without turning on the light, Osugi began fishing around noisily inside some shelves. After groping around, she pulled out a *yukata*.

"Could you turn the light on please? I can't do anything in this darkness."

Osugi simply replied "Yes" and made no effort to turn on the light. She stood apart from him. Sanki thought that she wouldn't turn on the light because she was ashamed to show her face. So he changed clothes and slumped down in silent exhaustion.

He thought about her reluctance to turn on the light even though she had waited so long for him, and he figured there were probably things in the room she did not want him to see. In any case, he had arrived unexpectedly; and now Osugi was a prostitute, unlike the time she stayed at his place. There may even have been a customer asleep beside him in the room. Sanki decided to be discreet and not embarrass Osugi about the light business. He turned toward where he thought she might be.

"Do you have any food? I haven't eaten all day."

"Oh no," she said, but made no attempt to speak or move any further.

"Then you don't have any either?"

"I had some just a while ago, but it's all gone now."

Sanki felt his remaining strength drain away. He figured that he would have to wait until tomorrow morning before he could get anything. Inside his head the empty sky he had been looking at all day began to spin round and round. But if he kept quiet he wouldn't be able to convey the joy he felt at meeting her after such a long absence.

"It really has been a long time, Osugi. I found out from Kōya just this morning that you were here. It's close to my place, isn't it. How come you didn't let me know before?"

In place of a reply he heard Osugi sobbing on a mat close to him. He was reminded of the way she cried in front of him the night Oryū fired her. He had definitely been at fault then. If he had just let Oryū have her way on that occasion, Osugi would not have suffered the wrath of Oryū's jealousy and been cut loose. And of course she would not have ended up as a prostitute.

"The night you left? Well . . . I was busy and couldn't be at home. But you were always welcome to stay at my place, Osugi. Didn't I tell you that when I left?"

Why did Osugi feel she had to leave his home like that? He thought about her leaving that day, and there were many explanations for her decision that he still did not comprehend. Had it been that Kōya had pursued her again that night? But if that were the case, wouldn't Osugi have been able to deal with it without resorting to selling herself? But no matter how much he tried to justify things this way, Sanki could not escape responsibility for having made Osugi a prostitute. Sanki felt, in the darkness of that night, he was receiving the lashes of a whip he had long ago forgotten. Perhaps her decision not to turn on the lights, to leave him in the dark, was really for his benefit.

"After that I saw you on the street once. I chased you in a rickshaw. Did you know that?"

"Yes."

"Then you were already here at the time, weren't you."

"Yes."

Sanki thought back on the way he was then, passionately losing himself over Qiu-lan. If he hadn't met Qiu-lan, then he might have continued pursuing Osugi. *Now everything was ruined. Even now I'm in love with Qiu-lan. It's not that I'm infatuated with her ideology. I love her eyes. Those are eyes that renounce all ideology. The gleam of her eyes is a gleam that makes fools of men.* In the midst of his joy at being near Osugi, he found himself still excited by Qiu-lan, allowing her to slip into his mind. He was puzzled about where to set the boundaries of his free-roaming thoughts, which traveled so endlessly at ease. Certainly this was a time to think about Osugi rather than Qiu-lan. Because of him, Osugi had been robbed of her livelihood by Oryū and had been victimized by Kōya. She had fallen into this melancholy alley. But what should he do for Osugi now? He thought about marrying her. It was not mere vanity to think that would make her happy. He remembered the anxiousness in his heart, which had been thrown into confusion by Osugi's innocent beauty the night she was fired. At the moment he learned that Kōya had got his claws into her at his place, he decided not to marry Osugi; and he had been happy at that same moment that he had not lost his freedom. Now he was hoping that in place of Kōya he would have his freedom taken by Osugi. He knew that his sentimentality was the result of giddiness caused by hunger and fatigue. Yet he could not help feeling that Osugi, whose body he could imagine crawling through the mud, was now more alluring than ever before. He thought that he could now reach out for her in the way that Kōya had. After all, that had been a pleasure he had secretly desired but had been unable to satisfy. *Should I become her customer?* But his heart came to a thudding halt, and he suddenly began to feel around for her knees. Once again his conscience, which reared up without fail whenever he touched Osugi, stunted his feelings. His thought of becoming a customer expressed the base sexual desire of a heart that tried to

211

avoid responsibility by thinking of Osugi as dirt.

"Osugi? I'm tired now, so do you mind if I rest here like this?"

"Please. There's bedding here, so go ahead and rest. I'll go fetch something to eat when dawn comes."

"Thank you."

"The electricity has been cut off tonight, so it's pitch dark in here. I hope you can put up with it."

"It's all right with me."

Sanki's hand groped toward Osugi's voice. The tip of his hand moved from the cool tatami and touched her knees, which were warmly swollen. Osugi led Sanki over to the bedding. She pulled the futon over him and said, "It's been dangerous on the streets recently. Are you injured?"

"I'm OK. How about you?"

"I don't leave this house. I go out once a day to fetch cooked rice from the Japanese Settlement. That's all. When will it end, I wonder? This disturbance."

"I wonder too. Tomorrow the Japanese army will arrive, so I suppose the uprising won't continue much longer."

"Really? The quicker it's over the better. Everyday I lose the spirit to go on living."

Sanki could feel her hand pulling back from his body, and he wondered where she would sleep.

"Where's your bed?"

"Don't worry, I'll be fine."

"If you don't have a place to sleep, then come here. I don't mind."

"No, you sleep there. I'll go to sleep when I'm ready."

"Really?"

Sanki could tell how hard Osugi was working to hide from him the whorish mannerisms she had acquired, and in response his heart was chilled by his own lewdness, which had made him consider the idea of becoming her customer. However, now that he was at last reunited with Osugi—the Osugi

212

who loved him so much, the Osugi who had fallen so deeply into the mire because of her love for him—how perverse was the working of his conscience, which kept him from making love to her here in the dark. He had previously refrained from having sex with Osugi because he did not want her to fall into prostitution. And now he couldn't make love to her because she had become a prostitute.

"Osugi? Don't you have a match? I'd like to see your face. OK?"

"I can't."

"But we haven't seen each other for so long. Talking in the dark like this without seeing your face, well . . . it's creepy. It's like talking to a ghost."

"Now that I'm living like this, I couldn't stand you looking at me."

He had guessed her feelings, but hearing it directly from her made his chest constrict.

"Does it really matter? The evening I left you I'd just been fired by my bank. And you had just been let go by Oryū. It's bad enough for a man, but when a woman loses her job, it's pretty hopeless."

Speaking such gentle words to Osugi, Sanki's desire continued to stir in his body, and he wanted to go to her. Then, with a single thought, he buried Osugi in the darkness and tried hard to fall asleep.

"Sanki? Are you seeing Oryū?"

"Oryū? No. I've haven't seen her at all since the night we quarreled."

"Oh? That night Oryū said something terrible to me."

"What was that?"

"I can't repeat such a thing."

Because Oryū was so jealous, Sanki figured she must have said something Osugi couldn't convey in a few words. On that occasion he had jokingly hinted that he loved Osugi by grabbing Oryū, who had come into the bath to give him a massage. The next thing he knew Oryū was dragging Osugi in and throwing her at his feet. He apologized for Osugi, but Oryū grew even more angry and fired her. All because of a joke, Sanki thought. Then he had gone and forgotten all about Osugi himself, and soon his heart was captured by Qiu-lan. Now, sensing that Osugi was gradually warming to him as before, naturally his heart leaped up in a sprightly dance.

"Osugi? I'm going to sleep now. I'm so tired I can't talk anymore. But I wonder if you would let me stay here with you from tomorrow? Do you mind?"

"Please stay as long as you want. But dirt is dirt, and tomorrow when it's light you'll understand everything."

"Dirt doesn't bother me. I'm beginning to like the idea of staying on here. If I'll be a bother to you, tell me now."

"You won't be a bother. However, this isn't a place for you to stay."

Sanki did not think that what he had said to Osugi would become a reality immediately on the morrow. But if what he said did become reality, that was all right too. "Right now it's more secure in an alley like this if there are two people instead of one. I can stay here, or you can come with me to my place. Either way is fine with me."

Thinking she would say something, he waited for Osugi's reply. But she said nothing. In the darkness he could hear her sobbing again. He remembered that when she first cried like that at Oryū's place, he had comforted her with words nearly identical to those he had used now. And each time she had trusted in his words, her misery had increased.

At that time he had nothing but words as a means of rescuing Osugi. If it were wrong to keep a woman who can no longer make a living in your house until she can, then what else could he do? The only thing he could be faulted for was not embracing Osugi and loving her. Sanki thought that of all his sins that was the worst.

To make love with her . . . What was wrong with that? It

would be better for Osugi than not embracing her at all. Despite his feelings, until the moment when he actually came to embrace Osugi, he would think of ever so many reasons to stop himself.

And yet he had to admit that all his excuses came down to the same thing. How long could he go on mistreating Osugi?

"Osugi? Come here. Don't think about anything. Just come here."

Sanki stretched his arms out to her. Her body fell heavily into them. At that moment Qiu-lan, in her aquamarine dress, vividly filled his arms.

Osugi quietly stretched and contracted her body, which overflowed with joy. She thought that all her regrets, all her pain would end there. She wouldn't go to sleep until tomorrow. If she slept, then like another evening at another time . . . Ah, that's right. Because she had been careless and fell asleep that night she was ravished in the dark. Was it Sanki or Kōya? Even today she was not absolutely sure. That night had been the very first night, and from then until now she had wondered who the man was—Sanki or Kōya? Kōya or Sanki?—dwelling on it constantly, every day and every night. But now tonight. It was dark, and just like that other night she could not see Sanki's face. But tonight there was only Sanki. And there was no mistaking that this really was Sanki. But what if the Sanki of that earlier night were the real Sanki? No, that man was very different from the Sanki here tonight. The man that night had a narrow chest, was more impetuous, had very long legs, and a lower temperature.

Like a young girl, Osugi tentatively touched Sanki's sleeping body here and there with her fingertips. She thought about how much she wanted to glimpse his face tomorrow. His various faces and shoulders from those days when she always watched him in fascination from a corner in Oryū's bathhouse came floating to her mind. But soon the coolly aloof face of Sanki, with its air of indifference, began to float, shimmering amid a wave of the long tongues, the oiled hair, the hard nails, the teeth that bit into her breasts, the rough, scaly skin, and the cold opium breath of all those customers who had come here night after night and left their money behind. She tossed in bed and unconsciously let out a sigh. What would Sanki think when he looked around the room tomorrow? Lined up on the desk under the southern window were a Hangchou doll left by a businessman from Suzhou, a mercurial, a withered saffron, and an empty bottle of snake liquor from Tibet. On the wall, in a gold frame, was a picture of a gentle-looking male actor. Most disgusting of all was the futon, shiny from the grime of men's necks. And the sheets hadn't been washed in days.

Osugi crept out of the futon. Groping around, she stuffed the Hangchou doll, the snake liquor, and the mercurial into a closet. She pulled some perfume out of a drawer and sprinkled it around the edge of the futon. Then she quietly curled up again, putting her forehead on Sanki's chest. This would probably be the only night when she would be able to do this sort of thing. With this in mind, Osugi felt compelled to pray that the riots on the streets would continue another day. Come tomorrow, if the Japanese army landed, the city would be as peaceful and safe as before. And when that happened, Sanki would leave, and it was not likely he would come again. Osugi took a deep breath, as though she were savoring Sanki's scent. She remembered the night she was fired. For a reason she never understood, Oryū had abruptly pulled her along by her collar and thrown her on Sanki's torso as he was lying in the rising steam. She continued to cry in the bath until Oryū dragged her out, chased after Sanki, and threw her once more on top of him. Now that same Sanki was with her here. *Here.* How many times had she thought about Sanki from that moment until now? *Ah, but he's here. Here.* That night she had trudged along to Sanki's house, crying, staring blankly up at his second-floor rooms where no one was home and no lights were on. Just when she thought that Sanki had finally returned, it was Kōya instead. Kōya had taken her up to the second floor and had gone to sleep without regard for her. She had been carelessly drawn in and fallen asleep in that condition. Then, in the middle of the night, Kōya took her in the dark. But when she woke up the next morning, weren't both Sanki and Kōya sleeping on the bed? Up to that moment she had been certain that Kōya had done it, but Sanki was also lying there and she was no longer sure. And so her suffering had continued until today. But now Sanki was here. No matter that it was as dark as it had been that other night. This was definitely Sanki, who resembled no one else. Osugi recalled the loneliness that followed the day Sanki left her behind in his house and did not return—a time she spent alone gazing absently at the surface of the water in the canal. On those occasions oil constantly floated beneath the fog like some design on the water. The bluish green growing on the sides of the crumbling mortar lapped up the oil on the surface. Beside it floated the yellowish corpse of a chick that drew toward it scraps of greens, socks, mango peels, and straw rubbish. Together with pitch-black bubbles that welled up from the depths, these items formed a little island in the middle of the canal. Osugi did nothing for two or three days but gaze at that little island and wait intently for Sanki to come home. If tomorrow the naval brigade landed and restored order to the city, wouldn't she once again have to continue on blankly, just as in those days. Then once more the men—their coarse, shark-like skin, their mouths reeking of garlic, the sticky oil plastered to their hair, the long fingernails, the sharp irregular teeth. Reflecting on these things, she stretched out like a patient who has given up and stared into the darkness spread across the ceiling.

Translator's Postscript

Yokomitsu Riichi (1898–1947) was a central figure in the generation of intellectuals and writers who rose to prominence in the 1920s. For Yokomitsu and his contemporaries the great transformation of the Meiji period (1868–1912), when a radical process of economic, cultural, and military modernization initiated Japan's march to great power status, was in many respects already a thing of the past. His was the first generation to grow up in a Japan that saw itself not simply as modernizing, but as modern. Such a self-image carried with it a feeling of confidence that Japan's potential was yet to be fully tapped; and that liberating sense of possibility was one source of the brilliant efflorescence of the arts, literature, philosophy, and film that marks the worldly culture of the Taishō period (1912–26).

If Taishō culture was sophisticated, however, it was also edgy and self-conscious. For the process of modernization had brought about economic and social dislocations that opened deep fissures in society. In particular, Taishō Japan was haunted by the original sin of Meiji—the decision to resist the power and cultural hegemony of the West by emulating Western material culture; by embarking on its own project of empire building in Asia; by acquiescing in the racial ideology that supported colonialism; and by constructing a modern myth of Japanese cultural uniqueness. For many in the 1920s the progress promised by modernization seemed ephemeral, since disparities in wealth and status were growing, and foreign threats appeared to be looming everywhere.

The Meiji cultural synthesis, that strange hybrid of Western modernity grafted onto a newly created imperial ideology of an essential, timeless Japan, appeared incapable of holding its center in an increasingly skeptical, self-conscious age. A wide-

219

spread sense of spiritual homelessness was as common to Yokomitsu's generation as the sense of potential noted above, and it
too inspired a burst of creative responses. Some artists reveled in
the breakdown of a sense of order and looked to new forms and
media, especially the cinema, as a means to escape the stultify-
ing Meiji legacy. Others followed the example set by some Western modernists and experimented with ways to pick up the pieces
of a fragmented tradition. Still others sought to escape through
the selfless objectivity promised by the historical materialism of
socialism or the mythic visions of nationalism.

The various roles Yokomitsu played in all these intellec-
tual and artistic cross-currents make him one of the most in-
triguing figures in the cultural history of Japan during the 1920s
and 1930s. He was born on March 17, 1898 in the hot springs
town of Higashiyama in Fukushima Prefecture. His father was
working there as an engineering contractor on a railway construction project, and the demands of that kind of work kept
the family on the move for much of Yokomitsu's early life. The
sense of rootlessness that is an important element of his later
writings may be traced at least in part to the circumstances of
his upbringing. When Yokomitsu was six his father went to work
on a railroad project in Korea, and so he moved with his mother
and older sister to live in his mother's home village of Tsuge in
Mie Prefecture. His schooling began in Tsuge, but he attended a
number of schools as the family moved around, and on occasion
lived away from home in boarding houses when he attended
school in Ōtsu (near Kyoto in Shiga Prefecture) and later in Mie
Prefecture.

Yokomitsu entered Waseda University in 1916, but after
a few months he suffered a nervous collapse and returned to his
parents' home in Yamashina, near Kyoto. During his stay at home
he began writing his first serious stories, and when he went
back to Waseda in 1918 he enrolled as a first-year student in the
English department. Yokomitsu began to make his most important literary acquaintances in 1920, and from that point on he

became more and more deeply involved, and prominent, in the Tokyo literary scene. He eventually counted among his peers some of the most powerful and influential figures of the literary establishment: the writer and publisher Kikuchi Kan, the polemicist Yasuda Yojūrō, and the writers Kawabata Yasunari, Kataoka Teppei, and Akutagawa Ryūnosuke. For the next two decades Yokomitsu was discussed by his peers in Japan in terms equal to those applied to some of the most important writers, such as Kawabata, and critics, such as Kobayashi Hideo.[1] Indeed, during this period he shared with the novelist Shiga Naoya the divine status conferred by the breathless epithet, *bungaku no kamisama* (a god of literature).[2]

Yokomitsu founded a literary magazine, *Tō* (Tower), in 1922, and over the next three years published a number of short stories, essays, and theoretical pieces in a variety of journals. His early period of intense activity culminated in 1924 when he joined with Kataoka and Kawabata to establish a new magazine, *Bungei jidai* (Literary age). Criticism of the work that appeared in this journal was sometimes harsh, and in response to this challenge Kataoka, Kawabata, and Yokomitsu chose to defend themselves by trying to systematize their aesthetic principles. The result was the creation of the Shinkankaku-ha, the New Sensation School, for which Yokomitsu served as chief theorist.

As a founding member of the New Sensation School Yokomitsu's call for a new sensibility—literally a new sensory capacity to perceive the world in an unmediated way—was initially motivated by his opposition to the narrow realism of the first-person narratives that characterized the work of the White Birch School. He was also strongly opposed to the narrow ideological aims of the Proletarian writers. However, in his criticisms of the Proletarian School Yokomitsu espoused neither a

1. *Bungei dokuhon: Yokomitsu Riichi* (Tokyo: Kawade Shobō, 1981), pp. 273–78.
2. Asami Fukashi, "Yokomitsu Riichi nyūmon," in *Yokomitsu Riichi shū*, vol. 65 of *Nihon gendai bungaku zenshū* (Tokyo: Kōdansha, 1961), p. 484.

simplistic anti-Marxism nor a return to traditional aesthetic values. Instead he voiced a particular version of a widespread, if often ill-defined, concern over the influence of the West in the formation of modern culture in Japan. He describes his own career as moving through several phases: from "a period of insubordination and absolutely desperate battle with the Japanese language, through a period of combat with Marxism, arriving at a period of submission and obedience to the national language."[3] These remarks have led some commentators to read into his early work a fundamental anti-realism common to many modernist movements around the world at the time. Yokomitsu, however, was no anti-realist. His aesthetics were motivated by an aspiration to create a culture that was modern and Asian, and through that cultural project to somehow overcome the modernity of the West. What Yokomitsu longed for was a culture that was at once parochial and universal—a culture that subsumed the West under an all but impossible synthesis of the national and the cosmopolitan.

This desire for synthesis is manifested in the formation of his theory of New Sensation. For example, near the end of his tract "Shinkankakuron" (A theory of the new sensation, 1925) he writes: "Futurism, Three-dimensionalism, Expressionism, Dadaism, Structuralism, Surrealism—all of these I recognize as belonging to the New Sensation School." The extreme inclusiveness of this definition makes the New Sensation School so universal in principle that its practices are all but impossible to isolate or distinguish. Indeed, when the diverse membership of the school is taken into consideration,[4] it is impossible to discern any elements that gave the movement a sense of unity or common purpose, especially when contrasted with the Prole-

3. Yokomitsu Riichi, "Kakikata sōshi," *Yokomitsu Riichi zenshū* (Complete works of Yokomitsu Riichi), vol. 16 (Tokyo: Kawade Shobō, 1987), p. 369.
4. For a full treatment in English of the history of the Shinkankaku-ha, see chapters 3 and 4 of Dennis Keene's study, *Yokomitsu Riichi: Modernist* (New York: Columbia University Press, 1980).

tarian School. However, to focus on the apparently diffuse aims of Yokomitsu is to miss the one vital element of his program, which is to create an overarching synthesis of literary praxis. Whatever problems arise in the formulation of his theory, the ambitious aims of his project of cultural renewal are unambiguous.

For Yokomitsu the term New Sensation was a broad marker intended to strip away ideology and modern historical consciousness from art and achieve immediate apprehension of reality through the senses. Here is his definition of the term:

> The general concept I call Sensation (*kankaku*) refers to the surface signs (or symbols, *hyōchō*) of perception; it refers to the intuitive triggering mechanism (*shokuhatsubutsu*) of subjectivity that strips away the external aspects of nature and merges with an object. This explanation is a bit extravagant and still does not quite get at the newness of the New Sensation. Thus we should acknowledge the importance of subjectivity. Subjectivity here refers to the capacity for the activity (*katsudō nōryoku*) by which an object is perceived as the thing itself. Such perception is of course a synthesis of intellect and emotion, though at the moment when subjectivity emerges, when the intellect and emotion that form the capacity to perceive an object merge with the object itself, then either the intellect or the emotion will take on a dynamic form as the dominant trigger of Sensation. It is very important to take this into account to explain the fundamental concept of the New Sensation. The representation (or signification, *hyōshō*) of an action that affects the capacity of representation of external, pure objectivity (*junsui kyakkan*) is Sensation. The concept of Sensation as it is used in literature is, to simplify, perception transformed to a surface sign.[5]

In Yokomitsu's formulation Sensation (*kankaku*) is defined not simply as perception, but as the representation of perception through surface signs, whether language, images, or music. His attempt to co-opt realism, symbolism, and futurism suggests that he was aware of the synthetic nature of his project;

5. Yokomitsu Riichi, *Ai no aisatsu, Basha, Junsui shōsetsu ron* (Tokyo: Kōdansha, 1993), pp. 245–46.

and the move he makes is noteworthy as an attempt to formulate an aesthetics of authenticity through a paradoxical fusion of perception, which is subjective, spatial, and immediate, with language, which in Yokomitsu's view is objectifying, temporal, and mediating. The motivation for his effort is the underlying problem of modernity for Yokomitsu: the self-consciousness of the modern subject identifies the need for authentic experience precisely because it recognizes itself as belated, unoriginal, and thus lacking the capacity of Sensation to perceive what is real, or genuine.

Yokomitsu explicitly addresses this problem of self-consciousness a decade after "Shinkankakuron" in another manifesto titled "Junsui shōsetsu ron" (Theory of the pure novel, 1935):

> I have looked at various assertions that advocate a revival of the literary arts, but I have yet to see any concrete theory. The spirit (*seishin*) needed to bring about such a revival is a problem I will have to leave for another occasion. However, we must recognize here the numerous underlying sources of the spirit of activism (*nōdō seishin*) and of romanticism (*romanshugi*) that have flourished since the start of this year. The specific assertions of these movements are issues that should be taken up after we have formulated a theory of the pure novel, for if we neglect the pure novel then neither activism nor romanticism have significance for literature. This is due to the excessive self-consciousness (*jiishikikajō*) of the intellectual class, which is the modern (*gendaiteki*) characteristic I mentioned earlier. Yet of the people involved in romanticism and activism (*nōdōshugi*), I have seen no one who can deal with the problem of self-consciousness, which is the most difficult to resolve.[6]

Yokomitsu goes to great pains in this essay to distinguish his term "pure novel" from the term *junbungaku*, pure literature, that gained currency in the 1920s. The distinction arises

6. Yamazaki Kuninori, *Yokomitsu Riichi ron* (Tokyo: Hokuyōsha, 1979), p. 265.

from his concern with the self-consciousness of modern intellectuals, exemplified by the notion of pure literature (*junbungaku*), which he sees as abstract and cut off from authentic aesthetic experience. His concept borrows from Kikuchi Kan's notion of content literature, which refers not just to popular literature but to literature accessible to the masses by virtue of its contact with the essential characteristics of Japanese culture. For Yokomitsu modern intellectuals are faced with a nearly intractable problem, which is that emphasis on the subject and on individual autonomy creates the critical distance, the epistemological skepticism, that is the defining feature of modern consciousness (what he calls the modern spirit). However, the heightened awareness of modern intellectuals of their belated historical position in an ongoing cultural tradition brings with it the realization that cultural values are relative and that the notion of personal autonomy, the constitutive element of the modern subject, is a fiction; that is, it is nothing more than an ideological commodity in a cultural marketplace that the individual is powerless to control.

The effort of so many intellectuals in the 1920s and 1930s—men such as Kuki Shūzō, Yanagi Sōetsu, and Yasuda Yojūrō—to explode the limits imposed by historical consciousness are apparent in the obsessive search for cultural origins and for essential cultural characteristics. In order to erase the temporal sense of belatedness vis-à-vis the West, or to contract the spatial distance from the cultural past, the focus turned to an exploration of the parochial elements of Japanese culture. For Yokomitsu, however, this parochialism was not quite enough; as noted above, his modernity was shaped by the desire to fuse the subjective, parochial qualities embodied in Japanese nationalism with the internationalist aspirations of modernist aesthetic movements.[7] In order to resolve his contradictory cultural aims, Yokomitsu had to enunciate his own version of the objective correlative, a surface sign that would contain the longed-for fusion of

7. Ibid., p. 164.

subjective experience and objective perception.

It was the search for a resolution to the conflicted consciousness of modernity that attracted Yokomitsu's interest in the city of Shanghai. As a colonized city Shanghai was Asian. As an exotic space where many cultures and races mixed, it was cosmopolitan. It was the creation of Western imperialism, a marketplace of rational materialism. It was at the same time a repository of the energy of an alternative Asian modernity that exposed the parochialism of the West and challenged its claim to cultural universality. Because it was both West and East and not wholly either one, Shanghai became for Yokomitsu a site onto which he could project a different vision of Japanese modernity—Japan as both colonialist power and liberator of Asia.

The origins of this vision can be traced to his one-month sojourn in Shanghai in April, 1928. The inspiration provided by this short visit is apparent in the ways in which he tries to clarify and reconcile his political beliefs and aesthetic practices. For example, the sharp political turn in his understanding of Japanese modernity is apparent in an essay, "Kūki sonota" (The air, etc.) he wrote soon after his return from China. In giving his initial impressions, he notes with considerable puzzlement that even though the people who are most cruel to the Chinese are the Americans, the Americans are nonetheless the people with whom the Chinese want the most contact. His puzzlement is expressed in strong terms when he writes, "For all that, if Japan does not cooperate with these Chinese, then the East (tōyō—Orient might be a better translation here) will be able to do nothing on the world stage." A few sentences later he adds, rather ominously, that "only Japanese militarism possesses enough power to rescue the subjugated East."[8]

The linkage between Yokomitsu's political and aesthetic ideas and the city of Shanghai is given a fuller treatment in a

8. Sugano Akimasa, "Samayou *Shanghai no Nihonjin*," in Yokomitsu Riichi, *Shanghai* (Tokyo: Kōdansha, 1991), p. 292.

miscellaneous essay written in 1939 called "Shinakai" (The China Sea). In this essay Yokomitsu tells of his second brief return to Shanghai, which was by then an occupied wartime city. Because of the war his itinerary is limited by the authorities, and so before he flies over he decides to make a brief stop in Kyushu to see Mt. Aso. This diversion provides him with a native site he can contrast with Shanghai. He argues that because of Japan's love of nature most foreigners remark that there is really nothing man-made worth seeing in Japan—and here he is obliquely referring to urban culture. He then stresses what he sees as the paradox of Japanese culture, which is that only spiritual beauty and nature exist—meaning that what defines Japanese culture is the lack of self-consciousness so crucial to urbane culture. This leads him to the following observation:

> I no longer think that there are any cities in Japan. It is hard to call Tokyo or Osaka a city. They are mere collections of country villages raked together, and so there is no formal need for a city. Put another way, we could say that the national entity (*kokuzentai*) is a single city. For the sake of nature the national entity maintains the form of a single city.
>
> Considering the current state of affairs, with the Japanese army spilling out over the continent, it seems to me that what is happening is that the one city that is Japan is gushing up and flowing out over the wilderness (*gen'ya*).[9]

The description of Japanese cities here seems a prescient description of the central role that large city-states would come to play in the globalizing economy. Nonetheless, this description is also very much the language of imperial destiny, where nature, that pure, unmediated source of Japanese culture, is equated with the political will that has led to war. The image of a flood moving across the landscape of China is disturbingly apt and morally reprehensible in the context of Yokomitsu's beliefs,

9. Yokomitsu Riichi, *Yokomitsu Riichi zenshū*, vol. 12 (Tokyo: Kawade Shobō, 1956), p. 196.

because the processes of nature burst asunder the temporal and spatial boundaries of human history. For all that, Yokomitsu is still very much aware of the move he is making, and so he tries to cover his tracks—to maintain, so to speak, the illusion of having escaped the trap of modern historical consciousness, which in turn allows him to justify Japan's imperialism on moral grounds: "Nature knows nothing at all of war. In that case, then, what does it know? Certainly the battle front has flowed through, and continues to flow on to distant Changsha. I gaze after it, thinking about it after the fact. Goethe once said that everything becomes complicated when we consider it after the fact."[10]

Yokomitsu continues his essay by arguing that we are all within the flow of history, and he tries to overcome the problem of historical consciousness by likening that consciousness to the sorts of recurring patterns he sees in the unconscious processes of nature. Here the significance of Shanghai to him is revealed in its boldest form, because he sees the city, especially the International Settlement, as "the birthplace (kokyō) of the problem that ever occupies my thoughts." He continues:

> The problem of the International Settlement is one of the most perplexing in the world. At the same time this location also represents the problem of the future. To some extent it is a very simple thing, but there is no other place on earth that so manifests the quality (seishitsu) that constitutes the modern (kindai). What is more, there exists no where in the world except the Settlement a site where all nations have created a common city. To think about this place is to think about the world in microcosm.[11]

Written almost a decade after the publication of *Shanghai*, this essay has the feel of a revisionist justification for the earlier work of fiction. Yokomitsu focuses on the future that Shanghai represents, a move that allows him to imagine a reso-

10. Ibid., p. 197.
11. Ibid.

lution of the dilemmas of modernity, or to at least defer the powerful sense of presentness Shanghai evokes in him, without having to deal with the inconvenience of the international political realities of his day. The essay is thus an extension of the political and aesthetic ideology that had already found its first and fullest expression in his novel. During the composition of *Shanghai*, Yokomitsu explicitly stated that his aim was to create a new realism to act as a counterweight to the Marxist literature of the Proletarian School of the 1920s, and the end result of his efforts was a historically informed, sharply ideological literature that simultaneously longed for the erasure of the historical consciousness that sustains political ideology. The paradox of his aims is manifest in the warring elements of both his political beliefs, which eventually settled into an uneasy mix of pan-Asianism and anti-leftist nationalism, and his aesthetics, which, as noted above, embraced cosmopolitan culture as an object of desire while trying to maintain a central place for authentic Japanese culture. Yokomitsu's cultural project, exemplified by *Shanghai*, was riven by a fault-line created by an essentialist politics and a radical aesthetics, the colliding tectonic plates of his modernism.

In order to fully appreciate the tensions inherent in Yokomitsu's project, it is helpful to read the novel within the context not only of his aesthetic practices, but also of the historical record. Because he set his fictional narrative of the lives of a group of Japanese expatriates against the backdrop of the May 30th Movement of 1925, a brief overview of the situation in Shanghai in the spring of that year is in order.

"Shanghai is China."

When Sun Yat-sen made this declaration to Japanese reporters in Shanghai in November, 1924 , his words shocked the foreign community and gave comfort to radical Chinese elements in the city. Though the proclamation now seems a statement of the obvious, sovereignty was a hotly contested issue complicated by the city's colonial origins. In the eyes of most foreigners at the time Shanghai was a unique place where the intermingling of cultures and economies had created a genuinely international city that was in China, but not of China.

Sun's death the following March left unresolved the question of his political successor and exacerbated the general uncertainty over the issue of sovereignty in China at large. The atmosphere of unrest and the increasing radicalism of the antiforeign movement, which was directed primarily at the British and the Japanese in Shanghai, resulted in a series of strikes against Japanese textile mills that began in February, 1925 and continued throughout much of the spring. The Japanese complained to the Municipal Police, but since most Japanese factories were on Chinese territory, the response of the authorities in the International Settlement was limited. The tension increased in April when the Municipal Council proposed a number of new by-laws that included measures to increase wharfage dues, reduce child labor, and license Shanghai's stock markets. These measures irritated many interests in Chinese Shanghai and were opposed by the General Chamber of Commerce, which claimed that foreigners had no right to impose such laws. The result was that for the first time in the city a common bond was forged between the radical politics of certain groups of workers and students and the financial interests of Chinese businesses and property owners.

This volatile atmosphere exploded on May 15, 1925 when several Japanese mills were struck yet again. Foremen opened fire on a crowd of rioters, wounding five and killing one. As the strikes widened, a number of groups began to organize resistance against the Municipal Council. On May 30th a group of student protesters was sent into the International Settlement. The protest turned violent in the afternoon, and the Louza Police Station was overrun. At that point the police opened fire, killing eleven and wounding twenty others. The crowd fled, but the event galvanized Chinese opposition. A general strike that included students, workers, and merchants brought Shanghai to a halt. Violence and looting erupted sporadically throughout the city and spread to other parts of China.

The foreign powers, Britain in particular, eventually restored control over the course of a long summer of disturbances; but the May 30th Movement was a watershed event that undercut the political, economic, and moral arguments used to support foreign domination and privilege in China. The Movement also coincided with the beginning of the civil war in China—a war that eventually drew Japan into a full-scale invasion, and ended only with the ascension to power of the Communists in 1949.[12]

In order to represent the complex swirl of historical events, Yokomitsu employs vivid, synaesthesic descriptions of the spectacle of the city, which he weaves into the story to amplify the personal lives and political beliefs of his characters. This technique exemplifies his literary modernism. In 1929, as he was in the midst of serializing *Shanghai*, Yokomitsu wrote of his aspirations in an essay titled "Mazu nagasa o" (First, the length). He stated: "I have once again returned to realism, and I think that I would like to settle in this mode for a while."[13] The word I have rendered as realism is *shajitsu*, a term that refers to exact, objective description, to representing things as they really are. The word also carries a secondary nuance of visual representation in the sense of the notion of copying or projecting reality. These nuances are significant for they suggest that Yokomitsu was pushing his literary experiments in the direction of merging language with the unmediated perceptions of the senses, especially the visual sense.

I want to suggest something of the visual quality of the novel by citing three passages and briefly cataloging elements in

12. For a compelling account of the May 30th Movement see Nicholas R. Clifford, *Spoilt Children of Empire: Westerners in Shanghai and the Chinese Revolution of the 1920s* (Hanover, NH: University Press of New England, 1991).
13. Cited in Yamazaki, *Yokomitsu Riichi ron,* p. 162.

those citations that illustrate the political implications of Yoko-mitsu's imagistic aesthetics. The first passage is taken from the opening pages of the novel:

> At high tide the river swelled and flowed backward. Prows of darkened motorboats lined up in a wave pattern. A row of rudders drawn up. Mountains of off-loaded cargo. The black legs of a wharf bound in chains. A signal show-ing calm winds raised atop a weather station tower. A customs house spire dimly visible through evening fog. Coolies on barrels stacked on the embankment, becom-ing soaked in the damp air. A black sail, torn and tilted, creaking along, adrift on brackish waves.
>
> Sanki, a man with the fair skin and intelligent face of some medieval hero, walked around the street and returned to the Bund. A group of exhausted Russian prostitutes was sitting on a bench along the strand. The blue lamp of a sampan moving against the current rotated interminably before their silent eyes.

After Sanki speaks with the prostitutes and shares a cigarette with them, the scene continues:

> The prostitutes stood and sauntered away one by one along an iron railing. A young woman at the end of the procession glanced back furtively at Sanki with her pallid eyes. Then, with a cigarette still between his lips, Sanki felt overwhelmed by a dream-like sadness. When Kyōko had announced that she would leave, she had looked back at him in the same way as this young woman now.
>
> Stepping over the black ropes that moored the boats, the hookers disappeared among the barrels. All they left behind was a banana peel, which had been stepped on and crushed, and some damp feathers. A pair of booted feet was sticking out from the entrance of the patrolman's tower at the end of the wharf.
>
> As soon as Sanki was alone he leaned back against the bench and recalled his mother back in his home village.

The most striking element of this opening scene is the scopic, camera-like movement of the narrative perspective. The novel opens with a kind of establishing shot: that is, an appar-ently objective list of external elements in the setting, which is

232

a technique Yokomitsu employed in some of his earlier short works like "Hae" (Flies, 1923) and "Haru wa, basha ni notte" (Spring rides in on a carriage, 1926). The introduction of Sanki and the Russian prostitutes brings alternative perspectives to the scene, which gradually becomes more subjective as these characters turn their gazes on one another, first as sexual commodities and then as figures for empathy, since all are strangers in a strange land. This scopic movement ends with the internal visualization by Sanki of the culturally/politically potent image of his mother back in Japan. This move from external visualization, which situates the narrative in a murky alien setting colored in misty blues, grays, and blacks, to Sanki's internal visualization, the gaze of the outsider that expresses the rootless expatriate's longing for the familiar, is equated at the outset with desire, nostalgia, and a mourning of loss.

The second passage appears about two-thirds into the novel. After some striking workers have been shot and killed, a series of protests and riots lead to a general strike. Sanki is attracted to one of the leaders of the strike, a beautiful woman named Fang Qiu-lan, a leader of a Communist cell. Although politically at odds with her, Sanki helps her get away at the time of the textile strike and is rewarded with a memorable kiss. She becomes an idealized substitute for his lost love, Kyōko, and an exotic and unattainable object of desire. He takes a risk in going out in the streets during the disturbances in hopes of seeing her again. The following passage is set during the fateful riot at a police station on May 30th:

> Sanki was forced back into the sunken entrance of a shop and could see only a pivoting transom opened horizontally above his head. The rioting crowd was reflected upside down in the transom glass. It was like being on the floor of an ocean that had lost its watery sky. Countless heads beneath shoulders, shoulders beneath feet. They described a weird, suspended canopy on the verge of falling, swaying like seaweed that drifted out, then drew back and drifted out again. As the riot continued swirling about,

Sanki searched for the face of Fang Qiu-lan in the crowd suspended over him. Then he heard more shots. He felt a tremor. He tried to reach out into the crowd on the ground, as if he were springing up. He disregarded his own equilibrium, which floated up into the confusion of the external world. His desire to fight that external world, which rose irresistibly in him, was like a sudden attack of a chronic disease. Simultaneously, he began to struggle to steal back his composure. He tried to watch intently the velocity of the bullets. A river made of waves of human beings sped past in front of him. These waves collided and rose up like spray. Banners fell, covering the waves. The cloth of the banners caught on the feet of the flowing crowd and seemed to be swallowed up into the buildings. Then, at that moment, he saw Qiu-lan. A Chinese patrolman attached to the Municipal Police had grabbed her arms and restrained her near one of the banners. Sanki's line of sight was blocked suddenly, so he fought his way through the wave and ran to the side of a building. He could still see Qiu-lan in the clutches of the policeman as she silently watched the riot swirling around her. Then she saw him. She smiled. He sensed death.

One of the elements of *Shanghai* that has most often been praised by Japanese critics is Yokomitsu's handling of the scenes of crowds and riots, and when we look at this particular passage in its context, we find the same kind of visual movement—from a wide external perspective to an internal one—as was employed in the opening. However, the passage also seems to be struggling with the conventional language of realism. For all its circumstantial detail, the scene is heightened, almost surrealistic: the inverted images in the glass, the water imagery (a kind of leitmotif in the novel), and the visualization of the velocity of the bullets. This heightened language is effective in this instance because it reveals the struggle of Sanki not to lose the consciousness of himself in the self-less crowd. There is a powerful tension between the unconscious tide of political revolution and the observing consciousness of the individual; and for Sanki the politically charged scene before him momentarily dissolves again to an image of sexual desire and death. As with the opening scene, the depiction of a particular historical site and moment collapse to an ostensibly nonideological vision that erases historical time and place and creates a space upon which universal images of desire may be projected.

The final passage I want to cite appears at the very end of the book in the scene where Sanki is reunited with another Japanese expatriate, the woman named Osugi. The first citation presents the scene from Sanki's perspective:

> Thinking she would say something, he waited for Osugi's reply. But she said nothing. In the darkness he could hear her sobbing again. He remembered that when she first cried like that at Oryū's place, he had comforted her with words nearly identical to those he had used now. And each time she had trusted in his words, her misery had increased.
>
> At that time he had nothing but words as a means of rescuing Osugi. If it were wrong to keep a woman who can no longer make a living in your house until she can, then what else could he do? The only thing he could be faulted for was not embracing Osugi and loving her. Sanki thought that of all his sins that was the worst.
>
> *To make love with her . . . What was wrong with that? It would be better for Osugi than not embracing her at all.* Despite his feelings, until the moment when he actually came to embrace Osugi, he would think of ever so many reasons to stop himself.
>
> And yet he had to admit that all his excuses came down to the same thing. How long could he go on mistreating Osugi?
>
> "Osugi? Come here. Don't think about anything. Just come here."
>
> Sanki stretched his arms out to her. Her body fell heavily into them. At that moment Qiu-lan, in her aquamarine dress, vividly filled his arms.

Shortly after this moment the perspective of the story shifts to Osugi:

> Osugi recalled the loneliness that followed the day Sanki left her behind in his house and did not return—a time

she spent alone gazing absently at the surface of the water in the canal. On those occasions oil constantly floated beneath the fog like some design on the water. The bluish green growing on the sides of the crumbling mortar lapped up the oil on the surface. Beside it floated the yellowish corpse of a chick that drew toward it scraps of greens, socks, mango peels, and straw rubbish. Together with pitch-black bubbles that welled up from the depths, these items formed a little island in the middle of the canal. Osugi did nothing for two or three days but gaze at that little island and wait intently for Sanki to come home. If tomorrow the naval brigade landed and restored order to the city, wouldn't she once again have to continue on blankly, just as in those days. Then once more the men— their coarse, shark-like skin, their mouths reeking of garlic, the sticky oil plastered to their hair, the long fingernails, the sharp irregular teeth. Reflecting on these things, she stretched out like a patient who has given up and stared into the darkness spread across the ceiling.

The most remarkable aspect of the closing pages of the novel is that the vivid imagistic descriptions of the city that are a significant recurring element of the narrative continue to appear prominently even though the scene itself is played out in utter darkness. In a sense Shanghai has been wholly colonized here, internalized as a site that acts as an objective correlative to express the states of mind of Osugi and Sanki. Of course, the differences between the visions they project into the dark are enormous. Sanki's vision is one of an idealized desire to possess Qiu-lan, a desire in which cultural and historical differences (including his own moral responsibility for the fates of both Qiu-lan and Osugi) are erased by an Orientalist image of exotic sexuality. Osugi's vision, in contrast, though not explicitly political, suggests the social and economic inequities, embodied by the squalor of a city, that are the causes of her terrible predicament. Though she never overtly discusses political ideology in the book, it seems politically significant that hers is the final perspective of the novel. Osugi, a young Japanese woman whose fate is sealed by her precarious economic position in capitalist Shanghai, is

236

degraded because of historical circumstances. Her gaze into a blank future suggests the costs of modernity, and this closing image of an utterly powerless woman, a stock figure in films and literature of this period, gives full expression to the sense of loss and desperation associated with the modern city.

These selected passages suggest how Yokomitsu uses Shanghai as both a historical site and an imaginary cityscape onto which his characters project their desires. And by relating the personal desires of his characters to political and social realities, Yokomitsu attempts to achieve the aesthetic aim of getting at unmediated experience through imagistic writing and the politically charged aim of resolving the conflicted historical consciousness of modern culture. The connection between politics and aesthetics in *Shanghai* is thus not simply a matter of the characters acting as mouthpieces for particular positions. The personal conflicts in Shanghai are an analogue to the political conflicts that racked Japan and China in the 1920s and 1930s. The desire to resolve that conflict in favor of a modernity that went beyond Western culture to a broader cosmopolitanism was a powerful ideological justification for Japan's colonial and military policies in the 1930s. In the long run this association of pan-Asian cosmopolitanism with the militarist dream that culminated in the Co-Prosperity Sphere was impossible to sustain. With military defeat came the collapse of that dream and of the dreams of men like Yokomitsu.

Despite the absolute failure of his ambitious cultural agenda (or perhaps because of its spectacular failure), Yokomitsu has never suffered from scholarly neglect. Numerous studies of his life and work have appeared since his death in 1947, suggesting that he remains a figure of considerable historical interest in Japan. Still, his reputation has lost much of the imposing stature it possessed in the 1930s. This diminution began with the critical failure of his self-styled masterwork *Ryoshū* (The melancholy of travel; serialized between 1937 and 1946) and accelerated in 1946 when the leftist journal *Shin Nihon bungaku* (New Japanese literature) charged him with responsibility for the war. The general atmosphere of remorse and recrimination following Japan's defeat put previously unquestioned critical assessments into play, and his death the following year, at the relatively young age of forty-nine, cut short a career that in retrospect seems never to have reached its full potential.

While the failures of Yokomitsu's later career, especially the moral responsibility he bears in supporting Japanese expansionism in Asia, have colored the reception of all his works, they help us to understand the peculiar nature of the achievement of *Shanghai*. Certainly the novel is something of an anomaly. Excluding fiction by Japanese expatriates and writers of other nationalities in Japan's colonies, *Shanghai* is one of the very few major novels of the period written by an establishment writer with a relatively large readership in which the story takes place wholly outside of Japan. Yokomitsu's preoccupation with his Japanese characters reflects not so much literary parochialism as the reality of Shanghai culture, which was born of imperialist desires and nurtured by colonial regimes. The book's depiction of the racial and political attitudes that were current at the time of its composition is deeply disturbing in part because these attitudes are so thoroughly aestheticized and eroticized, and in part because these fictionalized attitudes about the place of Japanese nationalism and militarism in Asia were later incorporated into the aesthetic ideology that Yokomitsu developed in the 1930s. In spite of all the troublesome aspects of the novel, however, Yokomitsu's work is not merely a historical curiosity. *Shanghai* is a stylistic tour de force that conveys a richly complex, sometimes contradictory mix of politics and aesthetics, revealing to us the contours of the imaginary cultural landscape of 1920s Japan.

A NOTE ON THE TEXT AND TRANSLATION

The text I used in preparing this translation is Kōdansha's *Bungei bunko* version, which is based on the version of *Shanghai* published in the *Teihon Yokomitsu Riichi zenshū* (Complete works of Yokomitsu Riichi: original texts) (Tokyo: Kawade Shobō, 1981). The only differences between the *Bungei bunko* version and the *Teihon* version are the substitution of current *kana* usage and the deletion of many of the *rubi* (glosses) that adorn the original. My reasons for choosing this text is that it is closest to the material Yokomitsu first wrote when he composed *Shanghai* in 1928 and 1929 and is a more complete text than other versions published by both Kōdansha and Shinchōsha. For example, the *Bungei bunko* version includes anti-foreign language, telegrams and letters, and an additional chapter (chapter 44) that were either edited out or not reproduced in the other versions. Chapters 29 and 32 are also in reverse order in the other texts. Unfortunately, while the version I chose is more complete, it is also more raw, containing numerous lacunae, grammatical errors, and instances of muddled writing that are corrected in the Kōdansha and Shinchōsha editions. For that reason I made use of these cleaner, more tightly edited texts when I needed help clarifying certain passages in the *Bungei bunko* version.

On the whole Yokomitsu kept to his program of returning to a realist mode in *Shanghai*, but traces of his experimental prose are evident throughout in a number of stylistic quirks. He uses catalogs of images as well as broken phrases and clauses to try to create a sense of immediacy and freshness in his diction and a sense of an objective camera eye. Dashes visually break up almost every page, setting off the internal thoughts of characters in order to allow the narrative to shift seamlessly between the perspectives of those characters and of the third-person narrator. I have on the whole indicated those thoughts by the use of italics.

The repetitive use of synaesthesic images gives the narrative a tight coherence by creating leitmotifs for both the city and the characters. The predominant images are related to water—images of flowing, dampness, fecundity, and decay; of shaking, swelling, rising, sliding. The images are reinforced by the repetitiveness of certain grammatical forms—the subordinate conjunction *to*, which marks a conditional temporal state; the conjunction *nagara*, which expresses simultaneity of action; the adverb *futo*, which suggests sudden, unexpected action; the conjunction *shikashi*, which is primarily used by Yokomitsu as a visual bridge to run sentences together—all of which combine with the visual quality of the narrative to create a visceral sense of movement and flux.

I have tried in this translation to recapture the effects created by these stylistic elements, and thus preserve the quirkiness of the original, by starting with as literal a version in English as I could manage. However, since a translation is by nature an analogue of the original, my work stands as an appropriation of Yokomitsu's story. Because I was aware throughout the process of translation that what I was producing is fundamentally different from the original, I consciously aimed throughout to replicate as best I could the strangeness of Yokomitsu's novel—a rather elusive quality that for me made the novel worth translating.

I would like to close by expressing my deep appreciation to Ikuko Watanabe, who assisted me in the initial stages of my work, and William Sibley, who painstakingly read through the manuscript and made many valuable suggestions and corrections.

About the Translator

Dennis Washburn teaches Japanese and Comparative Literature at Dartmouth College. He is the translator of Ōoka Shōhei's novel, *The Shade of Blossoms* (Michigan, 1998), coeditor of *Word and Image in the Japanese Cinema* (Cambridge, 2000) and *Studies in Modern Japanese Literature* (Michigan, 1997), and the author of *The Dilemma of the Modern in Japanese Fiction* (Yale, 1995).

CPSIA information can be obtained
at www.ICGtesting.com
Printed in the USA
BVHW071022230622
640493BV00001B/62

9 781929 280018